"Why, you insufferable beast!"

Mary took a deep breath, her hands going to her hips.

Ian's gaze slid down, pausing for a moment on her bosom before he looked back at her face. Only then did she recall that she had unbuttoned the neck of her dress. She knew that if she looked down there would be far more of her showing than she wished. Even as the thought swept through her mind, he smiled knowingly and she felt a deep flush of heat move down her throat and over her breasts. His next words drove all thought of retaining a pose of unconcern from her mind.

"If you keep standing there looking so completely desirable, Miss Fulton, I just might kiss you again."

Her arms came up to shield her bosom from his view. "You, my Lord Sinclair, are despicable. No wonder they call you Lord Sin."

Dear Reader,

Catherine Archer is fast gaining a reputation for her dramatic and emotional historical romances, and this month's *Lord Sin* with its brooding hero and Gothic overtones will surely add to it. Pressured by his estranged father to marry, a rakish nobleman, in an act of defiance, marries a vicar's daughter who is outspoken, educated and beautiful, but completely unsuitable, and gains a wife who can finally teach him the meaning of trust and love.

In Elizabeth Mayne's *Lady of the Lake*, a pagan princess surrenders her heritage and her heart to the Christian warrior who has been sent to marry her and unite their kingdoms. And *Cally and the Sheriff* by Cassandra Austin, is a lively Western about a Kansas sheriff who falls head over heels for the feisty young woman he's sworn to protect, even though she wants nothing to do with him.

Our fourth title for the month is *The Marriage Mishap* by Judith Stacy, the story of virtual strangers who wake up in bed together and discover they have gotten married.

Whatever your tastes in reading, we hope you enjoy all of our books, available wherever Harlequin Historicals are sold.

Sincerely,

Tracy Farrell
Senior Editor

Please address questions and book requests to:
Harlequin Reader Service
U.S.: 3010 Walden Ave., P.O. Box 1325, Buffalo, NY 14269
Canadian: P.O. Box 609, Fort Erie, Ont. L2A 5X3

Catherine Archer

Lord Sin

Harlequin Books

TORONTO • NEW YORK • LONDON
AMSTERDAM • PARIS • SYDNEY • HAMBURG
STOCKHOLM • ATHENS • TOKYO • MILAN
MADRID • WARSAW • BUDAPEST • AUCKLAND

ISBN 0-373-28979-0

LORD SIN

Copyright © 1997 by Catherine J. Archibald

All rights reserved. Except for use in any review, the reproduction or utilization of this work in whole or in part in any form by any electronic, mechanical or other means, now known or hereafter invented, including xerography, photocopying and recording, or in any information storage or retrieval system, is forbidden without the written permission of the publisher, Harlequin Enterprises Limited, 225 Duncan Mill Road, Don Mills, Ontario, Canada M3B 3K9.

Books by Catherine Archer

Harlequin Historicals

Rose Among Thorns #136
*Velvet Bond #282
*Velvet Touch #322
Lady Thorn #353
Lord Sin #379

*Velvet Series

CATHERINE ARCHER

has been hooked on historical romance since reading *Jane Eyre* at the age of twelve. She has an avid interest in history, particularly the Medieval period. A homemaker and mother, Catherine lives with her husband, three children and dog in Alberta, Canada, where the long winters give this American transplant plenty of time to write.

This book is dedicated to the children of my siblings with much love and the hope that they might each follow their own dreams. To Russell, Tricia, Matthew, Sofia, Samara, Alexander, Joseph, Jeremy, Arielle, Jason, Crystal and Jacob.

I would also like to add a word of thanks to the members of the RW—L, for their help with research information and moral support.

Lastly I must thank my editor, Karen Kosztolnyik, for her support and her valuable contributions to my work.

Chapter One

The wind tugged the hair loose from Mary Fulton's bun and whipped it across her pale face. She did not even bother to reach up and push it from her eyes. Mary was too intent on holding tightly to the straw bonnet she clutched over her slender midriff. It was as if that plain straw hat could hold her misery inside her, keep it from rising up to completely overwhelm her. She didn't notice the way the long, wide blue ribbon that was meant to tie the bonnet atop her head fluttered across the front of her lighter blue print dress as she walked, though she once came near to treading upon it.

Nor did she clearly see the heather, asphodel, campion and spotted orchids that bloomed amongst the short, coarse grass of the moorland. She had no appreciation for them, or the sun that occasionally peeked from the gray haze of clouds overhead, or anything else, for that matter. Nothing could get past the swelling ache of emptiness in her heart.

The two weeks that had passed since her father's funeral had done little to ease her sorrow. In this, the last year of her father's illness, she had known the end would come, had even realized it would be a release for him. Knowing this truth had not lessened the devastation of losing him.

From the time of her mother's death when she was five, Mary had taken over the care of her absentminded but brilliant parent.

Not that Robert Fulton had completely neglected his only child. The vicar had given unstintingly of himself and his time as far as her education was concerned. The simple truth was that he had had little thought for the ordinary things such as meals and clean clothing, of offering a hug when she fell down. It had been left to Mary to direct the series of housekeepers in their duties and help them with whatever needed doing, to dust off her own scraped knees.

Robert Fulton had spent his time in the pursuit of learning and knowledge. The bond between father and daughter had been forged on that path. Reverend Fulton had been proud of his Mary's quick mind, gladly teaching his daughter about any subject she seemed to take an interest in. He was a learned, broad-thinking and patient man, which stood him in good stead as a teacher.

Her father's abilities as a teacher had led Mary to meet Victoria Thorn, whose kind offer of a home had now brought her to her present state of indecision. Her uncertainty had sent her out onto the moor, for it had always had a soothing effect on her. But she found no comfort here.

Victoria was her dearest friend. Not long after the reverend had taken up the position of minister to the local church, Victoria's father, the Duke of Carlisle, had asked him to see to his daughter's education. He'd said he was impressed with Mary's knowledge. The moment Victoria had taken her place next to Mary in the book-filled study at the vicarage, Victoria's gray eyes had met Mary's golden brown ones. Victoria's gaze had been direct and curiously assessing without any of the condescension the minister's daughter had expected from the offspring of a duke. Mary had found herself smiling, and neither of the girls had ever wavered from the friendship begun on that day.

Unconsciously, Mary sighed, lifting her eyes to the grayness of the sky overhead. Somehow, something held her back from saying yes to Victoria's invitation. She was infinitely aware of her friend's own situation, the troubles she had so recently overcome.

In spite of her vast wealth and social position, life had been difficult for Victoria. Her father and mother had died several years ago and, along with their wealth, all their responsibilities had passed to their young daughter. Mary had done what she could to help Victoria through that horible time. And now Victoria and her husband, Jedidiah, were trying to do what they could to help Mary.

They had invited her to come and live with them at Brirwood, their enormous mansion. Though Mary knew the offer was made from the kindest of intentions, she was not sure she could say yes—in fact, did not see how she could do so.

Victoria and Jedidiah had been married only nine short months and were even now expecting their first child. Mary did not want to intrude on this special time between them. When the two of them had come to the vicarage yesterday afternoon to tell Mary of their invitation to live with them, she had seen the way they touched one another on the least excuse, the way their eyes met and held every few moments, the depth of passion neither could hide.

She did not wish to intrude on that. And a further truth was that their shared intimacy served only to make her own loneliness all the more obvious and painful.

Yet what was she to do? The new vicar and his family of six had lived in a rented house in the village since their arrival in Carlisle over a year ago. The family had a right to move into the comfortable two-story house next to the church. It was a measure of his kindness that Reverend Diller had insisted Robert Fulton stay in his own home through his illness.

Mary knew she absolutely must vacate the rectory as soon as she could. For the hundredth time she asked herself where else she could go if she did not say yes to Victoria. She raised a trembling hand to wipe it across her forehead, unable to think of any answer to her dilemma when her heart was so heavy.

She walked on, putting one foot in front of the other, forcing herself forward over the uneven ground, forcing herself not to look back. Yet she gained no insight, lost none of her sense of confusion.

Lifting her eyes heavenward, she whispered, "Please, God, send me a sign? Help me to know what I should do."

As if through a haze, the sound of galloping hooves penetrated her reverie. She looked up, her gaze scanning the moor. She saw a black stallion approaching at breakneck speed, its mane and tale flowing wildly in the wind. On its back was a man in dark clothing, bent low over the muscular neck, his lean thighs pressed tightly to his mount's sides.

Mary stopped still, in unconscious appreciation of the untamed beauty of man and beast. Yet as she watched, her appreciation changed to uncertainty, then apprehension. Her eyes grew round and her heart rose in her throat as the horse and rider continued to bear down upon her.

She felt frozen, incapable of moving. Something, perhaps the excesses of emotion she had experienced in the past weeks, kept her immobile, and she could only stare in growing fear. Only at the last minute did the man pull the horse up short, causing it to rear high in the air just scant feet from her. Released from her fixed state, Mary took a step backward with an involuntary gasp.

The horse spun around in what certainly must have been a dizzying arch. To her surprise she heard what sounded like a husky and decidedly irreverent laugh escape the rider.

Drawing herself up to her full five feet four inches, Mary put her hands on her hips. What sort of lunatic laughed at nearly running down a defenseless woman? She was just getting set to unleash her tongue on this madman when he brought the stallion around and turned to face her.

All the things she had been going to say flew from her mind, like leaves in a breeze. A pair of dark, dark eyes surrounded by a thick fringe of black lashes focused on her in open appreciation. Her heart stopped, then started again with a lurch as he smiled, his white teeth even and strong in his lean-jawed, tanned face. He lifted a hand to rake a tousled dark brown forelock from his eyes as he said, "A good day to you, Miss…?" There was a flirtatious charm in his voice that she could not help but hear.

Mary continued to stare up at him, wondering where this amazingly devastating man had come from, and if indeed he was some figment of her mind. For even in her distressed state Mary knew that physically this overconfident male was exactly what her fertile imagination would conjure in a man if it could do so.

"Miss…?" he prodded.

Suddenly Mary realized she was standing there staring like a fool. Giving herself a mental shake, she pulled the ragged ends of her dignity together. She raised her chin as she told herself that handsome features did not make a man, even while her rapidly beating pulse refused to quiet. Because of her lack of command over her own reactions, Mary spoke with more heat than she had meant to. "And why, may I ask, should I tell you who I am, sir? You have clearly displayed the fact that you are of questionable character by the way you nearly ran me down."

A look of complete dismay crossed his handsome face. "I? Dear lady, let me assure you that I would not have you think such a thing of me." He ran a caressing hand over the stallion's neck. "Balthazar is the most surefooted of mounts. He responds perfectly to the merest touch on the reins. He would never have touched you." He arched a contrite brow, seeming suddenly more schoolboy than man, as he said, "But I must beg your forgiveness if I caused you even a moment's concern for your safety. Please, do say you will forgive me?" The brilliant white smile he added was shocking in its power to catch her breath.

Mary recovered herself quickly and looked at him closely, not quite sure why but having the definite feeling that he was somehow making sport of her. Yet she could see no proof of this in either his expression or tone. She pushed the thought away, having been taught that she must believe the best of people unless they showed her otherwise. "Very well, sir. I accept your apology. I only hope you have more care in the future."

To her surprise he smiled again, leaning low over the horse's back, his gaze even with her own. "You have not told me your name."

She swallowed, feeling warm for no apparent reason at all. "I...Mary Fulton is my name." She raised her chin, irritated at her own hesitation. "Though it is not as if I owe you the courtesy of introducing myself when you have not done so. I would greatly appreciate it if you would be so good as to tell me to whom am I speaking, sir?"

He laughed, and the sound slipped down her spine like a trickle of warm oil. "I am Ian Sinclair, little spitfire, on my way to Briarwood Manor."

She gave a start. "Lord Ian Sinclair." This must be *the* Ian Sinclair. The one Victoria had told her about several months ago. The one they called "Lord Sin." The one who had asked Victoria to marry him. Victoria had in fact come very close to doing so, believing that Jedidiah did not want her. But they had worked out their differences and Victoria had rejected Sinclair's proposal.

So what, then, was he doing at Carlisle now?

He must have gained quite a bit of information from her reaction, for he seemed to scowl with chagrin for a moment before that expression of studied charm and unconcern masked the more vulnerable expression. "You seem to have me at a disadvantage, Miss Fulton. Am I to take your reaction as indication that you know of me?"

She nodded slowly, wondering why she felt even more drawn to him after having seen that momentary glimpse of vulnerability beneath the surface of his charm. "I am well acquainted with Lady Victoria. She has mentioned you in passing," she told him carefully. It was not precisely the truth, but for some reason Mary felt uncomfortable with having Ian Sinclair know she knew so much of his private affairs.

An inner voice told her that the more distance she kept between herself and this man, the better.

Blessedly unaware of her thoughts, he nodded, settling back on his horse. "Then I shall surely be seeing more of you this week while I am at Briarwood, Miss Fulton." Again there was that oddly intimate inflection in his voice that she could not fully define. It was also apparent in his mysterious dark eyes.

Self-consciously, she stepped backward and shrugged noncommittally. "Perhaps. Please, don't let me keep you. I'm sure they are expecting you."

Ian Sinclair looked down at her, the expression in his eyes now more clear as his admiring gaze moved slowly over her. Raising a dark brow, he indicated the empty space on the saddle before him. "I am not in such a great hurry.

I would be happy to take you wherever you might be going.''

Unaccustomed to such attention and unsure as to how to react, Mary was unable to meet that appreciative gaze. She flushed and ran unaccountably trembling fingers over the skirt of her blue cotton dress. ''No, really, I have not finished my walk.'' She waved a hand to indicate the open moor before her.

He looked at her closely. ''Are you sure? You would be no trouble to me—no trouble whatsoever.'' Again she heard that unexplainable something in his voice, a quality that made her think of summer nights that were too hot to lie beneath the covers.

For a breathless moment his eyes met hers and the world tilted. Now to that image of a hot night was added an unexpected vision of his face leaning over hers, his dark eyes seeming to see right into her soul. Mary took in a breath of shock.

He smiled, a dark, knowing smile that made her flush deepen as she blinked with disbelief at her own thoughts. ''Well?'' he prompted.

Quickly she answered, refusing to acknowledge any of what was happening. ''I am quite sure that I have no need of your assistance. I do very well on my own.''

A dark brow arched high. ''Do you, now? But just imagine how very well you might do with someone else.''

She did not want to even try to contemplate why he was persisting in talking this way. But Mary had had quite enough. ''Really, sir, I do not think it very good of you to make sport of me.''

He sobered abruptly, putting a hand over his heart. ''I assure you, Mary, I have no desire to make sport of you. At least, not with words.''

She frowned, feeling more and more out of her depth,

and not liking that in the least. But she tried her best to hold her own, dismissing him with as much disdain as she could muster. "That would be Miss Fulton, please. Now, good day, sir."

Ian Sinclair smiled again, seemingly unaffected by her hauteur. "As you wish, Miss *Mary* Fulton. Until we meet again." With that he spun his mount around and galloped off, the horse's hooves flashing.

She watched him, shaking her head. They would not be meeting again. She would make sure of that. He could not be up to any good with his lingering looks and innuendo that she could not quite understand. Men like Ian Sinclair, who she knew was the heir to an earldom, could only mean disaster to a young woman like her with no dowry and no prospects to recommend them for marriage.

Not that she wanted anything to do with the blackguard. He was not the kind of man one could depend on, with his flirtatious ways. And no one would deny that he was far too handsome for his own good.

Heaven help her, if a miracle did occur and Mary some-day met a suitable man and fell in love, he must certainly be a gentleman to depend on. Someone who would be a partner and soul mate. He would not be a man who would shed the light of his charm on every woman he met.

Squaring her shoulders, Mary set off across the moor once again, realizing as she did so that for the few moments she had been there, Ian Sinclair had made her forget the problems confronting her. With a sigh, Mary cast one last glance in the direction he had gone.

Ian barely felt the wind tugging at his hair as he rode away from the little country beauty. With her gold hair, and eyes that seemed to look right inside him, she had been enough to warm any man's blood. There had been no quaint demureness in her manner, stirring Ian's interest even further.

He was not at all surprised to learn that she was acquainted with Victoria Thorn. That lady was not one to simper and flutter her lashes like a schoolgirl. Lady Victoria faced a man directly, as had Miss Fulton—Mary. He laughed aloud at recalling her insistence on his using the formal address.

Mary. The name suited her, being somehow soft and strong at the same time, as he suspected its bearer was. For some reason he felt a growing curiosity about the young woman he had left behind him on the moors. She was not dressed at all fashionably, with her golden hair whipped to a wild disarray. Her plain straw bonnet could do little to protect that creamy complexion from the sun, clutched in her hand the way it had been. No hoops had shaped the skirt of her pale blue dress, and the wind had molded it quite distractingly to a slender and delicate but pleasingly rounded form.

Perhaps Victoria would be more willing to quench his curiosity about Miss Fulton than she herself had been. He spurred his mount forward.

Some time later Ian was riding down the well-tended, tree-lined drive. In the distance, through the veils of new leaves, he could see the enormous sandstone manor house where lived his host and hostess, the recently wedded Victoria and Jedidiah Thorn-McBride.

Ian had asked Victoria to marry him just under a year ago, and for a short while it had looked as if she might say yes. But it had been Jedidiah McBride whom she had loved. Jedidiah had been posing as her cousin from America at the time, though Ian had ultimately sensed there was something more than family devotion between the two. At the wedding, Victoria had admitted there was no family connection, only that they had agreed to do a favor for the other, and had ended up falling in love. He'd be lying if he said his heart was broken by her refusal, but he was disappointed, having felt they would deal very well together.

Having become even more friendly with the couple when they were in London right before Jedidiah's trip to America, Ian was content that Victoria had made the right choice for herself. It was more than obvious that the newlyweds were completely devoted to one another. How could he begrudge them such happiness?

As he came closer to the house, Ian could not help comparing it with his own family estate, a place he had not visited in two years. Briarwood was pale and bright, while Sinclair Hall seemed dark and austere in contrast. It was as if the exterior of his ancestral home reflected the stilted emotions and lack of forgiveness in the hearts of those inside.

Ian did not want to think about that. He had spent the eleven years since he was seventeen doing everything he could to keep himself from thinking about it. A fact that had left him with a less than savory reputation.

He drew his horse to a halt at the bottom of the wide steps. A liveried manservant came out to take his horse as soon as his feet touched the ground.

When he entered the high-ceilinged foyer, Victoria was coming across the marble floor, her hands outstretched. She smiled, and Ian could not help seeing what a beautiful woman she was in spite of her advancing pregnancy. Her creamy skin was touched by a delicate flush of health and her dark locks gleamed, as did her gray eyes. Victoria was favored with spirit and intelligence as well as beauty. It was with only the slightest twinge of regret that Ian told himself again that Jedidiah McBride was a very fortunate man.

For some reason he had a brief image of Mary Fulton's eyes, her wind-tousled golden hair. When Victoria took his hands and spoke, it disappeared. "We were surprised and so happy to receive your letter saying you would be in the district. It is good of you to come and visit us."

Ian smiled at her, kissing her offered cheek in a brotherly fashion. Usually with this woman, if no other, he felt completely at ease, with no need to play intricate sensual games. It was what had drawn him to her in the first place. Yet at this moment he had need to call upon his skills at acting.

Jedidiah had been the one to contact him, having decided to purchase one of Ian's finest mares as a birthday surprise for his wife. The mare was tied behind the carriage that was some hours behind him. Ian was not about to give away the secret. "How could I stay away?" he told her with exaggerated clutching at his chest. "You know you have stolen my heart, Lady Victoria."

She gave him a mocking reprimand. "Do please discontinue this kind of talk. Your heart is safely locked in your chest, where I believe it will continue to reside, Ian."

At his pained expression and declaration of "Now you've mortally wounded me," she laughed, as he had meant her to.

After taking his coat with a quelling glance, Victoria handed it to another footman. She said, "John, please have Mrs. Everard send tea into the sitting room."

"Very well, my lady." The young, dark-haired serving man bowed to each of them respectfully and moved off across the marble floor.

Victoria then linked her arm through Ian's and led him forward. "Now come into the sitting room and we'll have ea. Jedidiah is off showing one of the tenants how to set p an irrigation system. He should be back shortly.''

As they moved across the foyer Ian could not help thinking again what a charming home Briarwood Manor was. In pite of its size and grandeur, it reverberated a feeling of omfort and warmth. Through the open doorways on either ide of them he could see into rooms where the drapes had een drawn back to let in the light. He gained the impression of a pleasant mix of pale and vibrant colors that made ach chamber seem to beckon a welcome.

Once more Ian could not help comparing it to Sinclair Iall. He tried not to acknowledge the melancholy that igged at his heart on doing so. His own ancestral home e found lacking on every score. The rooms of that great ouse were kept dark and closed off, a fitting home for the hosts that roamed its halls. And there were ghosts—not nly the ghost of his mother, who had died giving birth to im, but also that of his brother, Malcolm.

The thought of his brother made his heart ache with loss. an had loved Malcolm with a devotion that was akin to ero-worship. Even Ian's very early understanding that his ather's love for himself would never come close to that of is older son had not changed Ian's feelings for Malcolm. Ie had been intelligent, loving and so full of life. How ould anyone begrudge him anything, least of all Ian? Malolm had been the sun they all orbited around. That was vhy his father had never been able to forgive Ian when he elieved his younger son had caused Malcolm's death.

It was a death that he had, in fact, not been responsible or.

Ian's lips thinned as he pushed the painful thoughts way. It was surprising how difficult this was to do, espeially when he had worked so diligently to forget in the ntervening years. Nothing—not drink, not women, not horse racing—had made him forget for more than brief hours. Realizing that living as Lord Sin was not making him forget had made Ian wish to change his life. He had thought Victoria would be part of that new life, but that had not come to pass.

Victoria led him into the sitting room, where they seated themselves on a pale green settee. Immediately Ian turned to her, needing to concentrate on something beyond his hurtful thoughts. "It seems Jed is keeping himself busy with the duties of running the estates."

She rested a hand on the swell of her stomach. Contentment and pride were clear in her tone and shining gray eyes. "Yes, he is. He never seems to resent the burdens marrying me has laid at his feet. He does in fact seem to thrive on the work and responsibility of looking after the welfare of so many." She smiled ruefully. "And I am grateful for him for more reasons than I can say. Not the least of which is that his care for our lands has freed me to be a mother to my child."

Ian heard her speak of Jedidiah's pleasure in his duties as overlord with a trace of regret. He would not be averse to taking up the duties of running the Sinclair estates. He did in fact wish that his father had ever seemed the least bit interested in having him do so. The one thing he appeared to expect from his son was an heir, and on that score he had been quite blunt. When last they'd spoken, the elder man had reiterated his desire for Ian to wed his cousin Barbara and get her with child. Ian had no intention of falling in with his father's wishes. He was not in the least attracted to Barbara, and would not have married her if he was. He would not allow the older man to rule his life. As long as he was earl Malcolm Sinclair had the power to keep Ian from having any say in how the estates were run. But he could not control the way Ian lived his own life.

As he replied, Ian could not help the unrest in his tone. "I'm sure the duties your husband performs offer more satisfaction than you know, Victoria. Seeing your own ideas implemented, improving conditions for the people who depend upon you. Those things would be reward enough to content any self-respecting man."

Having confided more of his unhappiness to Victoria than anyone else, Ian was not surprised when she laid a hand on his arm. "Ian, perhaps someday your father will allow you to take up your own rightful position as his heir. I know it is what you desire most."

Though he had told Victoria of his troubles with his father, Ian found he was somewhat uncomfortable with her concern. He gave a falsely bright smile. "I doubt the old fellow has any plans to do anything of the kind, but I shall not be losing any sleep over the matter. As you know, I have my horses and will continue to find satisfaction in that, for it does not look like I will inherit for many years to come. Not that I wish the earl any ill fortune. In spite of everything, he is my father."

"Are things no better between you?" she asked, cutting through his attempted facade easily. It was a knack she had possessed since the very beginning of their acquaintance.

Unable to keep up any pretext with this woman, who seemed to read him as if she had known him all his life, Ian shook his head, allowing the smile to fade. "No, I am afraid not. He has remained unceasing in his insistence that I marry. His every letter is a diatribe on the subject. He did in fact come up to London some months ago to reiterate his demands in person."

"Then why do you not marry, if only to make peace with him? You were prepared to do so some months ago."

He could not explain to her his own continued reticence,

and so replied dramatically, "The woman I wished to wed has taken another." Ian cast a mock tragic glance her way.

Her only answer was a delicately arched brow.

He grew more serious. "In all honesty I have met no one else whom I would seriously consider spending the rest of my life with. And I have no intention of doing as he wishes by marrying my cousin Barbara. It is unthinkable."

"If you made a real attempt, you might find someone of your own choosing," she told him stubbornly.

Ian shrugged. "You know how I feel about the young debs who are paraded before the bachelors of London society. They dance and flutter their eyelashes well enough, but not a thought about anything more interesting than how many dresses they own or how many servants a prospective bridegroom might provide passes through their minds. To marry one of them would be to condemn oneself to a life of abject boredom."

"Surely that is not true of all the young women you've met?" she said dryly.

Unexpectedly a vision crept into his mind. The vision had long golden hair and a pair of bewitchingly gold eyes, eyes like a hawk's. "I did meet a woman today not far from Carlisle," he told her with more uncertainty than he would have thought clouding his teasing tone. "She was...well...different."

Victoria leaned closer to him, her gray eyes sparkling with interest. "Different. And not far from Carlisle. This is quite exciting. Ian, you must tell me all. What is her name?"

He was surprised at his own reluctance to talk about the woman he'd met. He pushed it aside. This conversation was after all occurring only for amusement's sake. "I really know very little of her. The young woman seemed stimulatingly contrary and addressed me quite deprecatingly, in the manner of one quite accustomed to great deference. Though from her dress and the simple miss she attached to her name, she was certainly not of the nobility.''

So occupied was he in remembering how much he had enjoyed the exchange that Ian did not notice how very quiet Victoria had become. ''She was quite beautiful and I must admit that I would not be averse to getting to know her better, possibly much better.'' He glanced at Victoria then as he ended and found her biting her lip as she gazed down at her hands.

He finished with a dawning sense that something was wrong. ''By the way, she said she knew you, and that her name was Mary Fulton.''

Victoria sat back abruptly, her whole body stiff, one hand going to the mound of her stomach. ''Mary? I had feared as much.''

He scowled at her obviously unfavorable reaction. ''I resent your use of the term *fear.*''

She looked at him then, her gray eyes grown grave with warning. ''You must not speak of Mary that way, even in jest. I do in fact know her, and well. She is my dearest friend and has just lost her beloved father. He was the reverend of the church in Carlisle from the time I was quite small. Mary is in no way equal to your game, Ian.''

He felt as if she had slapped him, and a tightness gripped his chest as he looked away from her. So she thought he was not a suitable companion for her friend. His voice took on a condescending tone to cover his hurt. ''I do hope I have misunderstood what you are trying to say. Are you implying that I would seduce your little friend? I had no such intention. Now that you have told me of your association, I shall put her from my mind.''

Victoria was completely frank with him. ''Ian...forgive me, but you as well as anyone know of your reputation.

You have never pretended otherwise, even when you were courting me.''

He continued to hold himself stiffly. "And I also recall telling you that I had had enough of living up to my own reputation as Lord Sin. I meant it.''

A look of chagrin came over her fine-featured face. She spoke softly. "When you said you would like to know her better...I simply assumed...'' She drew herself up. "You know your father would never approve of your attachment to a simple vicar's daughter. And I love her so, as if she was my own sister. I could not bear to see her hurt in any way, even if it was inadvertent on your part. Jedidiah and I have asked her to come and live with us, though she has not said yes.'' Victoria paused before going on. "I will accept your assurances that she is in no danger from you.''

He glanced over to see that she was biting her lip again. Ian shook his head, meeting her eyes earnestly. "I told you when I asked you to marry me, Victoria. I am done with all that. I have no desire to seduce young innocents. And any that I might have gotten the credit for leading astray in the past were not as innocent as their families might have believed. Besides, you give me far too much credit.'' He gave a forced laugh. "There is no reason to believe the young woman would succumb even if I was to press her.''

She shrugged with a rueful smile. "Do not underestimate yourself, Ian. Because your heart is so carefully guarded it is difficult for you to see that others are not so adept at protecting their own.''

He felt he must defend himself here. "I was willing to love you.''

She shook her head sagely. "No, Ian, you were prepared to like me, even to respect me. That is not love. Love is the total giving of yourself into another's keeping. You did not love me.''

When he scowled, ready to deny what she had said, she held up her hand. "But enough of such talk. Forgive me. I believe you will act honorably. As I said, I spoke only out of my love for Mary and concern for the sadness and vulnerability she is feeling right now."

Ian nodded. He was no more interested in carrying on this conversation than she. He had no wish to examine the discomfort he felt at hearing her say he had locked his heart away. He knew he had learned to avoid thinking about how deeply his father's rejection of him hurt. That did not mean he could not love.

Just then the door opened and the maid entered with tea, effectively preventing any more such talk. And Ian was relieved. But as he watched the maid set the heavy tray down on the low table before them, Ian had a thought pass through his mind without his having called it forth.

He heard Victoria's voice telling him that his father would not approve of Mary Fulton. Indeed, Ian thought as he nodded for three sugars, Malcolm Sinclair would likely very much disapprove of the young woman, Mary Fulton. And not only because she was a minister's daughter. There had been an obvious measure of strength and determination in those direct golden eyes. She was quite unlikely to be led about by the nose. Which Ian believed was his father's major reason for approving of Barbara.

Ian and Barbara had been thrown together on every possible occasion since Ian was twenty. It seemed she had been a guest at Sinclair Hall on each of his infrequent visits. Barbara, being only four years his junior, could not have been anything but aware of what was happening, especially after his father had gone so far as to move her into Sinclair Hall just over a year ago. Though she had never actually expressed any desire to marry Ian, she seemed willing to go along with their parents' plans. Ian was not.

Again he saw Mary Fulton's face in his mind. Ian now knew what had caused that trace of sadness in her golden eyes. He was assaulted by unexpected feelings of protectiveness.

He gave himself a mental shake. Ian knew he must put these unwanted thoughts of Mary Fulton from his mind. He had given his promise not to seduce her. And he really could not offer marriage to a vicar's daughter even if he wanted to. It would be too far to go in his defiance of his father.

Any sense of protectiveness he was experiencing was brought on solely by his lack of compassion when he met her. It was regretful, really, that he had not known of her father's death.

Chapter Two

As she made her way out to the garden, Mary hesitated beside the table in the front hall and picked up her wide-brimmed straw hat. The last time she had seen Victoria, her friend had been adamant in telling her that she must remember to put the thing on her head when she was outside. She had then with affectionate admonition pointed out two light golden freckles on Mary's nose.

Yesterday when Mary had met Ian Sinclair she had not been wearing her bonnet. She suddenly wondered if he had noticed those freckles. Being an aristocrat himself, Ian Sinclair would certainly expect any well-bred young woman to take great care with her complexion. Yet when Mary thought back, she realized he had not appeared to be concerned about such things at all. Even now she flushed when she remembered the way he had looked at her. It was as if...as if he wanted to... Well, Mary didn't know what he wanted to do. Yet she did somehow know that the feeling of tightness in her belly was connected to that look.

In direct opposition to those feelings, Mary firmly told herself she did not care one way or another what the infamous ''Lord Sin'' thought of her. Then, in spite of her own declaration, she tied the bonnet ribbon securely beneath her chin as she made her way out the front door.

Mary had not done any work in her garden since before the funeral. There had simply seemed little point in tending plants that no one cared about. For some reason she had risen today with the overwhelming need to do so. Her mother had brought many of the seeds and cuttings here as a young wife and mother. Was it not Mary's duty to honor her memory by looking after the things that she had loved? Especially since that love of gardening had been passed on to Mary. One of the few clear memories she had of her mother was of her reaching up to give her a bloom from one of her own roses as she tended them.

Besides, the task would certainly give her something to do with her idle hands. Not to mention her mind, which obviously needed something worthwhile to occupy it if the number of times Ian Sinclair had popped into it since she met him was any indication.

The garden lay at the back of the red brick house, surrounded by a four-foot-high picket fence. An enormous weeping willow spread its branches over much of the yard, offering a portion of shade to her lilies of the valley during the hottest part of the summer days. Beneath the tree sat the lawn furniture where she and her father had often come to spend a warm evening before he had become too ill. She tried not to let her gaze linger too long on the rattan chaise where he had rested, most times reading a book. But even a glance was enough to jar her aching heart.

Mary squared her shoulders, fighting the wave of grief, refusing to let the misery overpower her again. She must get on with her life. It was what her father would want.

For several hours she managed to think of little besides the young plants she tended, which seemed to respond to her ministrations by reaching eager young leaves to the light. The earth was moist and dark, smelling rich and pleasantly musty in her hands. The few clouds that had lingered from the previous day cleared and the morning sun shone down with determined good cheer.

After a time, Mary grew warm. Absentmindedly she undid some of the buttons at her throat and with the handkerchief from her pocket wiped the perspiration that had beaded on the back of her neck and down the front of her dress. As she reached down between her breasts, Mary felt an odd prickling along the base of her neck. She looked toward the walk that led from the front of the house. No one was there. She told herself she was becoming too edgy from being alone so much, but she did take her hand from the front of her dress.

Telling herself this did not make the sensation of being watched go away. It in fact became overpowering, and she found herself turning around to look in the direction of the back gate.

Then she stopped in horror, still as the statue of St. George in the churchyard. For leaning against the top of the fence was none other than Ian Sinclair himself, looking every bit as handsome, confident and compellingly male as she had remembered him.

It was impossible.

Mary blinked to see if she was conjuring him up herself. But when she opened her lids, there he was, still smiling in that infuriatingly sardonic way of his, his dark eyes regarding her with that strangely unsettling expression of the previous day. It was almost as if he knew a secret about her, a secret that even she did not know.

That, Mary realized, was completely ridiculous. Ian Sinclair knew no secrets about her, because she had none. For some unknown reason this did not soothe her. She drew herself up, raising her chin high. "What are you doing here?"

He raised his brows in what she could only believe was feigned surprise and regret. "Am I to take that to mean you do not want me?" he asked. "Why? What have I done to offend you so greatly? We have only known each other since yesterday."

As he spoke his gaze drifted down to the open neck of her gown and she felt a flush rise to her cheeks. Mary had to resist the urge to look at what he might be seeing. With as much aplomb as she could manage, she drew the edges of the dress together with one hand, not at all pleased to note that her fingers were not quite steady.

Did not want him, indeed.

His smile widened as he watched her and she was even further chagrined, but she did not wish him to know that. "Is there something I can do for you, Mr.—Lord Sinclair?"

Unexpectedly his expression changed, growing decidedly more gentle, his dark eyes devastatingly intent with concern. "No, but there is something I wish to do. When I told Victoria of our meeting she informed me of your recent loss. It...I realized that you must have been somewhat distraught even before I came upon you yesterday. I thought I should..."

He indicated the black stallion, which she now saw he had tied farther along the fence toward the front of the house. "Well, I was out riding and decided it would only be common courtesy to come by and offer my condolences and apologize for upsetting you. It is the least I could do after giving you such a start."

She looked down at the ground, then back at him, nodding jerkily. His apology was rendered so endearingly, almost as if he was a recalcitrant schoolboy. It would have been nearly impossible to remain aloof, but her reaction to his care was stronger than she would have imagined, for it called forth a glowing warmth inside her. "I...thank you, that is very kind of you. I'm afraid I may have overreacted. I was never actually in any danger. It's just that it has been...so very difficult...." Mary halted, the lump in her throat preventing her from going on.

"And understandably so." He reached down and flipped the gate latch. The next thing she knew Mary was no longer standing alone in the garden. Ian Sinclair seemed to fill the space with the potency of his presence. He was too alive, too compellingly attractive to be real in the midst of this quiet garden. She watched as he moved forward—with the same grace as a tightrope walker she had once seen at a fair—and reached for her hand.

If some mystical fairy godmother had previously appeared and told her this would be happening, that this devastating man would so gently take her earth-stained hand in his, Mary would not have believed it possible. As it was, the event occurring without any hint of warning, her sense of unreality was numbing. She felt as if she was submerged in some thick fluid that hindered thought and speech.

She could only feel.

His hand was large and warm on hers, sparking a tingling current in her icy fingers. His dark eyes studied her with obvious concern as she looked up at him, not able to breathe properly around the tightness that gripped her throat as their glances grazed.

Mary looked down and found herself no more able to control her reactions to the rest of him. The dark brown fabric of his coat was molded perfectly over his wide shoulders and her fingers itched to trace them, to see if they were as hard as they appeared. Her gaze dipped lower, running over a paisley print vest that lay smoothly over a starched white shirt. His dark brown trousers were without even the

slightest unwanted crease on his long legs. Again she realized that Ian Sinclair was indeed the embodiment of her
every girlhood fantasy.

And that was what brought Mary to her senses. She was
not a girl, but a grown woman of twenty-three, long past
the age when most young women married. She was far too
mature to allow a man's physical presence to so overcome
her own natural reticence.

She suddenly became infinitely conscious of her own disheveled state, her faded dress, her tousled hair beneath the
old straw bonnet. A man like Ian Sinclair could not be
serious in his intentions toward her. She was the daughter
of a country vicar, he the son of a peer of the realm. Though
she could not fathom the reason for his interest, she must
not take his obvious concern to heart. It was only her own
vulnerability over her father's death that was confusing her.
Pride made her fight the tears that threatened to spill at this
thought.

Ian stood looking down at Mary Fulton and was surprised at the depth of compassion he felt as he saw the
tears glistening in her golden eyes. He'd not been able to
get her out of his mind since seeing her yesterday, and he'd
convinced himself it was because of his having frightened
her. He had decided that the preoccupation would go away
if he came and apologized, offered his condolences on the
loss of her father.

But as he studied her delicately lovely face now, Ian had
the strange feeling that there was something different about
Mary Fulton. That there was an unnamable force drawing
him to her. His gaze lingered on the pale curve of her cheek
as he watched her fight for control. For some reason her
battle for dignity moved him more than he dared admit to
himself.

He spoke gently. "Is there something I can do?"

She looked at him then, her expression bleak. "No. There is nothing anyone can do. I must simply learn to bear it."

"But you needn't do so alone," he reminded her. "Why do you not go up to Briarwood now? Victoria has told me that she has invited you to come and live with them. They would welcome you at any time."

She was shaking her head even before he finished. "I cannot do that. It would not be right."

Ian raised his hands in surprise. "But what do you mean? Victoria has made her affection for you clear to me. She is eager for your companionship."

Mary glanced up at him, then away, her eyes unseeing as she stared across the yard. "I could not do anything so thoughtless to Victoria and Jedidiah. They have only been married for less than a year and have already helped me more than anyone could hope for. They have a right to spend this time, with the baby coming, together without my problems to concern them." Her gaze flicked to his again and she raised her chin. "I shall seek a position as a governess, or…I don't know. I shall just have to find some suitable employment."

"But they are expecting—"

She halted him there. "Please. I have made up my mind. Victoria is not responsible for me. I wish to find my own way, to feel that I have not taken charity."

He watched her with growing admiration. What courage and pride it must have taken for Mary Fulton to make this decision. Few young women would reject such an overture as Victoria had made to her friend. The offer she had made had clearly come out of love alone, with no expectation of return.

He tried once more to convince Mary. "There is no need

for you to be so self-reliant. There is no harm in allowing
someone who loves you to care for and provide for you."

Still she did not look at him as she answered in a quiet
but steady voice. "We, my father and I, have lived in Carlisle since I was a very small girl. In that time we have
been dependent on the Thorn family's generosity, though
it was not given out of charity in the main. When my father
was the minister he earned his keep. But do you realize
that over the past year he had been able to perform none
of his duties? Victoria has been so kind in allowing us to
stay here. I love her more than I can say, but I cannot allow
her to keep giving so much to me. It would not be right."

He could hear the iron determination in her tone. Something told him that Mary Fulton would do exactly as she
had decided, no matter what anyone else thought best. Her
stubborn independence was a characteristic he could admire
even while he felt a sense of frustration toward her.

Telling himself he had no right to question this young
woman's decisions, Ian still found himself shaking his head
as he admitted, "I admire your will even though I cannot
agree that you have chosen in your own best interest. You
are very brave."

When she looked up at him, her golden eyes were glistening like wet topaz and Ian was hard-pressed to remember
he had no part in her affairs, that he had told Victoria he
had no designs on her friend. Almost as if it were against
her will, Mary whispered, "I do not feel very brave. I simply must make a life of my own somewhere. Staying here
would be too difficult with Father gone." Her voice broke
as he watched her fight to control her emotions. "I cannot
think of what life will be like without him."

One large tear fell from her eyes to glide across the
pearly surface of her cheek. His heart contracted painfully
in his chest. Ian could no more stop himself from reaching

ut to her than he could stop the moon from turning around
e earth.

There beneath the sheltering limbs of the weeping wil-
w, Mary's composure broke and she allowed Ian Sinclair
 draw her close to him. His chest was firm and strong
der her cheek. All her life she had longed for someone
 care for her this way. Her father had loved her, but he
d not been one to hold and comfort her. He would likely
ve spoken to her philosophically of the troubles she was
periencing, told her that the Lord sent the trials of life to
rengthen his flock. But she had loved him.

The tears began to flow in earnest when she felt a large
ndkerchief pressed into her hand. Now there was no stop-
ng the tide as she held the square of soft cotton to her
ce. It was as if she could no longer hold back the pain
at she'd bottled up inside her since her father's death.

Only when her sobs quieted did Ian Sinclair say anything
ore. Gently he patted her back, murmuring, "There, it's
 right. Sometimes a grief is just too big to keep inside.
u walk around feeling like you have it all under control
t it's there, someplace inside that aches just enough to
ep you from ever forgetting."

His voice was deep and comforting next to her ear, but
 the same time she could hear a strange current of pain
 his words. This man had suffered hurts of his own. Re-
zing this left her feeling unsettled and, much as she
shed to deny it, she sensed a change beginning to take
ce inside her—a change she did not quite understand.

Mary knew only that the tingle of awareness that traveled
m her ear to the pit of her stomach was in no way con-
cted to any memory of her father.

She became aware of Ian Sinclair's strong hand on her
ck, felt its warmth through the thin cotton of her dress
h a shiver that had nothing to do with being cold. And

at the same time it seemed he had grown very still, as i
he knew what she was feeling.

With bated breath, Mary glanced up at him from beneat
the thick fringe of her lashes. He was looking at her, hi
dark eyes intent with some emotion she could not name.

When Ian dipped his head and placed his firm but suppl
lips to hers, Mary thought she would surely faint from th
sweet pleasure that rippled through her. Unconsciously sh
tilted her head to allow him better access as his mout
caressed hers.

His arms tightened, pulling her even closer to the lor
length of him, and she gave a start as a foreign hardne
grew against her belly. Her eyes flew open wide and Mar
jerked back in shock.

She looked away from Ian Sinclair, her eyes focusing (
nothing, her hand going up to cover her mouth. How cou
she bring herself to face him after allowing him to kiss h(
after feeling his…? Crimson color stained her face a
neck. She did not even know this man. Whatever wou
her father say about this? What must Ian Sinclair himse
think of her?

She attempted to cover her shame with hauteur. "I thi
it would be best you go now."

He answered, drawing her gaze, though she could gau
nothing of his thoughts by his expressionless eyes nor
cool timbre of his voice. "I am very sorry for what I j
did, but let us not make more of this than there is. Y
were upset and I was comforting you, nothing else."

Mary felt a shaft of rebellion rise up inside her. Who v
he to tell her not to make too much of anything? He h
after all, been the one to kiss *her*. Her nose tilted hi;
"How very supercilious of you, my lord. Am I to und
stand that you always comfort women by kissing them?

that is the case, I very much pity any woman who might find herself attached to you.''

He seemed a bit taken aback, but only for a moment before a gleam of amusement and, dare she think it, admiration lit those dark eyes. ''My, but you are direct, Miss Fulton. To answer your question, I do not always kiss women when I am comforting them, but it has happened once or twice and I've had no complaints.''

She took a deep breath, her hands going to her hips. ''Why, you insufferable beast.''

His gaze slid down, pausing for a moment on her bosom before he looked back at her face. Mary only then recalled that she had unbuttoned the neck of her dress. She knew that if she looked down there would be far more of her showing than she wished. Only by an act of will did she keep herself from doing so. She would not allow him to see that she was embarrassed. Even as the thought swept through her mind, he smiled knowingly and she felt a deep flush of heat move down her throat and over her breasts.

His next words drove all thought of retaining a pose of unconcern from her mind. ''If you keep standing there looking so completely desirable, Miss Fulton, I just might kiss you again.''

Her arms came up to shield her bosom from his view. ''You, my lord Sinclair, are despicable. No wonder they call you 'Lord Sin.' ''

By the way his eyes narrowed and his lean jaw flexed she could see that this had struck a nerve. He spoke with slow deliberation. ''I will thank you not to call me that again.''

''And why should I do as you tell me?''

He took a step closer to her, and Mary took an involuntary step backward. His tone was dangerously controlled. ''Because I have asked you not to do so. If you will not

comply with a polite request—'' he shrugged meaningfully
''—I can take more drastic steps to gain your compliance.''

''Why...you...you... I can't think of anything despicable enough to call you. I'll not stand here for one more moment.'' With that she swung around and stalked away.

Ian watched her with irritation and a surprising amount of amusement and, to his further surprise, a grudging respect. What a little hellion she was. A man just did not know what she might say. Mary Fulton was the complete antithesis of his docile, obedient cousin Barbara. Unexpectedly Victoria's warnings that his father would never approve of a minister's daughter popped into his mind again. How very angry his father would be if he married someone like Mary Fulton, someone who would match and possibly even best the old fellow in a contest of wills.

And how very delicious she had tasted. How very much he would like to sip at those lips again, and even more, to learn if the skin on the curve of breast she had so unwittingly displayed was as smooth as it looked.

An idea was beginning to insinuate itself into his mind. The idea that Mary Fulton would make a very interesting selection as a wife. No. He could not even contemplate such a thing.

Besides, the woman obviously detested him. She had even gone so far as to call him ''Lord Sin'' to his face, something few men would have the temerity to do.

He pushed away the unthinkable notion that continued to prod at his consciousness. He would do well to ride straight back to Briarwood and enjoy the rest of his visit with Victoria and Jedidiah. In a few days he would be returning to London and his life there.

Not even to spite his father could Ian consider any union with that hoyden, no matter that her lips tasted of warm sweet woman and fresh air. Or even that she was delectabl rounded in all the right places despite her delicate form. He started toward his horse, which was still tied waiting for him. Yet he could not keep his gaze from straying to where one of the curtains fluttered at the upstairs window.

So she was watching him. An unconscious smile curved his lips as he rode toward Briarwood.

When the footman arrived at the rectory the next day with an invitation to dine at Briarwood, Mary told herself that she would not go. Never. Not as long as that man was staying there. With polite determination she gave the man her apology—she would not be able to attend dinner.

He bowed and left. Closing the door, she looked down at the card in her hand. With a disdainfully raised chin she promptly dropped the missive into the wastebasket.

She went back into the sitting room where she had been perusing several recent copies of *The Times* and *The Post*. Mary had circled several advertisements. Each was requesting a résumé from young women who would be interested in the post of governess. Sitting down beside the low table, she picked up her pen and continued down the columns. Her stomach churned with nervousness at the thought of what she was doing. Taking such a position would separate her from everything and everyone familiar to her. Determinedly she told herself she was only doing what was right.

Yet not thirty minutes later she found herself back in the front hall holding the invitation to dinner in her hand with a yearning expression on her face. Mary told herself she did so love Victoria and it might not be long before she was gone to make her living elsewhere.

Why should she allow Ian Sinclair to keep her from Victoria? Her friend's companionship was especially precious to her now when she was very likely going away.

Besides, a small voice inside her piped up, he had done

nothing but kiss her. Then apologized for that. Was she, as
he had implied, making too much of a little thing? The man
had made it very clear that he would not be losing any
sleep over the matter.

Yet she could not bring herself to go.

Half an hour later, unable to concentrate on anything,
Mary left the vicarage. A walk would surely clear her mind.
Until recent times, being out amongst the growing things
had always soothed her. Perhaps it would do so today.

But she was not soothed. She could not stop thinking
about the way Ian Sinclair had kissed her and how she had
reacted to that kiss. Why, oh, why did she feel this strange,
unfortunate attraction for the blackguard? Why had she no
more control over her own emotions and feelings?

A lush hawthorn hedge ran the length of the laneway.
She followed it to where it ran past the church that sat
beside the vicarage. Greeted by Matthew Brown as he used
a pair of hedge clippers to trim the new growth, she raised
a hand and smiled. The elderly gentleman had been looking
after the church grounds for as long as she could recall.
But Mary did not stop to chat with him as she usually did.

At the end of the hedge she paused and looked up at the
church. It was a welcoming-looking structure, deceptive in
its simplicity of design. No expense had been spared in the
quality of the stained glass windows that ran the length of
the building, nor in the highly polished woods, beautiful
statuary and tastefully used gilt trim inside.

But it was not to the inside of the church that her
thoughts turned today. It was to the bell tower. The enormous silver bell that pealed so purely every Sunday morning was silent and glistening in the sunlight far above her.

Just looking up at it caused a knot of tension in her
stomach.

It had not always been that way. She had loved that bell tower as a child. She had felt that she could get just a little closer to heaven and thus to her mother by going up there. Yet that had all changed when she was seven and two older boys from the village had discovered her up there alone. They'd teased her and said she was nothing but the lord's daughter's live doll. When she'd replied, haughtily telling them they were only jealous, they'd held her at the very edge of the tower platform, threatening to throw her off if she didn't retract her words. Pride had not allowed her to do so.

Luckily Victoria's father had come along. The boys had been punished, but Mary had not been able to go up into the tower nor to any other high place since. In all the years since that event, Mary had forgotten neither the fear nor the feeling of comfort she'd known as the gentle duke had carried her home. Not until yesterday when Ian Sinclair had taken her into his arms had she known those feelings again.

But she did not want to think of Ian Sinclair.

As she looked up, she felt frustrated and angry with herself for allowing someone else to rob her of the comfort she had known from being in the tower. And now that both her mother and father were gone from her, she was doubly cheated of any comfort she might find there. Why should she let anything, especially something that had happened so very long ago, to keep her from being close to her parents?

Just as she had allowed Ian Sinclair's presence at Briarwood to rob her of Victoria's company. Wasn't she made of sterner stuff?

Pushing her anxiety down with an act of will, Mary entered the church. Before she could change her mind she went quickly to the doorway that led to the tower.

At the bottom of the stairs she stopped. Her breath was

beginning to come more quickly as she looked up at the seemingly endless curve of the circular staircase. Dragging her gaze back, Mary took a deep, calming breath. She would not live in fear.

She closed her eyes, telling herself not to look, not to see how far it was. Taking hold of the bottom of the railing with shaking hands, she kept her eyes closed and put her foot on the first tread. Over and over again with each step upward she told herself not to think of where she was going, to pretend she was only walking up the stairs at home, that there was nothing to be afraid of.

And her determination might have worked, might actually have gotten her to the top. But she did not find out, for her foot caught on the hem of her dress and she stumbled. With a cry of fear she opened her eyes, at the same time clutching frantically at the railing.

Her horrified gaze lit on the floor so far beneath her. Vertigo swept her in sickening waves. Her heart pounding in her chest, Mary held on to the rail in abject desperation. Completely paralyzed by her terror, she could now move neither up nor down. The rail seemed the only stable force in a continually shifting world.

With a sob of self-defeat, she sank down, closing her eyes on the reality of her overwhelming fear. She'd solved nothing, proved nothing to herself.

How long she stayed there she did not know. Time felt as if it had melded to a pinpoint of fear, and paralysis. Forever she would be here frozen in this one moment of terror.

And then through the haze of her anxiety she heard the sound of a voice. It was a deep voice, rich and filled with concern.

Ian—where he had come from she had no idea, nor did she care. "Mary, what is it?"

She could not look up, could not speak, merely shaking her head in anguish. She was past even being ashamed that he should see her this way.

"Mary," he prodded softly. "You must tell me what has happened."

Without lifting her face from the crook of her arm, she whispered, "Too high, this is too high."

The next thing she knew she was being lifted, her hand being pulled from the security of that rail with gentle but unshakable insistence. It seemed the one thing she could do was cling to the only other stable object in her world.

Ian. His arms closed around her even as he pressed her face to his chest. Her own arms found their way around the solid strength of his shoulders and she clutched at him desperately as he started down the steps, the motion making her head spin anew even though she did not look.

Mary tried her very hardest to think of nothing, to make her mind a cloudless blue sky where the fear could not control her. It was not until Ian paused and lowered her to some soft object that she realized they had stopped.

She then heard him move away from her. For a moment Mary simply lay there with her eyes closed, making certain the feelings of vertigo had passed. As indeed they seemed to have done. Her head did not spin, nor her stomach.

At last, telling herself that she was quite safe now, Mary opened her eyes, and saw the cream-colored ceiling of her own sitting room. She saw also a decidedly anxious Ian Sinclair standing over her, his compelling dark eyes troubled.

He reached toward her with a glass in his hand. "Drink this," he told her.

Automatically Mary sat up and took it and drank the

water it contained. She was not entirely surprised to see how badly her hands were shaking, but now that the terror had passed she was beginning to feel a certain amount of embarrassment over what had occurred.

Why, of all people, had it been Ian Sinclair who had found her like that? How indeed had he found her?

Avoiding his gaze, Mary swung her boneless legs over the side of the settee. Still without looking at him, she put the glass on the table with exaggerated care. Taking a deep breath, she spoke, being not at all pleased at the huskiness of her voice. "How did you find me?"

He answered with a sigh. "I had come to the rectory looking for you. The man who was trimming the hedges told me you were in the church."

She glanced up at Ian, unable to keep from seeing the sheer masculine strength of him. In spite of her fear, Mary had felt so safe in those arms. Determinedly she kept her attention focused on the conversation. "Why were you looking for me?"

He scowled. "I was in the foyer when the footman was telling Victoria that you would not come to dine." His brows moved even farther together. "I had the distinct feeling that you had refused because of me. I could not allow you to do so."

Her incredulous reaction to this statement seemed to wash away the lingering traces of anxiety. "You would not allow, sir? How dare you!"

He halted her with a raised hand, shaking his head regretfully. "Mary, I did not mean to insult you. I have misspoken. I simply wanted to talk to you, to make you understand that you have no cause to avoid me. I know how much you must need your friends right now."

Mary could only stare at him, surprised by the seemingly genuine concern in his voice. The moment stretched on an she felt almost as if she was being pulled down into the dark, mysterious depths of his eyes.

Even as she watched, his expression changed. Those eyes became yet deeper, more sultry. Mary's pulse quickened in her veins, though she tried to calm it.

She knew this was wrong, knew with utter certainty that it was mad for her to allow Ian Sinclair to matter to her in any way. He was the son of an earl. Mustering every ounce of her will, she looked away. "I...thank you for what you did for me...in the church."

"What did happen in the church?" he asked, studying her closely. His face was set, making the fact that he refused to be put off quite evident.

She glanced over at him again, forcing herself to remain coolly polite. "I am simply afraid of heights. I had a bad experience in the bell tower as a child. I should not have tried to go up there."

His gaze was compelling. "Why did you, then?"

She wanted to lie, to make up some story that would salvage her pride, but her upbringing would not allow her to do so. Yet neither was she able to resist his will for her to answer. "I...know this must sound terribly silly, but I wanted to be closer to my parents. Before I was held at the edge and threatened with being tossed over by two ill-behaved boys from the village I would often go to the bell tower to speak with my mother. After that I could not go back."

"That is quite understandable," he answered with surprising kindness. "All of us live with the fear of something. And as far as thinking you silly for wanting to be closer to your parents, nothing could be further from the truth. I had my own special place to go in the wood at Sinclair Hall to speak with my mother. She died when I was born."

She nodded, somehow touched by his sharing this with

her. "It does seem as if they can hear you better in certain places, does it not?"

He nodded his own head. "I continued to go there until I was seventeen. That was when I went to live with my grandmother in London, after..." Ian stopped as if he had suddenly realized he was saying more than he wished to, his lean jaw working. "Well, enough of that," he concluded with studied charm. "It was you we were speaking about." In spite of the change of tone, Mary could see the tension in his stiffly held shoulders and neck. She wondered at the depth of unhappiness in him, as she had that day in the garden when he had spoken about the way unresolved hurts can influence one.

Looking at him from the outside, it seemed impossible that anything could so affect this man. He had wealth, social position and an undeniably handsome form and countenance. But each time she caught a glimpse of the man inside she sensed his hurt, and it drew her to him even more. What could possibly cause him such deep loneliness?

He went on, drawing her attention away from her thoughts, his gaze unwavering on hers. "Why today, Mary, when you are already under such constraint because of the loss of your father? Why would you try to overcome this fear now?"

Again she felt compelled to reply. "Today I just..." She looked down at her hands where they lay twisted together in her lap. "I just wanted to be free of my fear. I've never felt so afraid of things in my life as I have of late. I feel so uncertain about what will happen to me, about the decisions I am making." She unconsciously waved a hand over the London papers, which lay where she had left them.

The silence that greeted her admission made her look at him in surprise. Ian had bent forward and was reading the circled advertisements with a fixed expression. He raised his head to meet her gaze, and his lips thinned. "You are *seriously* looking for a domestic position."

Mary was confused at his obvious disapproval. She raised her chin. "I am considering taking a position, yes."

"But why, when there is no need for you to do anything so extreme?"

She stiffened, refusing to look at him again. Mary would not allow him to influence her with those eyes. "I will do as I think best."

His reply was cold. "I see. You may of course do as you will. But may I be so bold as to say that if this is really what you want to do, then it is doubly important for you to be with your friends now. For Victoria's sake as well as your own you should spend some time with her before leaving. I wish you would not stay away from Briarwood simply because I am a guest there."

Mary could think of no reply to this. She rose to her full height, albeit on trembling legs. "I appreciate your concern for me in the matter of Victoria. It is very kind of you. And now I must ask you to leave. There is no further need for you to stay. You have done more than anyone could have asked of you."

He bowed. "As you wish, Miss Fulton. Don't bother to see me out. I am quite capable of finding my way."

Chapter Three

As she heard the front door close behind Ian, Mary unhappily found herself recalling how she had clung to him as he carried her, how she had been more than willing to allow him to find the way for both of them. Mary gave herself a mental shake. She would not think about that. She must stand on her own feet. There was nothing to be gained in relying on this man. Nothing could come of a liaison between them, nothing but ruin for herself.

Yet his words about her last opportunities to be with Victoria kept ringing in her mind. She had not thought about the way her absence would feel to her friend. And it was quite unlike her to ignore the feelings of others. Much of her time was spent ministering to the poor and needy in the village. How could she ever forget to consider her dearest friend?

Should she then not spend what could possibly be her last remaining weeks at Carlisle wisely? To use Ian Sinclair's previous questionable behavior as reason to avoid going to Briarwood seemed unreasonable. He had not tried to take any untoward advantage of her at this meeting. He had been the soul of propriety. It was her own thoughts of him that had been inappropriate.

Should she allow her unacceptable attraction to this man to keep her from her friends? Mary had failed at conquering her fear of going up into the tower. Was she to fail in overcoming her fear of her own attraction to Ian Sinclair?

Before she could allow herself time to reconsider, Mary penned a note and gave one of the Anderson twins, who lived on the other side of the lane, a coin to take it up to the manor house for her.

She then went up to her room at the back of the house. It was a simple chamber, the only furnishings being the bed, a heavy oaken wardrobe, a night table and a chair. But the walls had been painted her favorite shade of pale pink and the counterpane was patterned with tiny red pansies. As she opened the door, the breeze from the open window brushed the ends of the lace curtains across the hardwood floor.

For a moment she paused in the narrow doorway, knowing she would miss this room very much. She had grown up here, conjured her own girlish fantasies of a happy future, a man to love her, children, a comfortable home with a garden, of course.

With a self-deprecating shake of her head she pushed the thoughts aside. None of that was to be, and she'd best get used to it.

With this thought fixed firmly in her mind, Mary went to the wardrobe and took out the one fashionable dress she owned. The rose pink gown with its full hooped skirts and low scooped neckline had been a completely impractical Christmas gift from Victoria. Though she wore the hooped confection only to Briarwood, she was secretly quite pleased to own it. Even a simple vicar's daughter felt the occasional need to look fashionable and attractive.

With an unmistakable flutter in her stomach, Mary alighted from the carriage Victoria had sent for her. She told herself that she was quite overreacting. This night was no different than any other she had spent at Briarwood. An image of Ian Sinclair's sardonic grin came to mind. Determinedly she pushed it away.

The footman opened the door immediately and reached for her wrap as she stepped into the grand foyer. As always, Mary sent a quick glance and prayer of thanks up to the cherub-painted ceiling. As a little girl she had thought those little angels were sent specially by God to look after her and her friend. Even though she now knew it was not true, they being the work of a gifted but mortal artist, Mary could not quite break the habit. And for some reason she had the sense that she needed their protection now as much as ever she had before.

Victoria came down the wide formal staircase at that very moment. She held out her hands. "Mary, I'm so glad you've come."

Mary nodded, taking her outstretched hands and kissing her taller, elegantly gowned and coiffured friend on the cheek. "You are beautiful, Victoria," she said. And it was true. The pregnancy had not detracted from Victoria's loveliness in the least. Her dark hair was shining with good health and her cheeks bore a fresh rosy tint.

Victoria hugged her and led her along the hall to her favorite sitting room. "Jedidiah and Ian are out in the stables admiring the mare Jedidiah bought from Ian for my birthday. Wait until you see her. She'll be a perfect mount after the baby comes. Until then you are more than welcome to ride her. It will be much easier for you to do so, of course, once you finish packing things up at the vicarage and come to us."

So Ian Sinclair had not told them of her decision. For some reason this made Mary feel a grudging gratitude to-

ard him. Obviously he was not one of those aristocrats
or whom gossip was a favorite sport.

But Mary did not wish to think favorably of Ian Sinclair,
or did she wish to discuss her future right now. She knew
Victoria was going to try to convince her to stay. Her kind
nature was one of the reasons Mary loved her. For this one
evening Mary wanted to forget her troubles. Thus she remained silent.

They went into the sitting room and settled themselves
in the pale green settee. Just as she turned to Mary again,
Victoria raised startled brows and placed a hand on her
swollen abdomen. "My, that was the strongest kick yet."

Mary gazed at her friend in awe as she watched the delicate fabric of Victoria's pale lilac gown bulge a moment
later. "Was that the baby?" What must it be like to have
something alive inside you? Mary marveled. To feel your
own child moving?

The ebony-haired woman gave a rueful laugh. "I'm
afraid it was." As if sensing her friend's question, she
asked, "Would you like to feel it?"

Mary's golden eyes widened. "Oh, Victoria, might I?"
At her friend's nod, she said, "I would like nothing better."
Placing her hand over the spot Victoria showed her, Mary
was rewarded a moment later as a firm thump met her palm.
She gave a startled laugh, tears springing to her eyes. "Vic-
toria, it is amazing."

Victoria smiled indulgently as she ran a loving hand over
her stomach, giving away the real emotions inside her even
as she spoke with irony. "You would not think so in the
middle of the night. The little one has even begun to wake
up Jedidiah." A look of loving contentment came into her
face. "But he does not seem to mind. He lights a candle
and talks to baby until it settles back down. Even if it takes
hours. He says he does not wish to miss another moment

Lord Sin

of my confinement, having already lost too much time in his trip to America. Oh, Mary, I am so fortunate to have him love me. I never thought life could be so perfect. Every moment with him is precious, especially when I thought we might never come together."

Mary knew the troubles the couple had faced, though Victoria had fully shared them only after they had been resolved. She was more certain than ever that she was making the right decision in going away. Jedidiah and Victoria deserved to have this time together—alone.

Mary realized she could not tell her friend of her plans. She did not want Victoria to know until it was too late to stop her. Once she had found a position and the arrangements had been made, it would be too late for discussion.

She was saved from having to hide her churning thought by the arrival of the two men. Mary's gaze went directly to Ian Sinclair as if drawn there by some inescapable force. She saw that the tall, dark man was also looking at her. She blushed and glanced away. Goodness, but he was every bit as handsome as she remembered, and more. The midnight blue of his perfectly tailored jacket and trousers full accentuated his height, the width of his shoulders and the narrowness of his hips. The crisp white of his shirt collar made his hair look even darker by contrast.

Her gaze flicked briefly to him again and she saw that he was still studying her, with those onyx dark eyes narrowed. As their gazes clashed for that brief moment he lifted one black brow high.

Heat suffused her. Was he remembering the fact that she had so abruptly asked him to leave her home and was now staring at him like some besotted fool?

Quickly Mary turned her attention to Jedidiah McBride as he said, "Good evening, Mary."

She nodded. "Good evening." Mary was genuinely fond of the American and felt he had been good for her friend.

He then came forward and kissed his wife on the cheek. Victoria was smiling at her tall, golden-haired husband with love. "How is the mare?"

Jedidiah laughed, the corners of his sea green eyes crinkling. "Settling in, but frisky. I think you'll get plenty of excitement out of her when you can ride again. Ian has produced a mare worth every pound of her exorbitant price."

Mary was infinitely aware of Ian Sinclair as he bowed and nodded modestly. Beneath his reticence she could tell he was proud of the horse they were discussing, as a parent might be of a praised child. His obvious fraternal affection for the animal surprised her and Mary realized there were many things about Ian Sinclair that she did not know.

What kind of father would he be, she wondered?

As soon as the thought entered her mind, Mary dismissed it. How Ian Sinclair might parent was not her concern.

Ian felt Mary Fulton's gaze rake him again, but this time he did not look at her. She'd made her feelings quite well known when she'd asked him to leave her house. And in all honesty, Ian could not truly blame her for resenting his interference in her affairs. He had as yet been incapable of coming up with any reasonable explanation for why he was so very interested in what she did with her life. He'd tried to convince himself it was because he knew how much Victoria cared for the other woman, but somehow it did not ring true.

Before Ian could stop it an image of Victoria's horrified face as she had listened to him talk about her friend flooded his mind. He clearly heard the discouraging words she'd said to him about his father's sure disapproval of his wedding a vicar's daughter.

Ian's lips thinned. To even contemplate the notion of marrying a woman simply because his father would be displeased was despicable. It was true that part of his desire to marry Victoria had been brought on by knowing she would greatly irritate the earl. But she had been one of his social class, the daughter of a duke. Mary was not. Not only his father but all of society would frown on such a union.

Unconsciously he found himself studying her again. She was looking quite delectable in a gown of rose satin. The dress was of the latest fashion and showed off her tiny waist above her wide hooped skirt, not to mention a bewitching hint of cleavage. She was without a doubt the most delectable morsel of womanhood he had seen in some time. There was no denying the attraction he felt toward her.

Yet what he had learned of Mary over the past days had taught him that she deserved better than he could offer. From what he'd seen of her, she had a quick mind and a strong spirit that prevented her from bowing to anyone. Ian could not but admire that, for it answered a like place within himself. He had spent most of the years of his adulthood flouting convention. It was what had earned him the appellation of "Lord Sin." But that was all behind him now, and fortunate that, for he might not have been able to resist the temptation to seduce the lovely Miss Fulton despite his assurances to Victoria.

His resistance to his desire was made doubly hard by her own reactions to him. For in spite of her anger toward him, he was not blind to the fact that Mary was not immune to him. Ian had experienced the charms of enough women to know mutual passion when he experienced it. Her response to his kiss, though brief and untutored, had been apparent. Her desire needed only a gentle and sensitive hand to call it to the fore.

Ian drew himself up and forced himself to concentrate on the conversation Jedidiah was having with his wife. He would not allow himself to think of Mary Fulton in any but the most appropriate of terms.

It was all he, with any honor, could do.

He was drawn from his thoughts by the servant who announced that dinner was ready to be served. Ian watched as Jedidiah offered Victoria his arm.

Mary stood and came forward with them. Ian told himself that his recent feelings for this young woman precluded his doing the polite thing and offering his own arm. But as she moved toward him, Mary glanced up from beneath the fringe of those thick dark lashes, her golden eyes uncertain. When she saw that he, too, was looking at her, she raised her head high.

He could not help thinking of the way he had found her that afternoon, quaking with terror on the bell tower steps. She was such a strange mixture of strength and softness, this Mary Fulton.

Without even realizing he was going to do so, Ian held out his arm. "May I?"

She hesitated, and Ian had to make an effort to hold back his annoyance. Why was he so drawn to this woman when she seemed to resent him despite the attraction she had not been able to hide? Could it be because she was the exact opposite of his cousin Barbara, who would never openly disagree with anything he said or did, as Mary was quite willing to do?

Finally she nodded, then reached out to place her hand on his arm. As she did so he was struck by a jolt of piercingly sweet awareness that moved from her to him. A delicately floral scent rose from her hair and Ian found himself wanting to take it down from the loose bun she wore, to see the glorious golden mass draped across her shoulders and naked...

He stopped in his tracks. What in God's name was he thinking here?

Mary looked up at him in question. "My lord."

He could see that Victoria had already reached the doorway that led to the dining room across the foyer. He had indeed been lost in thought. Knowing that Mary would be completely shocked to know what he had been thinking, Ian did not meet her puzzled gaze. "I beg your pardon. I fear I was not attending."

He made no comment on her suddenly closed expression. Releasing his arm and stepping away from him, she said, "I will leave you to your thoughts, then."

Ian nearly reached out to stop her, but he drew his hand back. He told himself that it was much better for both of them if she was annoyed with him. Hadn't he promised Victoria that he would not seduce her? Hadn't he promised himself?

As he had told himself before, Mary deserved better than that.

Victoria was watching him closely as he entered the elegantly furnished chamber behind the others. She raised her dark brows high as she glanced pointedly from Ian to Mary, who was already seated.

He quirked a brow in return, wondering how she would react to the turn of his thoughts.

Jedidiah interrupted this silent exchange. "Please be seated, Ian." He indicated the empty chair directly across from the vicar's daughter.

As he took his designated place, she flicked a glance toward him and Ian saw again that Mary was not immune to the strange attraction that existed between them. Her cheeks darkened to rose and her breath came more quickly from her slightly parted lips.

Victoria interrupted his contemplation, and though her tone was teasing, he could not but hear the chiding in it. "I hope, Ian, that you have not forgotten the promise you made to me."

He drew himself up, meeting her gaze directly. "I have not forgotten."

With a relaxed expression, which Ian knew belied the keen mind he possessed, Jedidiah asked, "What promise is that, my dear?"

Victoria turned to her husband with a smile. Ian knew she would not risk hurting Mary's feelings by making her reprimand of Ian known. "That answer you will not get from me, love. No more than you would tell me why Ian had come to visit before you had given me the mare. Torture would not have it from me."

For a moment Jedidiah said nothing, letting the heat of his gaze fall upon his now blushing wife. "I think we both know that you have your breaking point, my dear."

She flushed even more deeply and Ian looked away. What must it be like to be so close to another human being? Ian had never known.

Ian's gaze flicked to Mary. Though she flushed, she faced him squarely. He felt a wave of admiration.

As a notion he had been trying to reject for days set itself even more firmly in his consciousness, Ian's lips pressed to a line of determination. He would not seduce her.

But there was another way to have her. Was he not a man, free to do as he pleased? The act he was contemplating might very well garner enough disapproval from his father to see Ian disinherited, but he would not be ruled by the older man.

In the next breath Ian halted himself. What was he thinking? He could not marry this woman simply because he desired her, nor even because it would be the perfect act of rebellion toward his father. Had he not decided that he would no longer live up to his reputation as "Lord Sin"?

Mary Fulton was a young woman who had shown that she took much pride in ordering her own life. How could he not understand this sentiment when it was a right he valued so highly himself?

As a knock sounded on the front door, Mary looked up from the box of books she was packing. Still holding a volume in her hand, she went to answer it.

Deliberately she avoided looking at the letters waiting on the hall table to be posted. She had crossed a bridge by writing them, as each was an offer of her services for the position of governess. She had every hope that at least one reply would be favorable. Her problem lay in the fact that she had been assaulted by doubts as to the wisdom of her decision as soon as the missives were sealed. The idea of facing the unknown future had become suddenly over-whelming, but she knew she must do so, must have the courage to leave behind the only life she knew and strike out on her own.

She told herself they must be sent this very afternoon. Before she could change her mind. Why she was having such doubts she could not say, other than realizing that Ian Sinclair's face kept intruding on her thoughts. But that, she knew, was completely ridiculous. Lord Sinclair had nothing to do with her future. Even if she had wished to accept Victoria's generosity and live at Briarwood, she would not be seeing him. Sinclair was only visiting her friends and would soon be off to do…well…whatever a single man of his wealth and undeniable attractiveness did.

And beyond that he was not in the least interested in her. He had hardly spoken to her last eve at Briarwood.

It was true that Ian had kissed her the second time they'd met, but he had done nothing of the sort since. Oh, there had been times since when he looked at her...when she had thought... Obviously it was nothing more than her overactive imagination at work.

Realizing this only seemed to bring her a discomfort that she somehow feared to examine too closely. With these dismaying thoughts in mind, it was with little enthusiasm that she opened the front door.

To her utter amazement, Ian Sinclair himself stood on the stoop. A sudden nervous chill gripped her and she hesitated before speaking. Seeing him was especially unnerving considering her recent preoccupation with him. Telling herself she was being foolish, she opened the portal and said, with much more breathlessness than she would have hoped, "Good afternoon, Lord Sinclair. Is there something I can do for you?"

To her surprise he seemed somewhat hesitant, even agitated himself, turning his black silk hat in his hands. He stopped, his dark gaze meeting hers as his brows arched upward. "I...may I come in?"

She stepped back, realizing that she must seem somewhat foolish standing there gawking at him like some besotted schoolgirl. Determinedly Mary told herself she was not attracted to him, in spite of his undeniable good looks. She was simply overreacting to the fact that he had twice been there when she needed someone.

She would remain calm. Yet her heartbeat quickened as he stepped across the threshold to stand so near that she could see the fine shadow of mustache above his mobile lips. Would it, she wondered, feel rough if he should kiss her?

Mary's eyes flew wide with horror at her own thoughts. She certainly did not want Ian Sinclair to kiss her.

To her relief he did not appear to notice her agitation and continued to seem somewhat nervous as his gaze slid away from her to graze the tabletop. Then he appeared to frown with displeasure as his eyes alighted on the letters she had been thinking of only moments before. "Your requests for employment?"

She nodded, too surprised by his reaction to resent the prying question. "Yes."

His frown deepened for a moment before he straightened his already wide shoulders and took a deep breath. For some reason she had the distinct impression that he had come to a decision about something. His next words served only to confuse her further. "I have come to ask you a question."

"Oh," she replied, not at all certain as to what she should say. Studying him closely for a moment and judging him no less nervous, she began to think this was no ordinary question. What of import could Ian Sinclair have to say to her? Did he have some position in mind for her?

Ian continued to look down at her in the long, narrow hallway, and Mary glanced away, knowing that the light from the window that sat high in the door illuminated her own face much more clearly than his. In spite of the dim lighting she was very much aware of his being too tall and imposing for such humble surroundings.

Trying to still her sudden trembling, Mary reached out with her free hand. "May I take your hat?" She halted as she saw the traces of dust on her white fingers. With a self-conscious laugh, she wiped the hand on her apron, then indicated the book in her other hand. "I have been packing my father's books. I will be taking some of my favorites with me."

He glanced at the volume. "You read Greek?"

She looked down at the book. "Why...I...yes, father was a great scholar. He taught me everything he would have taught a son." She held her head high, knowing how most men disapproved of the practice of educating females and referred to them as bluestockings.

But Ian did not seem the least bit shocked or disapproving of her revelation as she reached out again and he gave her the silk hat. He said only, "I see."

How very nice for him, she thought with a trace of irony, for she certainly did not see. She hoped he came to the point soon, for she was growing more uncertain by the moment. With deliberate care Mary placed the hat on the rack along the wall and turned back to him.

"Would you care for some refreshment? I could make some tea."

He shook his head, his intense onyx eyes meeting hers again. "No, thank you." Once more she had the impression that this was no ordinary social call. She told herself she was imagining things.

In spite of her self-assurances, it was with growing unease that Mary motioned toward the open door of the study. The chamber was in a state of upheaval because she had been packing the books, but it was one of the few rooms that did not have dust covers over the furnishings. "Won't you come in and sit down?"

The answer that accompanied his polite nod only served to make her more unsure. "Yes, I think that would probably be best." She did her utmost not to worry herself over this last strange remark as they sat on the two matched navy blue wing chairs near the window.

With studied poise Mary folded her hands in her lap and waited for Ian Sinclair to begin. He did so after only a moment. "Miss Fulton, I realize that what I am about to say may seem somewhat precipitous to you, especially as we have only known one another for a very short time.''

She frowned, wondering where on earth this could be leading. ''Go on.''

He surprised her by reaching over and taking her cold hand in his warm one. Mary was too amazed to either comment or draw her hand away and she listened to him continue with only half her mind, as the touch of his warm skin made her own tingle with awareness. ''I know that the last months have been very difficult for you and that you find yourself in somewhat distressed circumstances. I want you to know that if the situation were otherwise I would not speak so hastily.'' His dark eyes were full of meaningful intent as she looked up into them, feeling herself drawn closer to him, though she made no physical movement.

She shook her head, her eyes wide. ''I cannot think what you might be talking about, sir.''

He squared his wide shoulders. ''I am asking, Miss Mary Fulton, if you would do me the honor of becoming my wife.''

The words had the effect of creating a thick haze of shock and confusion around her. She looked down at her hand in his, feeling as if it was miles from herself.

How—why was this happening? It could not be real. Ian Sinclair, eminently eligible bachelor and heir to an earldom, could not be asking her to marry him.

For heaven's sake, they did not even like one another. A sudden vivid memory of the kiss they had shared only days before in her own backyard insinuated itself into her mind. Even through the fog of her confusion Mary felt a tug in her lower belly.

She shook her head to drive the thought away. That kiss had not occurred because Ian liked her. He'd said himself that he was only trying to comfort her.

Was that possibly why he was doing this, she asked herself, because he felt sorry for her? Her sense of confusion cleared slightly at the thought. She looked at him closely and found that he was still watching her with that same intent expression he'd worn since entering the vicarage.

Forcing herself to speak calmly, she asked, "Why...why are you doing this? Is it because you feel—" she sat up straighter, forcing herself to go on "—sorry for me?"

The immediate and forceful tone of his reply made her believe him when he said, "No, absolutely not. I have no need to marry any woman out of sympathy."

A frown marred her brow as she wondered why, then, he *would* wish to marry her. "Tell me what has brought this about? I don't understand."

He leaned close to her, his tone intimate. "Don't you, Mary? You are a beautiful woman. I also think you would make just the kind of bride I have been searching for."

The words caused her heart to beat more quickly, even as she realized that for a moment there was something odd in his tone, almost a hint of bitterness. But as he went on looking at her that way she told herself she had imagined it.

As if sensing her uncertainty, Ian's fingers tightened on hers. "I desire you, Mary. I should think that even an innocent like you would know that."

A thrill of honeyed warmth suffused her even as she answered, "I don't know. I don't think it would be..." There had been times when he had looked at her as if...well, she'd been too afraid of her own reactions to really allow herself to understand what that look meant.

There was no denying it any longer. Mary had been attracted to Ian from the first moment she saw him riding across the moors toward her. Even the discovery that he was the infamous "Lord Sin" had not dulled her interest, no matter how she had tried to tell herself he was not an honorable man. And was he not disproving that even now, by asking her to marry him? It was completely honorable, this proposal he offered her. And did she not in her most secret heart rejoice that such a bold and handsome man would want her, Mary Fulton?

Still, a small voice inside her cried out in indecision. She shook her head and repeated, "I do not know."

He halted her with a finger on her lips. "Don't think, Mary. Just say yes."

When he saw her continued hesitation he went on, his tone rich and persuasive. "Or do you prefer the future you have told me of? Do you wish to spend your life in another woman's house, looking after her children? Is that what you really want for yourself, Mary? You were meant for so much more than that."

She pulled her hand away from the persuasive warmth of his touch and rubbed her forehead. "This is too sudden, too unexpected. I don't know how to answer you. I had not even thought."

To her utter amazement he stood and drew her, completely unresisting in her surprise, into his strong arms. His mouth, warm and pliant, descended to hers.

A current of heat swept her as his lips played over hers. It became a torrent as his mouth encouraged hers to open and his tongue flicked over hers. Mary moaned as the sensations pooled in her belly. Her breasts swelled against the hardness of his chest and she pressed herself closer to him to relieve their aching.

When Ian drew back, she looked up at him, her eyes heavy with languor. He spoke huskily. "Can you say you have not thought of that, Mary, of the way it feels when we touch, kiss? I have thought of little else since I first kissed you."

His frankness and her own innate honesty brought forth a truthful, albeit befuddled reply. "I have thought of it."

Ian placed his hand on the back of her head and drew her to him, kissing her again with a mastery that left her head swimming, her blood pounding in her veins. Weakly she leaned against him.

He felt so strong, so very solid in an unknown world. This was her opportunity to have her own home, a husband...perhaps children. Mary had always been strong, looked after those around her, behaved with a maturity far beyond her years. Was this her invitation to throw caution and common sense to the four winds?

His breath was hot on her forehead. "Say you will marry me." Again his mouth found hers. Those mobile lips sucked and played at her own until she could barely stand the depth of heat that washed through her and left her knees weak. He drew back only slightly, punctuating each word he uttered with a kiss. "Say...yes...Mary."

Unable to think of anything save being in his arms, of being held and kissed by this man, Mary nodded. When she replied, she was a little surprised by her own breathlessness, her own capitulation. "Yes, yes. I will marry you."

Chapter Four

Mary looked at herself in the gilt-edged mirror, hardly able to believe that the woman staring back at her was herself. Her hair had been arranged in an elaborate coiffure, with only a few soft tendrils left free to curl about her nape and temples. The eyes that stared back at her were luminous with an excitement she did not wish to acknowledge.

She was marrying Ian, but not because she loved him. Oh, no, Mary did not have any illusions as to that. She was doing it because it might be her one opportunity to have a home, a family. It also helped that Ian seemed to accept her as she was, to not fault her for her outspoken ways or education. The few men of her station whom she had chanced to meet had felt quite differently.

Behind her she heard Victoria say, "You may go now, Betty." She heard the door close behind the maid only a moment later.

Mary looked at her friend's reflection. Her eyes met Victoria's troubled ones as she asked, "Mary, are you sure this is what you want?"

Frowning, Mary turned to face her. "Yes. Why do you ask? I know it has been sudden, but I would think you would be pleased for me."

Victoria took Mary's ice-cold fingers in hers. "Yes, but *Ian*. Why him? That is the part I don't understand."

Rising, Mary began to pace the luxurious bedchamber where she had spent the previous night. The soft white carpet muffled her agitated footsteps. "Victoria, why would you be so surprised that I have agreed to this wedding? You even thought of marrying the man yourself." She looked closely at her friend. "You said that in spite of his reputation as 'Lord Sin,' Ian..." She paused, the name feeling strange and intimate on her lips. "You felt he was a good man, that he would have made a decent husband."

Victoria's gaze was beseeching. "But I was in love with Jedidiah."

Mary threw up her hands in exasperation. "Well, that has cleared up any confusion I might have over what you are trying to say to me."

Victoria laughed, though there was a sad quality to it. "That is the most like yourself you have sounded in weeks. You have been through so much I fear you have not been yourself. I wish you would think about that. You could at least consider waiting for a time before you marry. You are in mourning."

"As far as mourning is concerned, I know my father would not wish for me to wait because of any societal dictum. He felt that death is only a passing over into another, better place."

Victoria nodded. "After having been taught by your father I know that what you say is true. He would have been appalled at your doing that. It is your own state of loss that I am speaking of. You should wait until you are more yourself, Mary."

"But I do not want to wait." How could Mary explain that a part of her knew that what she was doing was completely out of character, that if she allowed herself to stop—

to think—she might not go through with the marriage? All her life Mary had done what she must, cared for her father, pushed her dreams to the back of her consciousness with unwavering determination.

Then Ian had come and offered her a shoulder to cry on. He had offered the prospect of security, not just monetarily—which was of little import to Mary—but in an emotional sense. In the few days she had known him, Ian had been irritating and male and quite maddening, but he had also held her when she needed someone. No one else had really ever done that, had ever seen past the wall of strength she presented to know how much she wanted that.

How could they, when she herself had not even realized it?

But Victoria did not know any of this and she continued with her train of thought. "Mary, I do not wish to badger you, but I hope you will reconsider. I'm sure Ian would understand if you decided to postpone the wedding. It is true that I considered marrying Ian, but there was a major difference in our situations. I was in love with Jedidiah at the time. You are not in love with someone else. What if you fall in love with Ian? He is charming and handsome, and although I am married, I would be blind not to see that there is a strange compelling sensuality about him. Can you tell me you do not see that?"

Mary could not stop the blush that rose to her hairline. She chose not to reply to the question, though she had indeed noticed that quality. Instead she shrugged and said, "I am still unsure as to what all this means. Would it be so very dreadful if I came to care for the man I am about to make my husband?"

Coming quickly across the floor, Victoria took Mary's hands in hers again, forcing her to meet her troubled gaze. "Ian will make you love him, Mary, without even trying.

But I do not know if he can truly love you or anyone else in return. There is pain inside him that can only be healed if he wishes it to be.''

Mary closed her eyes for a moment. She had sensed that there was something hurting in Ian, had been moved by his pain, even drawn to him. Surely it was not so deep it would prevent him from someday caring for her. Mary was not so foolish that she believed Ian was in love with her. He had never said any such thing, though he had been ready enough to admit his desire. Could that not become something more?

Remembering the heat of her responses to him, Mary could not help thinking that such passion might very well develop into a deeper bond, given time. How little Victoria understood that this might well be Mary's one opportunity to experience all of the things that she, as a happily married woman, took for granted.

When she opened her eyes once more her expression was determined. "Victoria, I know you love me. I also know you are concerned for my happiness. But let me be frank. We are both aware that I have no prospects. Before Ian offered for me I had come to the conclusion that I must seek a position as a governess. Had in fact written the letters of application.''

As Victoria opened her mouth in shock, Mary halted her by going on, "I know you want me to live here with you. But I cannot do that. I need to find my own life. I want a child, a home. Ian has given me that chance. I know he does not love me, nor do I love him, but I believe he has some degree of respect for me. I wish above all else that you might find it in your heart to allow me to take this chance, to make this decision for myself.''

For a long moment Victoria said nothing, then she smiled tremulously and there were tears in her eyes as she squeezed Mary's fingers gently. "Very well. I love you and must only pray that this marriage brings you nothing but happiness."

Mary reached out and put her arms around the taller woman. "Thank you, dear friend."

Victoria returned the embrace. "You have been with me through so much—the trials of girlhood, the loss of my family, the lonely years until I found Jedidiah. I shall miss you, Mary."

"And I you."

They embraced once more, then Victoria drew back, her expression serious. "Just remember that you have a home here with us any time you want it."

As she answered, Mary realized that she was unlikely to ever take up the offer, but she understood that it was given in the spirit of love. "I shall remember. And I want you to know it means more to me than I could ever say."

A soft knocking sounded at the door, before it was opened by a beaming Betty. "The carriage is ready to take you to the church, my lady, Miss Mary."

The ceremony was to take place at the little country church where her father had taken the pulpit every Sunday for most of her twenty-three years. Mary knew it was what he would want.

The previous night was the last she would spend at Carlisle for what would surely be a very long time. Ian had asked that they begin the journey to his home and she had agreed. Sinclair Hall—Mary felt the smooth, hard feel of the name in her mind. It was Ian's home, and soon to be her own.

With one last check of the ivory silk gown Victoria had insisted on giving her as a wedding present, Mary straightened her slender shoulders. "Shall we go?" Again she was shocked that the woman staring back at her was herself

The ivory silk skirt was decorated with hundreds of tiny rosebuds, as were the scooped neckline and the lace edging on the elbow-length sleeves. Mary felt like some princess in a fairy tale, and that only served to make what was happening even more unreal.

Ian's gaze moved over Mary's face as he leaned back against the dark blue velvet of the carriage seat. They had been traveling for some time, with only the most civil of exchanges, and he could see Mary's nervous agitation growing with each mile that passed.

She glanced toward him, then back out the window, and as she spoke he was infinitely aware of her fingers pleating the lush amber velvet fabric of her traveling gown, which had also been a gift from Victoria. "How many days until we arrive at Sinclair Hall?"

He answered evenly, "We should get there some time on the third day."

She nodded, her fingers now fidgeting with her lace-edged collar. His gaze was then drawn slightly lower to the provocative curve of her breast. Ian had to force himself to attend her words as she said, "I am most eager to meet your family. Tell me about them."

Ian stiffened. He did not want to talk about his family—not his father, nor Barbara. Yet he felt somewhat uncomfortable with taking Mary without some warning into what might very well be an unpleasant situation. "There is very little to tell. My cousin Barbara and my father are the only family living at Sinclair Hall. I...things are...difficult between myself and my father. He has long wanted me to marry."

She spoke up quickly. "Then perhaps things will be better between you now."

Ian smiled tightly. "Perhaps. But do not be surprised if

he does not seem over pleased with the matter in the beginning. Father does, very much, like to be in control of everything.''

Mary looked at him directly then, her gaze holding his own, a hopeful anticipation written clearly on her lovely features. "We shall weather any opposition together, and surely in the end he shall see that all is well."

He could not find it in his heart to apprise her of just how bad the situation might become. What if she was correct? What if his father did come around? Nodding jerkily, Ian replied earnestly, "If he will allow himself to see you as I do, Mary, he will be hard-pressed to find any fault with you."

She blushed and turned back to her contemplation of the passing scene. Thinking to forestall any more questions about his family for the moment, Ian closed his eyes and rested his head on the back of the seat.

Perhaps because he had discussed his father with Mary, the reality of what he had done was finally beginning to set in. He was married to Mary Fulton—Sinclair now—and on his way home to Sinclair Hall. He did not question his immediate need to take her home, to see what his father would say to him, to discover if Malcolm Sinclair would accept his son's selection of a bride. He only hoped that his wife's optimistic view of the future would indeed occur. Reason made him doubt the possibility greatly.

Mary's ready agreement to his suggestion that they begin the journey to Sinclair Hall immediately after the ceremony had surprised him. He did not have to open his eyes to know that she remained pale with nervousness, which he could understand. It was that discernible level of dubious excitement that somehow made him uncomfortable.

All through the two days leading up to the ceremony and even during it, Ian had not let himself think of anything other than that he had made the right decision. This had been made easier by the fact that there was much to do in a short time. He'd procured a special license, answered Victoria and Jedidiah's surprised queries with aplomb, made travel arrangements and hired men to see to the packing and moving of the rest of Mary's belongings.

He'd given no more than a passing thought to what his friends and acquaintances in London might say concerning his marriage. When they did learn of it they would surely be surprised, but would quickly immerse themselves in the many amusements that occupied their waking hours. He expected no more, having chosen his companions carefully. He wanted no one to ask unpleasant questions about his private life, and wanted no involvement in anyone else's personal concerns.

He was free to do as he pleased, had no need to consider what anyone might think but himself.

Yet now, after seeing that shy expectation on Mary's lovely face, in her golden eyes, doubt was beginning to cloud his mind. He had rushed into this marriage, but at the time it had seemed like the only thing to do. She was planning to leave Carlisle.

For the first time Ian wondered if he'd made a mistake in convincing her to marry him so quickly. Had he done the right thing for her? Could she be happy at Sinclair Hall?

It was true that he did not love Mary, but then, he had not professed to do so. When he had proposed, Ian had talked of nothing but his desire for her. And neither had she declared any such feelings for him. He had found the very sort of wife he was looking for, someone intelligent, beautiful and outspoken. She had clearly been in need of a more stable future, and marrying him had answered that need. The arrangement seemed almost predestined.

Still, her bridal nervousness and anticipation left him

feeling strangely uncomfortable, as if his skin did not quite fit him right. And Ian could not figure out why.

He pushed the doubts away. Of course he had done the right thing. He should be glad that she was not indifferent to him. Her responses to his kisses should encourage him that the approaching night would be a memorable one.

As for any worry over what his father would say, he was not going to allow it to rule him. Mary was his choice, and the elder Sinclair would simply have to accept that fact.

The carriage was casting a long, dark gray shadow over the road, hedges and trees they passed by the time they halted before the entrance of a well-kept inn. With polite consideration Ian helped Mary to alight from the carriage. He could not help giving her hand a gentle squeeze as he took it, for her trembling was readily apparent. She glanced up at him with marked uncertainty in those wide golden eyes. For a moment their gazes held, and Ian felt an unexpected tightening in his lower stomach. God, but she was beautiful with her perfect cream skin and delicate features, like some porcelain figure come to life.

Carefully he controlled his reaction to her beauty. For some reason he felt that any display of his own desire would only make her more agitated. Ian gave what he hoped was a reassuring smile. "I'm sure you'll find this inn comfortable."

Her lips curved upward hesitantly before she hurriedly looked away. "I have no doubt you are right, my…Ian."

Her hesitation in saying his name was not lost on him. Yet Ian did feel somewhat surprised to realize how much her doing so pleased him. His name, which he had never thought that much about, was soft and piercingly sweet as it passed her lips.

Once inside the inn, Ian signed the register. He then ascertained that there was a private dining chamber. "We shall require its use," he said to the obsequious innkeeper.

The man nodded his gray head. "Beggin' yer pardon, me lord, but that will cost ye extra. That is, if ye don't mind, me lord."

Ian shrugged and took a gold coin from his pocket. "That should take care of everything."

The man nodded again, this time with an even more ingratiating smile. "It will, me lord, it will. And don't hesitate to call on Jeremy Tucker for anything else ye might need."

Ian said, "I will be down to discuss the menu with you shortly. My wife and I will be expecting the very best you have to offer."

The man cast respectful brown eyes on Mary only briefly. "As you say, me lord. Only the best. My wife is a fine cook, me lord, of that you can be certain."

The corpulent innkeeper continued to be most deferential as he showed them up to a comfortably appointed chamber. Looking around himself, Ian was fairly certain it was the best he had to offer. The bed was huge and of dark-stained oak. A passably clean carpet covered most of the wood floor, and the night table, wardrobe and chairs were in good repair.

The man bowed himself from the room with a reminder that they should let him know of anything else they might require. Ian nodded in response, but his attention was focused on Mary where she stood in the center of the room, very obviously trying not to look at the bed.

Her agitation was now as tangible as the smoke from a wet fire. Her slender hands quivered as she smoothed the lush amber velvet of her skirt. Yet in spite of that he could not help noticing how lovely she was. The last dying rays of the sun slanted through the window behind her, outlining

Mary in a delicate gold, making her somehow seem to glow from within. She was all gold and warm and inviting, and she was his wife. When she raised one hand to press it against the hollow of her throat, his gaze was drawn to the perfect line of her profile, the sweetly erotic curve of her lips, the swell of her bosom beneath the close-fitting fabric of her jacket.

God, how beguiling she was, and so completely unaware of her own power. Even as he took a step toward her, her clouded glance flicked toward him and away. Ian halted himself in his tracks. He was not some green boy. He'd never had to take any woman by force or coercion. He would not start now with Mary. He would woo her gently. When they came together, she, too, would be desirous of the event.

Who could blame her for being apprehensive, he asked himself—this was her wedding night. The truth of it was that they were virtual strangers, in spite of the attraction that had drawn them together, in spite of the fact that they were now married. He spoke softly. "If you are agreeable, I will leave you to refresh yourself before dinner. As I told the landlord, we will have it in the private dining room downstairs."

She glanced at him shyly. "That would be fine."

He moved closer to her, wanting to reach out, to reassure her. But he stopped himself, though he was mere inches from doing so. "Would you like me to come and fetch you, or would you prefer to meet me below?"

Some of her anxiety seemed to be leaving her, for Mary's eyes met his as she answered, "Oh, don't bother to come and fetch me. I will find my way to you."

His own relaxed manner had obviously communicated itself to her. He could not help wondering if she had expected him to take her then and there. But he said nothing of his thoughts. "Very well, then. I will see you in, say, half an hour."

She nodded with a shy smile. "Yes. Half an hour." To his utter amazement, she blushed, then closed her eyes and tilted her face to his.

For a moment surprise held him immobile as he realized she awaited his kiss. Ian then chided himself for being surprised. She was just doing what she thought a dutiful wife should do.

She had no way of knowing how hard a battle he had just fought with his lust. His appreciative gaze ran over her delicate features before that sweetly curved pink mouth drew all his attention. Slowly, Ian leaned close to her and pressed his lips to hers. He had meant it to be no more than a brief touch, but she was so soft and he had been trying to quell his desire for her from the first moment they met. When she responded by sighing and tilting her head to allow him better access to her mouth, he lost the tenuous hold on his resistance. The change from dubious maiden to receptive woman was more than he could resist. His arms closed around his wife and the kiss deepened.

Mary pressed herself more fully to him, fitting her fragile form to his with a heady enthusiasm. Her arms moved up to his shoulders and her fingers tangled in the dark hair at his neck. Ian shivered as a tingle of awareness traveled from her cool fingers to the base of his spine.

"Ian." She sighed as his mouth left hers to press hot kisses to her throat.

He closed his eyes, dragging his will to the fore with a strength he had not known he possessed. Not now, not yet, not like this with the innkeeper expecting them downstairs. For some reason he could not understand, Ian did not want to subject Mary to the type of gossip that might engender.

He told himself it was because she was his wife, the

future Lady Sinclair. He owed her more due than the other women he had so lightly met in inns and even less respectable places, knowing full well what the proprietors would suspect and having not a care about it.

He held her close against him, his touch gentling as he focused on slowing the wild beating of his heart. "I will go downstairs now, Mary." He smiled into her passion-darkened eyes. "You will not be long?"

She flushed and offered a shy smile of her own. "I will not be long."

With one last kiss to the top of her golden head, he left the chamber. He was not completely surprised to see the slight shaking of his own hands as he made his way down the stairs. Again he willed himself to calm. In a matter of hours, no more, she would be his.

First Ian discussed the particulars of the meal with the innkeeper. He was pleased to learn they had some fresh oysters and mussels on hand, as well as a fairly respectable bottle of wine. This was, after all, to be Mary's wedding feast and he wanted it to be pleasant for her.

The next thing Ian did was go to the common room and order himself a mug of stout ale. He had need of something strong and bracing. It had been all he could do not to kiss Mary until she was weak and willing to have him throw her down on that bed and make love to her. And he had known that she would do so, for despite her maidenly reticence she had responded with gratifying heat the moment they kissed, had in fact done so from the first time he kissed her.

But he was glad that he had shown restraint. Mary was his wife, the woman he would take home to meet his father.

With that thought came a sardonic smile as he thought of how surprised the elder Sinclair would be to learn his son had married, and married the daughter of a country minister. It was unlikely that Malcolm Sinclair would be able to appreciate the ready sensuality and brightness of mind that made Mary attractive to his son. These thoughts were followed by more of that strange nagging doubt that had prodded the back of his mind in the carriage. Ian ordered another stout.

Mary washed her hands and face, took her nightclothes from her traveling valise and waited for the appointed time. She checked her pocket watch repeatedly, but the more often she did so, the more slowly the minutes seemed to drag by.

In the carriage she had been somewhat disheartened by Ian's warnings about his father's possible reaction to their marriage. She had felt the difference in their social status would prevent Ian from ever offering for her. But he had, so it could not be as great a barrier as she had thought. Surely, she told herself, Ian was only preparing her for the worst. It was not what he expected to occur. Else why would he take her to Sinclair Hall?

She had wanted to ask more questions, especially about his cousin Barbara, whom she hoped might become her friend. But Ian seemed to have fallen asleep. Mary had wished she could do the same, but it was beyond her powers of will. Over and over again she heard the minister pronounce them husband and wife.

Wife—heavens above. She, Mary Fulton, was someone's wife. Ian Sinclair's wife. As she realized it anew, an odd tingling of excitement raced through her.

All through the time of nursing her father in his illness she'd thought that any hope of such a thing happening to her was past. Who would want to marry her, penniless and without even her father's position as vicar to recommend her?

But someone had. Someone handsome, and strong, and intelligent, and—she blushed deeply—virile. She did not know what blessed state of grace had brought her such fortune, but Mary refused to question it.

If Ian's father was not immediately accepting of the union, he would surely come around. Even Victoria's warnings were pushed so far away that she could hear no more than a whisper.

Ian had married her, and she was going to do her utmost to be a good wife to him. And though she hardly dared contemplate such a thing, there was a remote hope that someday he might actually come to have some regard for her.

When the appointed time finally arrived, Mary stood and ran a hand over her velvet skirt as a wave of overwhelming uncertainty gripped her. She sat back down. The minutes had seemed to crawl, and now she was nervous about going down to Ian—her husband.

Telling herself to stop behaving like a foolish child, Mary stood again and went to the door with determined purpose. She had been enough of a fool earlier as they entered this chamber, when she'd been so nervous about what might happen now that she and Ian were actually man and wife. There was nothing to be so anxious about. Ian had been nothing but courteous and kind to her since making his proposal. He would continue to be so.

Chapter Five

Mary's husband was waiting in the inn's private dining room when she arrived. It was a small chamber with a low ceiling and was probably somewhat shabby in strong light, but the glow from the fire and the few candles that had been set on the table and mantel cast a warm, intimate glow on the dark-colored furnishings and hardwood floor.

Ian stood as she entered. "Mary, I see you've found your way."

She hesitated near the doorway. "I...yes, the innkeeper's wife directed me."

Ian indicated the table that had been set for two. "Are you ready to have the meal brought in, or would you prefer to wait?"

She replied quickly, "Now would be fine." Although she was too nervous for real hunger to have set in, it did occur to her that Ian might not feel the same. It had been many hours since they had eaten.

Ian went to the mantel and rang a small silver bell. A moment later a portly woman with a tidy iron gray bun entered carrying a heavily laden tray. Without looking directly at either of them, she set out the meal, then turned to face them with a quick curtsy. "Will there be anything else, m'lord?"

"Not at the moment," Ian told her in a voice that to Mary sounded somewhat distracted. "If we require anything more I shall ring for you."

The woman curtsied again, then left, though Mary barely took note of her exit as she wondered at Ian's distant tone. She looked to his strongly handsome features for an answer and found little to assist her. He did not look at her, but at the fire, and surely it did seem as if something was bothering him, if his intense concentration was any indication.

Mary drew herself up, pushing down her reluctance to question him. She was no callow girl. This man was her *husband.* Unfortunately the word caused more agitation instead of lessening it, but she forced that agitation down. "Is something troubling you...Ian?"

He looked at her then, as if suddenly recalling her presence, visibly collecting his thoughts. "No, nothing is troubling me. I was simply thinking of tomorrow's journey."

She looked at her hands, his talk of tomorrow sending all other thoughts fleeing from her mind. By tomorrow everything would be different. By then she would be Ian's wife in the full sense of the word. Again Mary was assaulted by that strange sense of anticipation, which served only to make her feel even more shy. For it must surely be somewhat unmaidenly for her to be looking forward to what was to come.

She was grateful for the fact that Ian seemed unaware of her feelings as he indicated the laden table. "Shall we?" he asked.

Mary looked more closely at the fare provided. There was fresh bread, a shellfish soup of some sort, roast quail and strawberries with cream.

Taking her place, Mary searched desperately for a suitable topic of conversation, anything to take her wayward mind from the memory of the kiss they had shared only a short time ago in the chamber where they would soon spend their wedding night.

As he poured her a glass of wine she said, "I do hope that the journey does not take us any longer than you have indicated. The cuttings I brought from the garden at Carlisle will need watering. I would not wish for anything to happen to them, because they are taken from the roses my mother brought with her when she arrived at the parsonage."

Ian smiled politely as he began to eat the delectable-looking meal. "There is no reason to believe we will not arrive on schedule, but in the event that we are delayed I will do whatever is required to make you content."

She smiled shyly in return. "Thank you. Those roses mean a great deal to me. I hope that my daughter can some-day take cuttings from them for her own home."

Giving her an inscrutable look, Ian then turned his attention to his plate, seeming uncomfortable with her mention of a child. Mary flushed, feeling she had gone too far in mentioning children, especially with the wedding night still ahead of her. The silence stretched on, but she was far too embarrassed to be the one to break it as she pushed the food around on her plate with her fork.

Unexpectedly he spoke, drawing her gaze to his face. "Do you, Mary, remember your mother?"

She shook her head, wondering at his abrupt change of topic even as she replied, "No, not really. Nothing more than impressions of warmth and the scent of roses, gentle-ness."

He went on, his voice sounding distant, leaving her with the impression that he might have forgotten her presence. "I don't even recall that much. My mother died giving birth to me. I've often wondered if my father...well, he might have been a different person if that had not happened." He looked at her then and shrugged. "Might have reacted differently to...many things."

"What things?" she ventured gently.

He seemed totally unaware of her as he answered. "My brother's death. Though who could blame Father for mourning his loss? He was...well, Malcolm—fleeter of foot, quicker of wit, more outgoing and giving than anyone I have ever known. His death left a void that could never be filled by anyone."

When he spoke of his brother, she couldn't mistake the deep pain in Ian. Clearly the ghost of Malcolm continued to haunt this strangely enigmatic man who was now her husband. Mary found it hard to believe that anyone could be more handsome or charmingly virile than the man sitting across from her. He was simply recalling his brother with the hero-worship a younger boy might feel for a loving and strong sibling.

Ian went on, his lips tight with regret, "Who, really, could find it in their heart to fault my father for hating the sight of the very one he holds responsible for taking what meant the most to him?"

Mary blanched at his pain. She had not felt she had a right to ask him about any of this before. But now she was Ian's wife. Did that not give her some right, even obligation, to know about the things that tormented him so?

Yet it was with uncharacteristic caution that she said, "Ian, I do not understand what you are saying. Do you believe your father blames you for his death?"

He stiffened, his eyes clouded as he looked at her. Yet to her surprise he did answer. "Do I believe he blames me for Malcolm's death? In a word, yes."

"But why? Can you not tell me what happened?"

He was silent for a long time, gazing into the flame of

the lit candle. Finally he said, "I can see nothing to be gained by talking to you of what happened. It is long over and best forgotten. Suffice it to say that there was an accident. As a result of that accident I was unconscious for two days. When I awoke, certain assumptions had already been made. My explanation of the events was not asked for then, and I feel it is far too late to give it now."

"But, Ian, if I knew, if there is something your father should know that would make things better between you…"

His face grew hard and cold as he cut her off. "It was an accident and that is all I will say. It is not something I am willing to discuss with you or…anyone else, either now or in the future."

She stiffened, stung that he would be so abrupt. As she rose she tried not to allow him to see the hurt his words had caused. "Very well, then, I will not trouble you by asking about it again. If you don't mind, I am feeling somewhat tired now. I believe I will go to my room."

Ian stood, too, clearly struggling with some dark emotion. "Mary, forgive me. You simply do not understand. There are some things that cannot be discussed. They evoke memories I prefer to put behind me and forget."

She nodded without looking at him. "As you wish." She tried to tell herself that it did not matter, that she really had no right to press him about anything. But inside a stinging bruise remained. Although she was newly wed, it did not seem to her that there should be very many things that a husband and wife would keep from one another. Ian seemed to have many secrets.

How well did it bode for the future of their marriage if such matters were already coming between them?

When Ian moved around the table to stand before her, effectively blocking her intended exit, Mary could not stop herself from looking up into his beckoning gaze. His expression was now soft, reasoning. "Mary, I am sorry for having hurt you. I have no desire to upset you over something that is long dead in all minds but two. It is a subject which is completely unworthy of your tender consideration."

She found herself lost in those dark pools, which were surrounded by a fringe of thick black lashes that only served to make them more compelling. She could not prevent herself from saying the words that rose up in answer to his. "I care what makes you unhappy, Ian. Your troubles are mine."

He took her hand and drew it to his chest. "You are such a mix of gentleness and strength. I never know what you are going to say, Mary, and find myself on guard lest you cut too close to the quick of a matter I wish to keep undisturbed. Yet the softness of your heart tempers every perceived wound. You are worthy of only the very best in return. Why ever did you agree to marry me?"

She felt her heart lurch in her chest. Might he actually be coming to care for her? She could hardly credit that such a thing could be true. But the hope of it made her blood sing, nonetheless. She replied without thinking, unknowingly giving away more than she wished to. "Because I needed someone, Ian, someone I could look after, who would look after me in return. I ask you about these things because I want to understand, to be a part of your life, your family."

Ian looked at Mary. He heard the lonely yearning in her words, saw the light of longing in her eyes and realized what had been prodding at the back of his mind this whole day. She was going to be hurt here. Now he knew why he could not bring himself to discuss his family with her, and the deep state of unrest that existed between himself and his father. How could he talk to Mary about his family when he knew that their reaction to his marriage was not likely to be positive, would in fact probably be the exact opposite? It was highly unlikely that she would be readily accepted as a member of the family.

He now could no longer deny that he had wanted to test his father, to see if Malcolm would accept him and his choice. What a ridiculous notion that had been. The conversation he and Mary had had concerning his brother's death was a vivid reminder of just how judgmental the earl could be. He would not respect Ian's decision to wed Mary any more than he had ever respected any of his choices.

Ian knew he had been wrong, so very wrong, to marry her.

What he had just said to her was true. She did deserve the very best. And he was not it. He realized that he must set her free. They must get an annulment. Then he would see that she was settled somewhere with a comfortable income of her own. It was the only way he could rectify this situation. Mary's independent streak had been part of what had drawn him to her from the beginning.

Ian ignored the unexpected stab of regret he felt at knowing that her future would best be built away from him. He told himself that his discomfort was caused by the shame he was experiencing at realizing he had misled her.

He tried not to think about how beautiful she was, nor of the gentle sweetness of her scent, nor of the warmth in her amber eyes.

Drawing her hand away from his chest with deliberate care, he said, "Let us go up to our room, Mary. There is something I must tell you."

Her lashes fluttered down and he saw by the wash of color along the delicate lines of her cheeks that she was blushing. He gave her hand a gentle squeeze as he realized what she must be thinking. He had no intention of taking her now, no matter how much disappointment he might feel about not fulfilling the promise of passion between them.

Her voice seemed huskier when she replied, "Would you be so good as to give me a few moments before you come up?"

Ian nodded quickly. It would give him some time to put his thoughts into words that Mary, hopefully, would understand.

When he reached their room some fifteen minutes later, he knocked and waited for her reply. She called out in a voice he could barely hear. Ian entered, then carefully closed the door as he prepared to tell Mary what he had come to say.

As his gaze found her, he hesitated.

Mary stood looking out the window into the darkness and made no move to indicate that she had heard him. But he knew she had. What made him pause was the fact that she was no longer dressed in the gown of amber velvet. She was now wearing a diaphanous robe of white, and if his eyes did not play pranks on him, very little beneath. For he could just make out the creamy line of her slender legs and hips. Her gold-streaked hair tumbled down her back in rippling waves that seemed to steal every bit of warmth the candlelight had to offer. It was a scene to strike passion in the blood of any man, and Ian had had little reason to deny that part of himself since he was a boy.

Yet he knew he must do so now. For Mary's good, he ignored the pull of need in his lower belly.

In his determination to tell her the truth and set her free, he'd not thought that she might ready herself for bed—their marriage bed. He could not prevent his wayward gaze from straying to that object, and found the covers turned down invitingly.

Deliberately Ian took a deep breath. He'd not considered the fact that to see this matter accomplished he would have to overcome his own desire for her. But that was just what he would do, he reminded himself firmly.

He knew he was doing the right thing in telling her he wanted to end their brief marriage. Yet he felt he must be careful to make Mary understand it was through no fault of hers. Still, the thought of sending her away tugged painfully at his chest.

The slender line of her back and the proud tilt of her head held his gaze as he moved to stand behind her. As he came to a halt, Mary turned unexpectedly to face him. Her eyes were closed and her head tilted, her thick hair falling back over her shoulders to expose the full curves of her breasts, which were visible above the low neckline of her garments. Ian could not deny the ripple of desire that swept through him at her loveliness. His heated gaze was drawn upward as if by divine guidance as those lush pink lips pursed.

Good heavens, she wanted him to kiss her. A fierce rush of heat streaked through him and tightened his loins. He could not move, could not speak lest he lose the tight hold he had on his desire for her. Since the first time he had seen her walking the moors alone, Ian had wanted this woman, had imagined himself buried deeply within her willing body.

When he did not move she opened those heavily lashed golden eyes and looked up at him. Her expression of hesitant encouragement made his belly quiver. When she reached out and put her delicate hand over his and spoke his name, "Ian," and said with soft but unmistakable urging, "There is no need to hold back any longer. I am not afraid to be your wife," he was lost. He told himself he could not shame her by rejecting her tentative advances, that Mary was speaking out of her own need and he could not deny her desire or his own.

His arms closed around her and he drew her slim form close to his. She sighed and melted into him, all soft and inviting woman—his woman, his wife.

Mary pressed herself closer to the hard length of Ian's body. The very fact that he was holding her like this seemed so unreal that she felt she must surely be caught in some dream. She reminded herself that it was true—the very real singing of her blood was evidence of it. The hard contours of his chest beneath her fingers was even further proof.

During the few minutes she had spent readying herself for her wedding night, Mary had thought about their conversation downstairs. Ian had been very abrupt in telling her he would not discuss his problems with her. Yet he had apologized so sweetly. Was that not a sign that he was coming to have some regard for her?

Slowly her sense of anticipation had returned as she'd wondered with both nervousness and curiosity what the coming night would bring. Would she feel again the same sensations she had when he'd kissed her?

Yet when she had heard her husband come in, known that the moment of discovery had arrived, she'd been overcome with shyness. Only when Ian had come to her had she been able to act on the feelings inside her, telling herself she must show that she was prepared to be his wife in every way.

His avid response now swept away the nervousness brought on by lack of experience. When his lips softened above hers, pulling and sucking delicately at her own, she found her own mouth responding.

He muttered softly in encouragement, "Oh, yes, my Mary. You learn so quickly."

A shiver of pleasure coursed down her spine at the husky sensuousness of his words and tone. She rose to place her arms around his neck, pressing herself more fully to him. "Ian," she breathed.

"Mmm." Ian sighed, running his hands down her back, his long fingers tracing the delicate length with slow deliberation. She shivered from the delightful tingling his touch engendered. When he reached her hips he held her to him firmly, his fingers molding her gentle curves with just the right mixture of strength and care. She was made fully aware of his arousal on her lower belly. Mary gasped as a heavy fluid warmth swelled up from between her thighs in response to his hardness.

Never changing that same sweet pressure, he traced up her back until he reached her shoulders. He leaned away, his eyes dark as onyx as he ran his heavily lidded gaze over her. The heat from his gaze made her so weak Mary had to close her eyes to keep from swooning.

When she felt him tug gently at the ribbon that held her robe closed, her lids flew open and she looked down, overcome with sudden shyness. Her surprised glance took in the fact that Ian's quick fingers had made effortless work of that barrier, for she now had only the sheer fabric of her night rail to guard her from that scorching gaze. Her nipples hardened even as she watched, and Mary blushed to the tips of her toes, looking down at the floor in embarrassment.

In the next moment she felt a gentle hand on her chin, lifting her face tenderly but inexorably until she met Ian's eyes. "Never be ashamed of your reactions to my look, my touch, my kisses. They please me. You please me, Mary Sinclair."

For a long moment her gaze was held by Ian's as his eyes seemed to draw the very soul from her. He made her feel beautiful, desirable, wanted, as if she was the only woman in all the world. Not breaking that contact, Mary shrugged her robe from her shoulders and stepped back to let it fall to the floor. She then leaned toward him and pressed her lips to his, unable to give voice to the things his words made her feel.

Ian swung her up into his arms and carried her toward the bed. Gently he laid her down, bending over her to nuzzle her throat. Mary's head fell backward, allowing him better access as she sighed with pleasure. She closed her eyes, opening them only when his lips left her skin.

Briefly he leaned back and shrugged out of his coat, then his cream lawn shirt. Mary's gaze fell on his masculine chest with its smattering of dark hair. He was beautiful and so very male. She continued to be overcome with this uncharacteristic silence.

All she could do was hold out her arms, and sigh with pleasure when Ian came back to her. She felt his hot mouth dip lower to brush the upper curves of her breasts, and trembled with anticipation. When he flicked his tongue against one turgid nipple she gasped and reached for him. Then somehow her breasts were bare and he found the naked tip. She held him against her, completely overwhelmed by the tug of hot longing that raced through her body to her stomach.

His hand closed around her other breast and she felt the tip harden even more against his palm as another wave of heat swept through her. Gently he stroked it with his thumb while he continued to suckle the other. The longing inside her moved lower, settling in that secret place between her thighs. She felt a dampness growing there, a softening, though the rest of her seemed to become more tense with each caress.

A strange sort of heightened expectation had gripped her,

as if her body knew something that she herself did not. The band of tension around her chest tightened further as he then laid a hand over her quivering stomach.

His fingers dipped lower, tracing delicately through the tangle of curls that hid the now aching core of her.

He stroked her inner thighs and she quivered, her body heating even more fiercely at every caress. Ian replaced his hand with his lips and she cried out, her fingers tangling in his hair. His hair slid pleasantly along the delicate flesh, adding to the sensations engendered by his warm lips.

When his mouth moved higher and pressed against the moist core of her, Mary sobbed his name, her hips rearing. "Ian, oh, Ian."

And then as he began to ply her there with the velvet raspiness of his tongue she knew no more of where Ian left off and Mary began. His body had become part of hers, his caresses sending her spiraling ever upward toward some goal she could not name. And then she stiffened as the ascent broke and she dissolved into rippling waves of pleasure that washed over and through her in an all-encompassing flood of ecstasy.

As she slowly came back to a realization of herself, Mary discovered that Ian was holding her close against him. Gently he stroked her hair.

She sighed and opened her eyes to find him looking down at her. To her surprise, Mary was neither embarrassed nor discomfited by what had occurred, for there was nothing but tender consideration in his dark eyes.

He reached out to touch her face. "So very lovely with the light of fulfillment in your eyes. Just as I knew you would be."

She blushed, but tried to express the emotions inside her nonetheless. "Ian, you have made me feel so... I did not know it would be..."

He hushed her with a finger on her lips, his eyes knowing. "It is far from done, sweet. I have only warmed your body for what is to come."

Her eyes grew wide. "Do you mean there is more? But how can I bear it?"

He leaned over to kiss her lips. "I shall show you."

And as the kiss deepened, Mary realized to her great amazement and delight that she felt that heat in her belly begin to grow anew.

In moments she was weak and breathless with passion, ready for that moment of release that had come to her before with such intensity. When Ian rose up above her, his own breath coming more quickly, his eyes dark with need, Mary instinctively opened her legs to receive him.

Somewhere she had gained the vague notion that there would be pain in this act. But he slipped into her body with barely a hint of discomfort.

He held himself still above her, the effort it was costing him to hold back making the perspiration bead on his upper lip. "Are you all right?"

Mary raised her head to kiss him. "Completely, Ian. Do not hold yourself back from me."

Then he was moving inside her, and soon Mary found the rhythm of this primeval dance. It seemed only moments later that she was exploding again, dazzled by the brilliance of the pleasure bursting inside her. At nearly the same instant she felt Ian stiffen above her and heard his own gasp of release.

Mary opened her eyes as he sagged forward, keeping his weight on his hands. She wanted to wrap her arms around him and pull him down upon her own bare breasts, but he rolled to the side.

Next time she would tell him she wanted to hold him,

Mary promised herself. She and Ian were married, and he would always be there to care for and pleasure her.

She sighed as he pulled her close against him, her head settling on Ian's shoulder. His heart beat strongly beneath her cheek and his breath was still coming quickly. He reached down and drew her leg up across his own thighs, stroking her tender skin gently.

Her fingers curled in the surprisingly silky hair at the base of his neck. This small act seemed somehow even more intimate than the one they had just shared. During their lovemaking she had felt driven by some primitive force inside her.

Now with his dark hair clinging to her own fingers did Mary realize that she was truly Ian's wife. She had the right to touch him.

The knowledge brought a strange, pleasurable ache to her chest. With that sweet ache warming her from the inside out, Mary's eyes closed and she knew no more.

Chapter Six

When Mary awoke the next morning, Ian was not in her bed, but the memory of his lovemaking and how she had reacted to it was heartrendingly vivid. Though she did feel a certain shyness about what they had done together and about seeing him again, she also felt a sense of eagerness that she could not deny. The thought of being with him, of having the right to touch him, of having him touch her for the rest of their lives together was overwhelming.

Mary was just tying her bonnet under her chin when there was a knock at the door. She swung around with a flutter of her heart. "Ian?"

His deep voice answered her breathless query. "Mary, may I come in?"

She wondered at his formality, but called out shyly, "Please do."

The door opened and Ian stood hesitantly on the threshold. "The innkeeper has laid out breakfast in the small dining room, if you are ready." There was a certain reserve in his tone that gave her a brief niggling of unease.

Mary looked at her husband more closely, but could not define exactly what was troubling her. His dark eyes regarded her levelly in return, yet she could not disregard the feeling that something was wrong. She could not stop herself from asking, "Is something the matter, Ian? Have I done something to displease you?"

He grimaced and glanced down, then back at her, and when he did his expression was earnest. "No, you have done nothing wrong, Mary. I am simply preoccupied with the journey to Sinclair Hall. Forgive me if I have given you the wrong impression. I find absolutely no fault in you." He rubbed a hand over his nape.

Mary watched him for a moment, her eyes drawn to the base of his neck by his action. Last night she had felt no compunction about putting her hands there and running her fingers through the baby-fine hair. A blush stole over her cheeks as she recalled the other things passion had driven her to do.

She dropped her gaze, hoping to hide her flush. It now seemed nearly impossible that they had been so intimate only hours ago. Ian stood so stiffly across the room, and she felt so shy.

Was it always so when people had shared such a night? Mary had no basis for comparison, and she certainly was not going to query Ian. One thing she did know was that standing here feeling awkward with one another was not going to change anything. She spoke without looking at him. "I can accompany you down now."

He replied politely, drawing her gaze to his face. "I will have your baggage loaded. Then we can be on our way when you are ready."

His words and expression should have reassured her, but for some unexplainable reason they did not. Perhaps, she told herself as she followed him from the chamber, he was more concerned about the journey than she had previously thought. Then again, it might be their coming arrival at their destination that was troubling him, not the traveling.

He had revealed just enough about his relationship with
his father to tell her that. Mary resolved to let the matter
drop for the time being.

For the next two days they traveled east from Carlisle,
away from the only life she could remember. Ian was polite, and he told her something of the fishing community
he had grown up in on the opposite side of England. But
he did not touch her again.

He was attentive to her needs, making sure she was comfortable and well looked after at each stop along the road.
He simply took two rooms, one for himself and one for
her. Perhaps, she thought, he was being mindful of her.

Ian had told her Sinclair Hall lay along the coast in Lin-
colnshire, thus she was not surprised to smell the sharp tang
of salt in the air as they neared their destination. Other than
that, she knew very little of her new home and was anxious
to see it.

Ian talked of the village a little, but he made it clear that
his memories were, for the most part, just that—memories.
He had left home to live with his grandmother in London
when he was seventeen. Though Mary had the distinct impression that this was connected to his brother's death and
his subsequent estrangement from his father, he did not say
so.

Mary wanted to ask, but did not. Instead she said, "I
will be very happy to meet the people of your community.
I have always enjoyed attending to the needs of those in
my father's parish. I'm sure such work will be doubly fulfilling now that I am your...wife." She smiled hesitantly.
"I am looking forward to our arrival."

Ian watched her for a long, long moment. "Mary, there
is something I believe you should know before we arrive
at Sinclair Hall."

She nodded, wondering at his odd demeanor. "Yes."

"It is about my cousin Barbara." At her puzzled frown he rushed on. "My father has...had the mistaken impression that I would someday marry her."

Mary felt as if she'd been hit by a cold gust of wind. "Heavens, Ian. And what was her understanding of this matter? Did *she* believe you would marry her?"

He reassured her quickly and with absolute sincerity. "No, I gave her no indication that I would." His lips tightened. "It is my father who will be angry at having his plans thwarted. Barbara cannot be mistaken in that she is a cousin to me and nothing more."

His certainty reassured Mary somewhat, and his disclosure about his father's plans helped to explain some of Ian's obvious agitation. If their own relationship had been less formal, Mary would have questioned her husband further, but in an uncharacteristic show of reticence, she remained silent. The past few days had passed in a blur, and Mary felt numb with all the emotions that had tugged her this way and that.

She could only hope that once they reached Sinclair Hall and settled in, they would get to know one another better. Mary felt that Ian's decision to take her to Sinclair Hall rather than London was surely a sign that he was ready to settle down, that he had given up being "Lord Sin." Surely that would help his father to see that the marriage was not a mistake.

They traveled on quietly for a time. Ian had told her that he planned to stop at an inn along the way, yet as evening drew near he had changed his mind.

When he asked Mary if she would have any objection to their going on, she looked at him with a puzzled frown. "I thought you said we would be stopping for the night so we might arrive in the daylight."

Ian did not meet her gaze. "It is not yet late, and we are quite close now. Under the circumstances it seems foolish to sleep at an inn."

"I have no objection if you think it is best," Mary told him. She tried not to let her disappointment show in her voice. She had wanted to make as good an impression as she could. Now she would arrive tired and coated in travel dust.

She need not have worried, for Ian did not appear to notice her reluctance. He opened the window and called to the driver to hasten his pace.

Mary looked at her husband closely, but he did not meet her gaze. Soon the light in the carriage became too dim to make out his features and he did not light the lantern. Instead Ian leaned back against the seat with his eyes closed and she thought he must have gone to sleep.

Mary closed her own eyes, but she was unable to rest. She could not stop wondering what the greeting at Sinclair Hall might be.

Soon that worry was replaced by other even more disturbing thoughts. The carriage lurched as they drove over a rut, and Ian's knee brushed hers. Abruptly her mind was flooded with memories of the night she had spent in her husband's arms. Even now she felt tingling warmth in her thighs at the mere thought of how he had touched her, kissed her, held her. Never in her wildest imaginings had Mary Fulton ever thought a man would do those things to her.

She and Ian were married, and he had the right to do all of those things to her. It was their duty as man and wife to produce children. For that she was secretly very glad indeed.

Soon they would reach their new home, and their new life together would start. Certainly it seemed there might be problems, but they were overshadowed by the fact that never again would Mary feel alone. She would have Ian and a family to call her own.

Ian was not sleeping. It was all he could do to sit across from the woman he called wife and not take her right there in the intimate darkness of the carriage. The brush of her leg against his had served only to fan the flames of desire that grew with every moment they spent together.

Yet he would not allow himself to unleash his passions.

He had wronged Mary, dreadfully, in what he had already done to her. He had no right to slake his seemly boundless lust on her. For that was exactly how he felt. He had thought of her—the taste, feel and scent of her—unceasingly since the night they'd made love. Their coming together had been more than he would ever have thought possible.

Even now the tugging at his loins caused a wave of self-castigation. He'd had no right to touch her, but the moment she'd so sweetly offered herself to him, Ian had been lost.

His weakness had forever ruined his plans to set her free. Her talk of her eagerness to start her new life had only added to the guilt he felt. He had known he must tell her of his father's plans for himself and Barbara. He could not allow Mary to go into this with no warning whatsoever.

The only thing Ian could do to assuage his guilt even a little was to live by his determination not to use her again. That much he owed Mary. It was true she was strong as he had thought, but she was also vulnerable, and lonely.

Thus he'd done his utmost to set aside his desire, treat her with the respect she was due in the past two days. The task had not grown easier with time. In fact, quite the opposite had occurred, and Ian felt as if he would surely lose this tight rein on his control if she looked into his eyes with her own wide with concern for him one more time.

For years he had wanted someone to care for him, to treat him with some regard for his feelings. Her genuine solicitude as he had talked of his brother's death had shown him that Mary was a woman who held a deep care for others.

That was why he had not stopped for the night. He could see her uncertainty and vulnerability, as he had on the night he'd made love to her. Ian was afraid he would not be able to resist her or himself.

The carriage lurched again, and as once more her leg brushed against his, Ian started, pulling away. He opened his lids, searching desperately for something to distract him from the heat that touch engendered, opened his lids and met his wife's glowing gaze. Mary's golden eyes shone like two limpid pools of liquid gold, even in the dimness. He found himself unable to turn away.

Softly she whispered, "Ian, what is it? What is wrong? Have I done something?" He could hear the hurt in her voice, though it was obvious she was trying to hide it.

Ian knew he could not remain silent. Never had he wished to hurt her. "Mary, there is something I must explain, if you are to understand."

Her confusion was apparent, but she nodded. "Go on."

He looked away from her, hoping he could somehow make his position clear without causing her further pain. "I have for many years led a…less than exemplary life." He heard the bitterness in his own voice and tried to curb it. "You know that I have been called 'Lord Sin' by enemy and friend alike. I fear the appellation was justified."

He faced her then earnestly. "I have told you that I am done with that. I wish to start anew."

"Yes, but what…?"

He held up his hand to forestall her. "Please, what I am about to say is very difficult. I have had...well...numerous romantic experiences."

She interrupted him then, her voice barely audible. "I see, and you find me less than satisfactory in this area."

Ian did not have to see her blush to know it was there. He rushed in to dissuade her from this thinking. "On the contrary. You are most pleasing to me, Mary Sinclair." Still she did not meet his gaze, and he went on, "You must believe that if nothing else. What I am trying to say is that being with you was more than I would have imagined or hoped for."

She did meet his eyes then, her own more luminous than before. He went on. "You are so very special, Mary, that I want our joining to reflect that. I do not wish to use you for nothing more than physical gratification. I want to treat you with the honor you deserve. You are my wife, but before we continue on with a physical relationship I would like to show you that you mean much more to me than the other women I have known."

Ian continued to watch her face, and though he felt she was listening, he did not think she fully understood what he was trying to impart. How could she, he asked himself with a trace of bitterness. Mary did not know the whole truth—that he had used her.

That was the one thing he could not tell her. He could not bear to see the pain and hatred she would surely feel if she learned of it. For reasons he could not even begin to fathom, the idea that she would come to hate him brought a knot of pain to his belly.

Though he could not tell her of his less-than-honorable motives for marrying her, Ian knew without having to be told that Mary would not wish him to touch her if the truth was known to her. Thus he must do what was right even if it meant denying himself the thing he most wanted, to hold her in his arms. He concluded gently, "I hope you can see that I mean to show you only the utmost respect in this and all matters."

She nodded stiffly, looking down at her hands. "If that is what you intend, how can I be other than honored?"

Though she said the words, the frown marring Mary's smooth brow told him she was as confused as before, if not more so. Ian could think of nothing more to say. He was living in a hell of his own making, with no idea of how to resolve the situation.

He leaned back against the seat and closed his eyes once more. They would go on to Sinclair Hall. He had set this farce in motion. Ian would face his father—and his own actions.

When they slowed some hours later and turned sharply to the right, Ian sat up. He cast a quick glance at Mary and saw the perturbation on her face. Guilt stabbed him afresh as he reassured her, "We are nearly there."

Her only reply was a nod, but she held her head high. Ian was aware of a wave of admiration for her courage.

Mary pushed down the nervousness that rose inside her in nauseating waves. This was her new home and she would begin with fortitude, as she meant to go on.

Yet the task of doing so was not made easy by Ian's revelation to her. She was still not completely sure she understood what he had been saying. It did seem as if he had said that, out of respect for her, he did not wish to have a physical relationship with her.

Mary had hardly known what to reply to this. It was so very unexpected. Rather than being pleased that he felt differently about her than the other women he had been with, Mary was left with a sensation of confusion and a nagging impression that something was not quite right. For the past hours she had tried without success to determine the cause of this unease.

She had no more time to contemplate the matter now, for the carriage was stopping. Ian alighted first and turned to take her hand. She inhaled a deep, calming breath, then let it out slowly before stepping from the vehicle and looking up at Sinclair Hall for the very first time. It was quite dark and she had only an impression of immense size before the door opened and a tall, very slim man dressed in black came out onto the stoop, holding a glowing candelabra high. He peered toward them as Ian led her forward, the light making his features appear gaunt and mysterious in the darkness.

As they ascended the steps, Ian's hand riding low on her back, he said, "Good evening, Winslow."

The man frowned and held the light higher still. "Master Ian."

"Yes."

The man's watery gaze swept Mary before he said, "Welcome home, sir. We weren't expecting you."

Ian answered cryptically, "No, I know you weren't. Is my father at home?"

"Yes, sir, he is." Again the man looked to Mary, and still Ian said nothing as to who she might be. Mary was certain he wished to first tell his father of their marriage.

Without giving any of his thoughts away, Ian said, "Take me to him. Would you then please ask Mrs. Morgan to see that my room and the adjoining one are readied for the night."

"As you wish, my lord." The servant cast another quick glance toward Mary but still said nothing. Obviously in this household the help were not on familiar terms with the family.

They were led down a darkened hallway to a door. The servant knocked gently, then opened it. From her position behind her husband Mary saw that the chamber was a sitting room, decorated in dark colors and illuminated by the light of several lanterns. It appeared to be occupied by two people, an older man and a dark-haired woman.

As the man looked up and saw Ian, he came forward. She had an impression of height, squared shoulders and dark eyes as he said, "Ian!" There was both astonishment and something else Mary felt might be guarded pleasure in his tone.

But as her husband continued to stand there without smiling, the other man's expression changed, hardened. His craggy gray brows rose in question. "What a surprise to see you, Ian. You haven't deigned to grace Sinclair Hall with your presence for quite some time now."

Mary felt her husband stiffen. "Father, it is good to see you, as well." His voice held a mocking quality that could not be lost on the elder Sinclair.

Malcolm Sinclair faltered for a moment, then continued toward them. It was only when Ian reached behind himself and drew Mary closer to his side that the older man seemed to notice her. His eyes raked her coolly, but she refused to be unnerved by that gaze.

Ian smiled with forced amenity. "Father, I would like you to meet Mary—my wife."

The elder Sinclair halted, his shocked gaze going back to his son. "Your wife?"

Ian's smile widened, and Mary felt a decided sense of unrest as she looked at her husband. He seemed to be enjoying his father's obvious perturbation far too much for her liking. Though she did have to admit that the elder Sinclair was being somewhat unpleasant, she had seen that glimmer of happiness in his eyes when he'd first seen Ian, no matter how he tried to hide it.

The older man frowned then, staring at his son with an expression that Mary could not even begin to read. He was a tall man, and still as straight of carriage and flat bellied as his son. But his dark hair was laced with gray, as were his brows, and his voice held a slightly rougher quality than the rich deepness of Ian's. He seemed almost angry, but there again was that hint of melancholy in his eyes. It drew an unexpected wave of sympathy from Mary.

It was only when an incredulous female voice drew her attention that Mary was able to wrench her gaze from Ian's father. "Your wife, Ian? What do you mean, your wife?"

Her gaze alighted on a narrow-faced woman in a dark blue gown as she came around the end of the settee. Her dark hair was arranged in a tight bun at the nape of her neck and her dark eyes held shock and what appeared to be betrayal. Mary realized this must be Ian's cousin Barbara. But what might have brought a reaction of betrayal Mary could not imagine. She knew the earl had wished for Ian to marry his cousin, but her husband had assured her that the woman in question had no such expectation that a marriage would occur. Her reaction now made Mary think Ian had been quite mistaken.

Mary looked to Ian and saw that he seemed not to be aware of his cousin. His attention was all on his father.

Malcolm Sinclair moved toward his son again, his stance tall and proud. "When did this marriage take place? When I last saw you in London only three weeks ago you made no mention of it or the lady."

"Mary and I were married three days ago."

"I see."

Mary was not oblivious to the fact that Ian had not bothered to answer his father's other statement.

Well, Mary told herself, nothing was stopping her from making a reply. She had no intention of remaining silent while they spoke of her as if she was not even present. Calmly she said, "Ian and I have not known one another long, sir, but I am sure we will do quite well together."

Malcolm Sinclair looked at her then, his gaze assessing. "So the girl has a tongue of her own."

"I do, indeed," Mary assured him.

"And where did you come from, Mary?" he asked, studying her closely. "How did you meet my son?"

She raised her chin. "Ian and I met in Carlisle."

Ian interrupted. "Mary is a close friend of Victoria Thorn, the daughter of the Duke of Carlisle. I had gone to Carlisle to deliver a horse Victoria's husband had purchased for her birthday. I had personally assumed the task, as the couple are friends of my own."

"Carlisle." The earl frowned thoughtfully. "And your own family name would be...?"

Mary raised her chin even higher. "Fulton. My father was the vicar in Carlisle for many years before his recent death." She said the last word with an unwanted catch in her throat. She did not wish to appear weak before this man. For he was formidable in spite of his obvious unhappiness over his relationship with his son.

She heard a barely stifled gasp. "A vicar's daughter?" Looking up, Mary saw that Barbara was standing with her slender white hand over her mouth as her devastated gaze went to Ian.

Mary felt the penetrating displeasure of her father-in-law's gaze as he focused his frowning attention on his son. A wave of indignation shot through her. Mary had known that she and Ian were not social equals. She would have had to be incredibly daft not to. But never had she expected her new family to be so very direct in their disapproval of the match.

She was wordless with shock.

Ian spoke into the ensuing silence, his tone cool. "If you don't mind, Father, I'd like to get Mary settled before either of you may insult her further. It has been a very long day and I know she is tired."

Mary felt a warm sense of gratitude for her husband's intervention. She was tired, and newly married, and uncertain of her relationship with Ian. This cold reception was more painful than she would ever care to admit to anyone, even herself.

Ian turned to his cousin Barbara. "Would you mind asking Mrs. Morgan if she's readied a room for my wife?"

She shook her head. "Ian, I..."

It was clear to Mary that she had not recovered from her shock at learning he was married. Just then a matronly voice spoke up from the doorway. "I have indeed readied a room, Master Ian. And as you requested, I've put your wife next to your own chamber."

Mary turned to a see fresh-faced older woman dressed in black except for the enveloping white apron she wore. When her gaze met Mary's she smiled blithely. "And let me say, sir, how happy I am to see you come home with a wife. A most joyous day this is." *At last,* Mary thought as she nodded in return, *one welcoming face.*

Ian turned to the housekeeper with a forced smile. "Thank you so much, Mrs. Morgan. I'm glad to see someone approves."

"Indeed I do, and of that you can make no mistake." The woman moved to Mary's side with a respectful nod. "Now, if you'll come with me, my lady, I'll take you on up."

Mary gave her a hesitant smile and blinked to clear her

eyes of the sheen of tears she would not shed. She was nearly done in by the woman's friendliness after having kept her composure in the midst of all this tension, and she would not give them the satisfaction of seeing her hurt.

Ian seemed to feel some of the strain, too, for he said, "If you don't mind, Father, I think I'll go on up to my own chamber."

Without waiting for a reply he took his wife's arm, and the two of them followed Mrs. Morgan from the room. Mary had more impressions of dark colors, heavy furnishings and portraits of stern-looking ancestors as Mrs. Morgan led them back to the foyer, then up a set of wide, dark stairs. A carpeted landing branched to the right and left at the top. They turned left.

The housekeeper stopped just moments later in front of a dark-paneled door. "This chamber will be yours, my lady." She opened the door and stood back for them to enter.

Mary went first, seeing that the chamber was well lit and the bed turned down. Her gaze fell upon the lush appointments with some amazement. Here, as in the rest of the house, the furnishings were heavy, but they had been painted white and bore much gold inlay. The coverlet was a light blue brocade. The wallpaper, of the same blue, was patterned with gold ivy. The carpet was cream and blue, the chairs a cream brocade. Gold tassels held back the blue-and-ivory draperies.

It wasn't the fineness of the chamber that gave her pause. It was the marked difference from what she had viewed of the house thus far.

Ian seemed to sense her surprise, for he said, "It is beautiful, is it not? This and the room adjoining it—" he indicated the connecting door "—are two of the ones my mother redecorated before her death. My father's mother had originally furnished the house when it was built, and preferred more somber tones.''

Mary could only nod. ''I see. It is beautiful.''

Mrs. Morgan interrupted them politely. ''Your luggage has been unpacked, my lady. I can send Miss Barbara's maid to help you undress, if you wish.''

Mary shook her head immediately. ''No, thank you, that will not be necessary.'' She had no wish to have the woman's maid wait upon her. She was quite capable of seeing to her own needs.

The housekeeper nodded. ''Will there be anything else, my lady?''

''No, I'm sure I can manage now. Thank you so much,'' Mary replied distractedly, knowing she would soon be alone with her husband.

''Master Ian?''

''No, Mrs. Morgan. I will be fine. Thank you for your assistance.''

Neither of them said any more as she curtsied and left.

Mary stood hesitant and uncertain. Ian's defense of her downstairs had warmed her, but he seemed somehow distant again now that they were alone. How long, she wondered, would it be before they had a true marriage again? Only Ian knew the answer to that, and she found herself strangely reluctant to ask him.

When he spoke it was with polite civility, his expression giving away nothing of his inner feelings. ''We will set about getting you a maid in the morning, and anything else you might require.''

Mary began, ''But I don't require a—''

''Nonsense. You will have need of a maid.'' He looked at her then. ''Mary, I know this evening has been difficult for you, and I can only apologize for my family's rudeness.''

She moved to stand looking up at him, her gaze earnest. "It is not your fault, Ian. You do not have to answer for them."

He blanched, and his voice was husky as he replied, "I only wish that were true."

She stepped closer still, feeling the heat of his body near hers. Surely if he saw that she had no liking for this distance between them, they could begin their relationship afresh. There was no need for him to prove anything to her. His desire to do so was proof enough that he felt she was different from his previous amours. "I could never blame you for the way your father and cousin behaved. You defended me, Ian. What more could you do?" She closed the space between them, putting her head on his strong shoulder.

She felt his quick intake of breath beneath her cheek and looked up to see that his eyes were shut and his hands clenched at his sides. His face was set in a pained expression. He stood like that for what seemed an eternity before he slowly reached up and put his hands on her shoulders. Carefully he set her away from him, then leaned down to press a chaste kiss upon her temple. "It has been a long day, Mary. I know you are tired. I will leave you now to rest."

Before she could say anything to dissuade him, Ian was gone, the door between their two chambers firmly closed. For a brief instant she considered going to him and telling him she was not tired, that she wished, above all things, just to be with him. But the clicking of the lock stopped her with the force of a slap.

Mary rose the next morning and donned the best of her day gowns. She could not wear the pink evening dress, and her traveling costume was sadly in need of cleaning, as well as being inappropriate. The dark green dress with its high, starched cream lace collar seemed somehow shabby in the midst of so much wealth, but she refused to allow herself to be intimidated. She doubted that fine garments would make her suitable in her in-law's eyes.

She was just going to open the door to see if she could find her way down to breakfast when there was a knock upon it. Turning the knob, Mary discovered Ian standing there.

He bowed politely. "May I escort you down to breakfast?"

She bit her lip and nodded, not sure what to say to him after the previous night. For hours she had lain awake wondering how this impasse could be ended.

He reached for her hand with courtly grace, his touch making her heart quicken. "I trust you slept well."

Mary nodded, knowing she was telling a falsehood even as she replied, "Yes, fine, thank you." She would rather he did not know how unhappy she had been over his pronouncement in the carriage yesterday, not to mention his abrupt departure last night.

He patted her hand. "I'm glad. I had hoped you would be able to rest. It will be difficult enough for you here without having to face it all in such an exhausted state."

Mary looked at him closely, seeing the concern in his dark eyes with some gladness. Ian did seem genuinely worried for her and had treated her with nothing but gentle courtesy. Surely he would soon feel that he had proven his respect and consideration. The thought buoyed her somewhat and she felt some of the weight of sadness lift from her heart.

Ian spoke softly as they came to the staircase at the end of the corridor. "My father's rooms are on the southern end of this floor. You probably won't have any need to venture in that direction. He guards his privacy somewhat jealously.'' He nodded off toward the right.

Mary looked down the darkened hallway, seeing no more than dim shadows even now in the daylight. She shook her head. ''No, I would imagine I won't.''

Ian led her down the stairs, across the foyer and then into another chamber, which she saw was a breakfast room. It, too, was decorated in dark colors—forest green and a red so deep it was nearly purple. The table and enormous carved sideboard were fashioned from a dark varnished walnut, beautiful to be sure, but heavy. She looked at the green velvet draperies, which were closed. Letting in the light would bring a major improvement, she thought, but it was not her right to do so.

As she and Ian moved to sit at the table, which had already been set, a female voice spoke from behind them. Mary turned to see Ian's cousin coming toward them. Her dark gray gown was simply made and lacked adornment, but the silk was of the finest quality. Her dark hair was again arranged in an elegant and neat bun. She was an attractive woman, if somewhat solemn of manner for one of her years, for Mary was sure she could not be above five and twenty. Her almond-shaped dark eyes were in fact quite notable with their long fringe of black lashes.

But what made Mary really look at her was the fact that this morning she wore an expression of studied welcome, which was a surprise after her reaction the previous night.

She held out her hand to Mary first. ''Welcome, Mary. I am so sorry that I was not more forthcoming with my congratulations last evening. I...we were simply shocked to learn of the marriage when we had not even known of your existence.''

Mary took the hand briefly. The words Ian's cousin

spoke were civil enough, but Mary still sensed a hint of resentment hidden behind them.

Ian seemed not to hear it, for he took the offered hand with a smile. "Thank you so much, cousin. Your congratulation means a great deal to us, doesn't it, Mary?"

Mary smiled with as much enthusiasm as she could summon. "Of course. Thank you."

"Please sit down," Barbara added, then laughed with what Mary thought was a trace of bitterness. "I suppose I have no need to tell you to sit in your own home." She looked to Mary.

Again Ian appeared to be oblivious to this. "Mary would not take offense at such a thing. In fact," Ian went on, "I'm sure Mary would be very grateful if you assisted her in settling in here, wouldn't you, Mary? That way you can take over the running of the house gradually."

Mary had not given the notion of running this house even a moment's thought, so it was not difficult for her to reply in the affirmative. "I would thank you for instructing me on what must be done."

When Barbara looked at Mary, her smile seemed forced. "I will do whatever I can." She then rang the bell next to her plate.

A young woman appeared through a doorway at the far end of the room. She approached the table cautiously, for she carried an obviously heavy tray. When she had finally set the burden down upon the table with a clatter, she heaved an audible sigh of relief.

Barbara looked at her with a grimace. "You'll have to forgive Frances for her lack of grace. She's just been promoted from her former position as scullery maid. Mildred, our other housemaid, is having a child."

"I'm sorry, miss." The maid blinked back a sheen of tears.

"Just please fetch breakfast," Barbara instructed.

Mary met the maid's unhappy gaze with a sympathetic one of her own. She looked to Ian and saw that he was pouring himself a cup of tea, but his gaze was trained on the open doorway.

Barbara looked at Mary as she poured out tea for both of them. "It is best to handle servants with a firm hand. It is what Cousin Malcolm expects."

Mary wondered if she always did exactly as Cousin Malcolm expected. Mary could not help answering herself affirmatively. Well, she had no intention of acting against her own principles, and deliberately humiliating anyone, including a servant who was nervous and inexperienced, would be doing just that. Mary met the dark-haired woman's gaze with a level one of her own. She did not think she and Ian's cousin would become friends.

Ian changed the topic abruptly, making Mary realize why he seemed so distracted. "Have you seen my father?"

Barbara answered. "Cousin Malcolm has left for the village. He had some business to attend. I believe he will not be back for some hours."

To Mary, Ian seemed both relieved and disappointed. He took a sip of his tea. Wishing she could do something to comfort him, but knowing she could not, Mary was relieved when they were interrupted by the arrival of the butler.

"Yes, Winslow," Barbara greeted him.

The butler bowed. "I've a message for Lord Ian. It seems there is some trouble in the stables. His attention is graciously requested."

Ian stood immediately. "If you will excuse me, Mary."

She nodded. Mary knew how much his horses meant to him.

He paused then as he passed his cousin's chair. "Cousin Barbara, I was intending to show Mary around the house.

If you are not too busy, would you mind doing that? I wish for her to see everything so she can become accustomed to thinking of this as her home.''

She spoke without looking around. "I would be happy to do so, Ian.''

He reached out and briefly pressed a hand to her shoulder. "Thank you.''

Only Mary saw the way Barbara's lids came down to mask her eyes and the sharp rise of her breathing as he touched her. Quickly Mary glanced down at her own meal. Her impressions the previous evening had not been wrong. The other woman's feelings for Ian could not be more obvious.

Barbara and Mary finished breakfast in silence. Mary was not sorry, for she could think of nothing to say. She only wished there was some way to avoid the coming tour. It would not be pleasant for either of them.

When Barbara did finally address her, Mary had to restrain a start. "Shall we have a look at the house, then?'' Her voice and expression were carefully polite.

Perhaps it would not be too unbearable if they could keep it on such a civil footing. After all, Mary could not completely avoid the woman. They were now living in the same house.

As they made the rounds of the downstairs, Mary gained more impressions of dark furniture and colors. Only in three rooms did Mary sense the same hand that had decorated her own bedchamber. There was the conservatory, which was a spacious room with hundreds of lush and beautiful plants, a small sitting room, done in pale peaches and greens, and lastly the ballroom, which was awash with gilt and creamy colors. Their footsteps echoed hollowly as they crossed the marble floor, and the room had a ghostly vacant air, giving Mary the feeling this chamber had seen no dancing in many years.

What, she wondered, had happened to take all the joy from this house? For surely there must have been some glimmers of happiness at one time. The woman who had begun to redecorate Sinclair Hall had obviously been blessed with a lightness of spirit and love of life.

As they left the library, which was filled with hundreds of books that made Mary itch to return as soon as she had an opportunity, she asked, "Is there some reason none of the drapes are drawn back to let in the sun?"

Barbara looked at her with surprise. "The sunlight is not good for the carpets and furniture, not to mention the wall coverings. It washes the color from them."

"But what good are any of those things if no one is enjoying them?"

Ian's cousin shook her head pityingly. "Cousin Malcolm prefers them closed, and that is the way my own mother keeps her home. It is the way to keep such valuable treasures as you find in this house from suffering unnecessary damage. I think you will find that it is best to leave things as they are. The earl would not welcome any change."

Mary decided to allow that matter to drop for the moment, though she did believe that the woman's thinking was flawed. Victoria's home was even finer than this, and she insisted on having the curtains pulled to let in the light. It made her home seem welcoming and lived-in despite its grandeur.

What Mary did want to talk about was Barbara's family. "How are you related to Ian?"

Barbara continued to lead her forward as she answered, "My grandmother and Cousin Malcolm's father were siblings. My mother is his first cousin. Cousin Malcolm and my parents agreed that I should come to live here a year ago. There was some hope... Well, never mind that.''

Mary heard the strain in her voice. Why hadn't any of them consulted Ian before putting this poor woman through what must surely be an embarrassing situation? The sympathy in Mary's voice when she spoke was genuine. ''Don't they miss you, your parents? And surely you miss them?''

Barbara stiffened. ''I...I do not know. It is not something I have ever discussed with them. I am the eldest of five sisters. We have one brother, the middle child. He will inherit what little...from my father.'' Her nose rose to a haughty angle and her cool gaze now turned to Mary. ''I was...to marry first. I do not think they are any of them going to be overly glad to see me return home.''

Mary spoke softly. ''I am sorry. I had no idea.''

Barbara answered coldly, ''I neither require nor want your sympathy. I assure you I will be quite all right.''

Before Mary could say any more, Barbara stopped and Mary saw that they had arrived back in the foyer. The dark-haired woman smiled stiffly. ''I'm very sorry, but you will have to excuse me now. I find that we have taken longer than I had anticipated. There really are a few things I must see to.''

Mary did not have to be told that Ian's cousin had revealed all she was going to and was indeed sorry for what she had said.

Chapter Seven

Mary explored the rest of the house on her own. Though there were several areas where she did not go, she saw enough to gain a general impression. It was large, expensively furnished and for the most part dark and too quiet.

Not at all the sort of home she wanted her children to grow up in. That was if she ever had any children, she thought, ever aware of Ian's decision to treat her with special care, which clearly excluded any marital relations.

Surely that would soon change now that they were at Sinclair Hall and settled in.

She did not see Ian at luncheon, nor his father. Stiltedly Barbara informed her that the earl had not returned from his business appointment. When Mary inquired about Ian, Barbara discouraged Mary from going to the stables where Ian was still trying to save the life of a mare that was having a very difficult birth. The dark-haired woman had pointedly told Mary that she could not wish to put herself in the way.

Mary had refrained from making any comment, though the directive prickled somewhat. They had not stayed long in one another's presence.

The afternoon had passed slowly and Mary was eager

for evening to arrive, for she was certain Ian would dine with them. As the hour approached, Mary removed the pink gown from her wardrobe and laid it on the bed. She bit her lip as she wondered how she was going to manage the row of tiny pearl buttons at the back. Perhaps Ian was right about her needing a lady's maid.

As a knock came softly on her door she turned, her heart beating more quickly as she wondered if it could be her husband. She called out, "Enter."

It was Frances, the maid whom Barbara had been so displeased with that morning. She dipped a curtsy, not meeting Mary's gaze. "May I light the candles for you, my lady?"

Mary nodded. "Thank you." She frowned. "I thought you had been asked to serve at table."

The maid moved across the room to begin lighting the candles. "Miss Barbara has changed her mind, my lady. One of the other scullery maids has been given the position." There was no way of mistaking the sadness in Frances's voice, though she tried to hide it.

"I see," Mary told her, scowling. How humiliating it would be to be demoted without a fair trial. The maid had been no more than a trifle overcareful and awkward.

Mary looked from the dress to Frances's slender back, her expression thoughtful. "Frances, would you be so good as to assist me for a moment?"

Mary met Ian at the entrance to the dining room and paused with a smile. As always, she felt a compelling wave of awareness. The dark gray trousers and matching coat he wore only emphasized his height and masculine elegance. He ran a long-fingered hand through his hair and she was swept by a heated memory of having his hands tangled in her own hair, touching her skin.

Surely he would wish to resume their marital relationship soon. Ian's demeanor and actions had already shown her he was greatly changed from the man they had called "Lord Sin." He had been kind and considerate of her, making every effort to defend her in the face of his father's displeasure. She had no further need for him to demonstrate his sincerity.

Clearly unaware of her thoughts, Ian hesitated before returning her smile with a brief one of his own. "I trust you have had a good day."

She nodded, though it had not been what she would call a good day. "I was informed that you were helping a mare to deliver her foal. I hope all went well for you."

He nodded with unmistakable satisfaction, and again she was reminded of how much pride and pleasure he took in his horses. "The foal has been delivered safely. The mare is very young and had been allowed to escape into a field where a large draft horse had been grazing." He shrugged. "The horse was a stallion. The resulting foal was quite large and difficult for her to birth, but all has turned out fine. I left mother and babe eating."

Mary felt a poignant sort of pleasure at standing here with her husband discussing his day. She was not certain how he would react to what she wished to say to him. Her decision to tell Ian that she had realized she did indeed require a lady's maid and that she wanted the serving girl Frances to fill that position made her nervous. The girl was more ignorant than herself as far as these matters went. But Mary felt she was agile of wit and would learn quickly.

Mary could think of no way to present the request other than to do so. Thus she squared her shoulders and said, "Ian, there is something I wish to ask. You have told me that I have need of a lady's maid. I have a suggestion as to who might fill that role."

He looked at her with surprise. "Mary, you don't have to ask my permission on these matters. As I said, this is your home. You must do whatever you wish."

She nodded, her heart warmed by his words. Her home. In spite of the problems with Ian's father not accepting her and Barbara's obvious dislike of her, Ian wanted her here. Now, if only he would forget this nonsense about proving himself to her. An unknowingly wistful smile curved her mouth. "I am so happy to have you say that. I wish to have Frances, the young girl we met this morning at breakfast. I think we would do quite well together, and what she doesn't know about being a personal servant I am sure she would learn quickly."

A shocked voice interrupted her. "Frances! Why, she is totally unsuited to such a position. She could not adequately fill the duties of serving woman. How can you imagine that she would be able to help care for your clothing and such? Arrange your hair?"

Mary stiffened as she turned to face Barbara. "I have made my decision."

"Ian, can you not dissuade her?" The other woman turned to Ian. "It is obvious that Mary is simply feeling sorry for this girl. She would not be able to fulfill the duties required of your...the wife of an earl. You must think of that when making these decisions. The way you present yourself will reflect on your husband." She raised her arched brows as her gaze swept Mary's pink gown.

Mary looked at Barbara's own gown and saw that she was dressed well, but very sedately as usual. The pink confection Victoria had given her and which she had been convinced could not cause offense was obviously not to the other woman's liking. Mary shrugged. It was the only remotely suitable gown she possessed. The ivory satin wedding gown was even more elaborate.

She felt that Barbara was quite overreacting to her decision to have Frances as her maid. The dark-haired woman must be embarrassed at their conversation earlier in the day, and trying to hide it behind this mask of superiority. Yet Mary was not going to allow anyone to intimidate her. She would have the maid of her own choosing. "I am sure I can teach Frances. She seems extremely bright."

Barbara laughed. "Oh, dear..."

Ian spoke up, halting his cousin before she could continue. "I am sure you are only trying to help, cousin. But Mary may do as she wishes."

Again Mary's heart was warmed by her husband's support of her.

Barbara stood still for a long moment, then to Mary's surprise replied in a very contrite tone, "As you wish, Ian. I meant only to be helpful."

He smiled at her. "Your concern is appreciated. I do hope that you continue to help Mary to adjust to living here at Sinclair Hall."

"I am happy to do whatever I can for you, Ian...and of course Mary," Barbara told him. Barbara then swung around to face Mary and she knew that Ian could not be aware of the look of disdain that was cast her way.

Later that night Mary lay awake. Ian had remained in the salon when she had risen and said she was going to bed.

Confusion continued to dominate Mary's thoughts in regard to her husband. In spite of his championing of her over the matter of Frances, he had grown progressively more distant as the evening wore on. He had barely acknowledged her leaving, seeming as preoccupied as he had that morning.

Barbara's expression had appeared relieved as Mary left

them. This Mary dismissed quickly. Though she would have preferred to be on friendly terms with Ian's cousin, Mary did not require her friendship or approval.

Mary stared up at the corniced ceiling in the darkness, feeling oddly unsettled. Time passed and still she heard no sound from Ian's room. Where could he be?

How long would he continue to avoid being alone with her, for that was surely what he was doing, was it not? What was causing that unmistakable deep preoccupation?

Why did he think that avoiding the physical aspects of their relationship would help him show that he respected and honored her? Spending her nights alone in this enormous bed was not improving her opinion of Ian.

At last Mary could stand it no more. She did not know where her husband was, nor did she really understand why he had determined to follow this course, but she'd had enough.

Mary rose and donned her robe. On the off chance that Ian had gone to his chamber without her having heard him, she went to the connecting door, gathered her courage and knocked softly.

Without thinking, she reached down and turned the knob, the very fact that Ian had locked it filling her with vexation. To her surprise, the door opened. It was immediately obvious that the room, which was done in varying shades of green, was not occupied. The enormous carved-oak bed had been readied for his arrival, his robe laid out across the turned-down sheets. The crisp, snowy sheets were a sharp contrast to the green-and-white-striped bed hangings.

She closed the connecting door and swung around to face her own door. Before she could stop to consider what she was doing, Mary was on her way to the lower floor.

The house was silent. No one was in the salon, nor in the sitting room, nor any of the others she looked in. And with each vacant chamber her determination lagged, as Mary began to wonder if she did indeed have the courage to face Ian so directly about such a...delicate subject.

As she was just getting ready to give up and go back to her room, Mary realized that there was a light coming from beneath the library door. She took a deep breath and squared her shoulders. And though her hands felt damp with nervousness, Mary approached the closed door with resolve.

Just as she was reaching for the knob, she halted as she heard Ian's father's voice say her name. But it was the rest of what he said that held her immobile with shock. "You cannot love this girl, Ian, which would not excuse your poor judgment in marrying the daughter of a *vicar,* but it would at least serve as a reasoning point, however invalid. By your own admission you barely know her. I can only conclude that you have carried out this foolishness in order to shock and spite me."

There was a long silence, so heavy Mary felt her shoulders sag beneath the weight of it. Why did Ian not deny this accusation? She knew he did not love her, but he had not married her to spite anyone. Then finally Ian replied, his words falling like boulders upon her already tumultuous emotions. "Yes, Father. I did marry her for those reasons. I can't pretend otherwise."

Mary's heart shattered inside her chest, flinging sharp splinters up to sting eyes and throat. Covering her mouth with her hand to deafen the sound of her misery, Mary turned and ran down the hall.

The reason for Ian's odd behavior was now abundantly clear. He had not discontinued their relationship out of a need to prove anything to her, or himself, but because he had never wanted her from the outset. Her face flamed as she remembered how she had offered herself to him on their wedding night. Ian had not made any advances toward her.

Shame twisted her stomach into a tight knot of anguish. She was aware of nothing besides the pain of her disillusionment as she stumbled her way up the stairs. She had to steady herself by holding tightly to the railing, for it seemed the one stable object in her reeling world.

It was as she reached the upper floor and started down the hall that she nearly ran into Ian's cousin Barbara. Mary drew herself up short, cursing the coincidence that had brought her directly into the path of this woman.

She had no wish to face her now, not with the agony of Ian's admission ringing in her ears.

Mary could not help seeing the satisfaction on the other woman's face as she took in Mary's tears. Battered anew by this unsympathetic reaction, she made to go around Barbara, but was halted as the dark-haired woman stepped deliberately into her path.

Looking at her in confusion, Mary spoke in a hoarse whisper as she fought to control herself before this wall of coldness. "Please let me pass."

Barbara Howard stared at her for a long moment, then replied, "I will do so, but only after I have had my say. I can only assume from the state you are in that there are problems between yourself and Ian. Because of this, I find I must put aside my reticence and tell you the truth." She paused for a long moment, then said, "You may have married Ian, but he does not love you."

Another shaft of pain laced through her. Was the woman inside her head, so that she knew what Mary had just overheard? Hurriedly she told herself Ian's cousin could not know. She was simply able to see Mary's hurt and was saying the one thing she thought would wound the most.

It was nothing but ill fate that the words hit so close to the truth.

Unaware of Mary's thoughts, Barbara went on, her brown eyes hard, though Mary could see the pain she tried to hide there, as well. "It is myself Ian loves. We were to be married, and you have ruined all. His family welcomed the idea, as did mine. I don't know why he did marry you, but he loves me. And his father will never accept you, make no mistake on that." She pressed her hand over her heart, her expression fierce.

She should not be surprised to learn of this. Obviously Ian was not above playing her false. Unable to make any reply to this, Mary had had enough. Fully prepared to force her way by if need be, she moved forward. She need not have worried. The other woman had said what she wished to, and now stepped out of her path.

From his seat at the head of the table Malcolm Sinclair frowned at Mary the next morning as she stood in the doorway of the breakfast room. His disapproval was obvious as his gaze raked her from head to toe.

Mary raised her chin and moved into the austere chamber without being invited. She refused to be intimidated by this cold older man. She now knew that she was not wanted here, by her husband or his family, but she would not allow them to cow her.

Belatedly Malcolm stood and motioned to the seat at his right. "Sit here, gel."

Pointedly she took the one next to it. "Good morning," she said with stilted politeness.

"Have a mind of your own, do you? Well, that doesn't impress me any." He cut off a thick slice of ham and ate it.

Pouring tea from the silver pot into the blue patterned

china cup at her place, Mary ignored the remark, though it was not easy. All she'd wanted was a little happiness to call her own, someone to care for and protect her. The reality was as far from her ideal as possible.

It felt as though her hopes for happiness had become a caged bird inside her and she must ignore its fluttering bursts of sorrow or give up entirely. She was here, for good or ill, and meant to stay. There was no way she was going to let them chase her back to Carlisle. Though she knew Victoria would take her gladly, Mary could not allow herself to contemplate the idea, especially after her own refusal to heed Victoria's warnings about Ian.

No matter how uneasy she was at this encounter with her father-in-law, Mary knew it was negligible in comparison to the apprehension and pain she felt at the thought of facing Ian after what she had heard him say the previous night.

The thought of meeting him had nearly kept her in her room this morning. But she would not let him see how hurt she was.

Mary's lips tightened with bitter irony. Considering his purposeful avoidance of being alone with her, it would likely not prove difficult to keep her secret.

A female voice intruded upon her thoughts. "Good morning, Cousin Malcolm...Mary." She looked up to see Barbara on the opposite side of the table.

Mary nodded briefly without meeting the other's gaze. Whatever was she to say to the woman after being told Barbara herself was the one Mary's husband really cared for?

A knifepoint of sorrow sliced through her breast at the renewed realization that the words might indeed be true, and then again as she attempted to tell herself that it mattered little if it was the truth. Ian cared nothing for her.

For a moment the whole situation was nearly too much for her, and her throat constricted with misery. Mary took a deep breath and managed to hold herself together. Never, not ever, could they know how devastated she was by the turn her life had taken. Barbara would not again see Mary laid bare for her barbs as she had last night.

Squaring her shoulders, Mary looked up at the other woman coolly. "Good morning."

Barbara gave what Mary could only describe as a condescending smile. "Ian won't be joining us. He has already gone out to the stables. He says there is much work to be done there." To Mary it seemed as if the woman was making a great effort to display the fact that it was she who was in Ian's confidence.

Malcolm Sinclair made a rough sound in his throat, drawing Mary's gaze to his face. For a moment Mary felt that there was a hint of disappointment in his eyes as he made a great show of stirring his tea. When he spoke, the cold disapproval in his tone told her she must have been mistaken. "I would have thought he'd show some interest in getting his wife settled in here. That boy is..."

Mary drew herself up. "Forgive me for interrupting, my lord, but Ian has no need to see me settled in. I am quite capable of seeing to myself."

"Are you, then?" His dark gaze, so surprisingly like his son's, ran over her, assessing her, clearly not approving what he saw. "If that is so, then there is something I would appreciate your doing."

She faced him evenly. "Yes."

"When you married my son your circumstances, shall we say, improved somewhat. If the garment you are wearing is any indication, you will have need for a wardrobe that is more befitting the wife of a future earl."

Mary resisted the urge to look down at her plain green

gown, which she had worn the day before, as well Stiffly she replied, "I do not require a new wardrobe. That is not why I married your son."

His dark eyes held hers. "Why did you marry my son?"

"That sir, is a personal matter. Suffice it to say that it was not for his position or material goods." Mary was not about to admit that she had so desperately clung to Ian when he had behaved as if he would care for her that she had married a man she did not even know.

She continued to hold that skeptical gaze, until finally Malcolm Sinclair, the Earl of Dryden, sat back with an expression of what she would have described as grudging respect had she not known that was impossible. The impression was quickly forgotten as he said, "Nonetheless, you will have a new wardrobe. As a member of my family it is your responsibility to uphold not only your husband's but also my position. You are far more than a simple minister's daughter now, my dear."

Mary wanted to refuse, but could not think of a way to do so without giving away the fact that she knew what Ian had told him about their marriage. Yesterday she would have agreed to this plan without argument. As Ian's wife, she was required to represent him properly. But now, knowing that she was unwanted by him, she felt wrong about taking anything from him or his father.

Before she could think of any plausible rebuttal, Malcolm stood. "Barbara, I will expect you to lend your assistance to Ian's wife in this matter. The dressmaker will be here this afternoon."

Barbara nodded and replied submissively, "Of course, Cousin Malcolm." But when she looked at Mary her expression was anything but submissive. Her resentment was more than obvious as her dark eyes found and held Mary's own.

Yet she clearly had no courage to openly defy the earl's wishes.

Ian turned to the stable boy and held out his hand for the ointment. He then salved a generous amount on the dappled gelding's leg.

"Will it heal, my lord?" came the anxious question.

Ian swung around to meet the youngster's brown gaze. "I believe so, but he'll never be the jumper he was." He then reached for clean wrappings to cover the strain.

Ian could understand why Lester was so worried about the horse. He had been the one riding it when it stepped into a rabbit hole. He had done his best to reassure the thirteen-year-old that he was convinced of the events being an accident, but Lester, to his credit, continued to show his concern.

When the horse's leg was wrapped he exited the stall and went down the row until he reached the one that contained the mare, Portia. Her foal, a hearty little colt, frisked around her legs at Ian's presence. The mare moved to nuzzle his hand. He'd been concerned for her in the hours it had taken the foal to arrive. Not yet ready for breeding with a suitable stud, the mare's adventure with the draft horse had nearly cost her her life.

He patted her neck gently. Luckily she seemed none the worse for her ordeal.

Even as he examined the horse, his mind was filled with Mary. The night before last he had waited for his father, knowing he must explain to the older man that he was home for good, that he planned to make a life at Sinclair Hall. And that life would include Mary.

He did not yet know how he would ever reconcile his guilt over what he had done to his wife. He only knew that he had to act with honor from now on. Telling his father the complete truth when he had asked if Ian had married her to spite him had come from the decision to act with honor.

He would not face Mary, or even his father, without the integrity that he now wished to live by. How could he ever hope to be worthy of the woman he had taken as his wife if he did not behave this way?

Inside him there was a piece of himself that wanted to tell her the truth, to purge himself and try to begin again. But he knew he could not do this. Telling Mary the truth would only bring her shame. It was he who must conquer his own feelings of self-recrimination, by being the man she had thought he was.

Never in his adult life had Ian cared as much about a woman's feelings as he did Mary's. What he'd told her about wanting to show her that she was different from the other women he'd known was true.

Yet following through with his intentions was not as easily done as said. His desire for his wife was still as alive as it had been the first moment he saw her.

Knowing that Mary lay sleeping on the other side of that door between their two chambers was a torment. The memory of her uninhibited responses to his lovemaking on their wedding night served only to make the temptation all the more difficult to resist.

Ian left the stall and strode down the center aisle of the neatly kept building. He felt a need to expend some of the tension growing inside him. A ride might help.

As he was approaching Balthazar's stall he heard a commotion out in the courtyard. Quickly he changed direction, going to investigate. Out in the cobbled courtyard a small group of onlookers was gathered around a mounted man, whom Ian recognized immediately as an acquaintance of his father's, Squire Cedric Barnaby. He was a stout, gray-

haired gentleman who wore his waistcoats tight and enjoyed his port. He reached into his pocket and extracted a
handkerchief, which he swabbed over his red, perspiration-
dampened face.

What Ian focused on, though, was the young white stallion he was leading. He had no trouble recalling the origin
of the horse. It had been foaled from one of his favorite
gray Arabian sires and a very pretty white Thoroughbred
mare.

Spying Ian, the squire climbed awkwardly from his bay.
"Sinclair. I'm surprised to see you here at Sinclair Hall."

Ian approached him with reserve. He did not care for the
man's overbearing attitude. He had sold him the horse in
the first place only because he admired the trainer who
would have charge of the animal. He had since learned that
the trainer had left the squire's employ. The man who was
reputed to have been hired in his stead was not someone
Ian respected.

Ian tried his best to show a polite face. "Squire Barnaby,
is there some way I can be of assistance to you?"

The squire gestured over his shoulder with his crop.
"You certainly can. I'll thank you to be taking this beast
back from me and returning my money. It's robbed I've
been, and no mistake."

Ian balked. He cheated no one. His gaze was hard as he
met that of the other man. "I'll thank *you* to have a care
about any accusations you might make."

The squire blanched, his gaze dropping to the ground as
he wiped his face again. "I, of course, meant no offense."
The white stallion snorted as if sensing the man's unease
and finding pleasure in it. The squire obviously felt this,
too, for he looked back at Ian, scowling.

"I've paid for a horse that can be ridden, but got this
wild beast. My trainer has been working with him for far

longer than is reasonable, and he's able to do no more than put a saddle on his back. The horse won't let anyone, including myself—'' he lifted his double chin ''—who have some experience with horses, to ride him. Threw me right on my backside this morning.''

His grimace told Ian clearly that that portion of him was still smarting, though likely more from embarrassment than injury.

Although he knew that the problem was very likely in the way the horse had been handled, he was more than willing to take the animal back. He hated to see potential such as the stallion displayed go to waste because of inept training. He replied evenly, ''I will gladly refund the price you paid.''

The man frowned more deeply. ''I have fed and kept that beast for two years. Surely you owe me for that?''

Ian had had enough. He moved close to the much shorter squire. ''It is you who should be paying me. The work and time that will be required to undo the harm that has been done him, if it can be undone, are uncountable.''

The shorter man puffed up his chest. ''Is that so, now, young Ian? Are you saying that the beast's bad nature is my fault?''

Ian raised his dark brows. ''In a word, yes.''

The older man was not about to back down. ''I'll tell you what I will do. If you, yourself, Ian Sinclair, can ride that demon, he is yours, free of charge. He will be my gift to you.'' He paused, then went on with a superior smile, ''But it will be done today. Surely a man of your reputed skill with horses can accomplish that small feat? If you fail, you will refund double what I originally paid.''

Ian felt the thrill of challenge go through him like a bracing October breeze even as he faced the little man with disdain. The days when he had thrived on such moments were not so very far behind him.

Without breaking the contact of their eyes he replied, "I agree."

Ian swung around and discovered that not only was the stable boy right behind him, but quite a large number of people had gathered. Speaking coolly, Ian told the boy, "Bring the horse around to the training enclosure."

Mary left the manor house and started off across the cobbled courtyard. She had had quite enough of Barbara's fair company. That woman had not mentioned her relationship with Ian again, thankfully, but at every opportunity she did make it clear that she felt Mary was beneath her.

She never did so in Malcolm Sinclair's presence, keeping up a pretense of polite solicitude. It was when the two women were alone, which had been far too much for Mary's liking in the past two days, that she showed her true feelings.

As Malcolm had asked, Barbara had been present when Madame Marie Fleur, the dressmaker, had come the previous afternoon bearing bolts of fabric and drawings taken from Godey's. Ian's cousin had at first tried to take over the whole proceeding, telling the woman exactly what would be needed and how much.

That was until Mary had politely but firmly stepped in. She had decided that if she was to wear the garments the dressmaker was preparing, she would be the one to choose them.

Her rebellion had been made easier by the fact that Marie Fleur had supported her choices wholeheartedly. She had in fact praised Mary for her excellent taste.

Barbara had seemed less than happy, but she had not made an exit. Obviously she was afraid of displeasing her cousin Malcolm, whom she clearly obeyed in even the smallest of matters.

She'd not seen Ian at all since the night two days ago when she had heard him say the words that had forever destroyed any hopes that she and her husband might ever have a real marriage. She told herself she had no wish to see Ian, but the heaviness of her heart gave the lie to her self-assurances.

It was a gentle day, the sky blue, the breeze barely ruffling the hair at her temples, but Mary had little enthusiasm for the fine weather. As she crossed the courtyard, she became aware of the hum of voices off to her left. Glancing that way, she noted that a small crowd had gathered at the far end of the stone stables, which sat directly across the cobbled courtyard.

Without even realizing that she had changed direction, Mary soon found herself on the outer fringe of this gathering. Rising on tiptoe, she tried to see over the shoulders of people in front of her.

Glancing behind him, the man directly ahead of Mary took note of her presence and moved respectfully out of her way. At his urging for attention, others did the same, bowing and curtsying as they did so.

Clearly, word of Ian's marriage had circulated.

She was soon standing directly against a sturdy wooden fence. It enclosed a fairly small paddock. Inside was a horse, its eyes wide, lips curled as it pulled on the end of a lead rope. On the end of that rope was Ian.

"What is he doing?" she whispered, completely unaware that she had spoken aloud.

A large, dark-haired man with his sleeves rolled back on his suntanned forearms answered her. "Squire Barnaby—" he nodded briefly toward a stout well-dressed gentleman on the other side of the crowd "—has come to return a horse he purchased from the master some time ago, my lady. He says the stallion is too ill-tempered to work with. Says no one has been able to mount him at all. It seems he threw the squire this very morning.''

There was no mistaking the secret glee in the man's voice, before he went on with some pride, ''The squire has made a wager with Lord Ian. If he can ride the stallion, he doesn't have to pay to have the horse back.''

It wasn't much of an explanation but, knowing how Ian felt about his animals, Mary could guess at the rest. She looked at the wild-eyed stallion. He did appear quite ill-tempered to her.

Her unknowingly avid gaze went to her husband, ran over the smooth skin exposed by the open neck of his white shirt. The rope was wrapped securely around the palm of his leather riding glove. His long legs were encased in tight-fitting, buff-colored riding breeches, and the hard muscles in his thighs flexed as he moved with deliberate control around the dusty enclosure.

She watched as Ian's gaze met the horse's wild one and, as if by some magic, held it. Then as he began to draw on the rope, bringing the horse ever closer to him, she felt tension in herself and the people gathered around her.

Slowly Ian reached out his hand and allowed the stallion to sniff at his fingers. When the animal drew back its lips as if to nip, Mary held her breath, but her husband's hand remained steady, and the bite never came. He spoke softly in words that only he and the horse could hear, and moved ever closer until he was stroking the long elegant neck, then rubbing the tapering muzzle. With a flick of a glance Ian attracted the attention of a boy who stood just inside the closed gate. With all the care of a tightrope walker, he took Ian a bridle. With surprisingly little trouble, Ian soon had the bridle in place and secure.

Watching him, Mary could not help recalling the feel of those strong, sensitive hands on her own flesh, drawing the very life force from deep inside her and setting her aflame. She closed her eyes on the erotic images that were conjured up watching him master the wild animal with such skill and patience. So had he mastered her, drawn out responses from the deepest part of herself.

He made another motion with his hand, and the young boy approached him with the same deliberation as before, a saddle in his hands. He gave it to Ian, who continued to watch the stallion.

Still using soothing words, Ian stroked along the animal's back, then gently slipped the blanket and saddle into place. Mary glanced at the squire and saw that his face did not mirror the pride of the folk of Sinclair Hall.

Ian continued to stroke and soothe the horse, his voice a husky murmur that further warmed Mary's senses. When at last the moment came for him to mount, her mouth was dry from watching those long-fingered hands and recalling the feel of them upon her own heated flesh.

Her breath caught as Ian swung up into the saddle and the animal reared. He gripped the horse's sides with his long strong legs, thus keeping his lean hips firmly planted in the saddle, even though the horse tossed about beneath him.

Her heart jumped in her chest as the animal reared even higher. Her hands went to her breast, as if that would somehow calm her now-racing organ.

It did not.

Mary felt a tingling along her spine that had nothing to do with fear. Why, oh, why did Ian have to be so handsome, so strong, so seductively appealing to her?

Mary wanted to turn away, to deny the unsettling truth within herself. But she could not. In spite of the fact he did

not want her, Ian was just as compelling and devastating
to her senses as he had ever been.

She watched mesmerized as Ian held his seat, never stopping that sweet encouraging dialogue. An audible sigh escaped her then as the unexpected took place. The stallion
grew quiet and raised his head to the man on his back. As
the dust settled around them, Ian leaned forward and
stroked the animal's white neck and she heard the words
he spoke. "Good boy, what a fine boy."

He was so strong and capable, a man who you might
think could be depended upon to take charge of every situation, conquer every problem, make things right where
they were wrong. Ian appeared, in fact, to be everything a
woman could desire in a man. She'd thought he would be
someone to lean on, someone to take care of her.

He had not been.

A rough growl drew her attention from her own painful
thoughts, and Mary saw the man named Squire Barnaby
throw down his crop and stalk away. His anger should not
rest solely with Ian, she thought, for from what the large
man had told her, she knew he had insisted on the wager.

One of the several housekeepers they'd had at the vicarage in Carlisle had been a woman who readily shared her
homespun wisdoms. Mary could recall her saying that one
should never put themselves in a position of losing what
they could not afford to lose.

Suddenly Mary realized that this was exactly what she
had done. She had taken the gamble of marrying Ian, who
was a virtual stranger to her, and thus had a part in her
own sorrow. She'd married Ian for the wrong reasons. All
her life she'd taken care of her father and the parishioners,
anyone who needed her. In Ian she'd thought she'd found
someone who would do that for her.

It had been a terrible mistake to put such faith and power

in the hands of a man she barely knew. That was why she did not want to tell Ian she knew what he had done. She knew deep inside herself that she was as much to blame for her present circumstances as he. She had wanted the wrong things from this man. Mary had not married him out of love and respect as she should have, but out of need.

When she opened her eyes again, Ian was turning the horse toward the gate. He looked up then over the horse's proud head, as he headed toward where she stood with the others. Their gazes met, and a strange flash of awareness passed between them.

It was almost, Mary thought, as if he read her mind, felt her emotions, knew and understood her better than anyone ever had. But this was only an illusion caused by her own desire for him. By his own admission he cared nothing for her.

With a silent cry of frustration, Mary turned away, and the crowd parted as if moved by some magic force. Allowing her gaze to rest on the faces around her for no more than the briefest of moments, she tried to get away without having to speak to anyone.

But that was not to be. The tall man who had spoken to her earlier stood in her path. He clutched his cap close against his middle as he bowed to her. Mary was forced, by kindness and courtesy, to address him. "Yes."

"Beggin' your pardon, my lady, for making myself so bold earlier. I was carried away by the excitement of what was happening and thought you might want to know what Lord Ian was about."

She nodded. "I took no offense."

He went on. "Thank you, my lady. And if you don't mind, I want to say, and I think I speak for all of us—" His glance swept the eager faces around them and she saw many of them nod. "I just wanted to say how glad we all are that Lord Sinclair has married and come back to live at the Hall.''

Mary did not know what to say. The truth of her circumstances felt even more painful in the midst of such goodwill.

It was then that the man who haunted not only her dreams but her waking hours spoke from behind her. ''My wife and I thank you for your good wishes, Frank Goodwin.''

She swung around and saw that Ian was now standing at the fence just inside the enclosure. He was watching her with that strange enigmatic expression that so deftly hid his thoughts. Mary looked away from him, her heart hammering inside her chest. ''I thank you, Mr. Goodwin.'' Her gaze skittered over the faces, resting upon none, as she thought only of escape. ''Thank you all. And now I must go.''

With that she turned and made her way toward the house, uncaring in that moment what they would make of her hasty exit. She could not listen to their heartfelt congratulations with Ian standing there, not while she knew how he really felt about her and their marriage.

How she was going to go on with this, Mary did not know. The one thing she was certain of was that she did not want Ian to know how much of a fool she had been.

Her only chance of salvaging any of her own pride was to keep him from learning that she knew the truth. Let him think what he would about why she would now avoid being alone with him.

What she felt for Ian was a simple attraction that could surely be overcome in time. Mary knew that marriage was a lifelong commitment and that she was firmly stuck in a mire of her own making. But that did not mean she should wish to share her bed with a man who had deceived her.

Chapter Eight

Ian strode across the terrace and down the steps to the garden.

He'd met Barbara in the house and she had indicated that his father was in consultation with the head gardener. Ian knew he could wait to discuss the matter of the gelding being sold, but he was too angry. Why did his father have to question his every action as if he was a child, unable to make any rational decision?

Yet even in his outrage he'd had to still a sense of disappointment at not catching any sight of Mary. He knew that keeping himself away from her was best for both of them. When he was with her it was only more difficult for him to deny his desire for her.

Ian ran an agitated hand through his hair.

Judging from the cool expression on Mary's face and her hasty departure the previous day, she had no desire to be with him. He'd not seen her for two days and, perversely, her coldness had shocked and wounded him. The people of the estate had only been trying to congratulate them on their marriage. Why Mary had reacted that way he did not know, other than that being at Sinclair Hall had shown her that she'd made a poor bargain in marrying him.

The pain he felt at her rejection he refused to examine. What he could not ignore was his own guilt in her unhappiness. He should have told her the truth from the beginning. He in fact should not have married her at all. But he had done so. And then, to make matters worse, he had given in to his desire to have her and completely eradicated any possibility of setting her free.

What if there was a child on the way? Ian found that the thought was more appealing than he would have imagined.

The thought of having a child served only to make Ian all the more determined to do right by his wife now. He would be a better father than his own had been to him.

He pushed those thoughts away, forcing himself to remember that he was looking for his father. If he was to do what was right for himself and his wife, he had to move forward with his wish to take some of the responsibilities of running the estates upon himself.

Why, Ian wondered again, did his father have to question every decision he made? When the stable master had told him that his father had ordered him to delay the sale of the horse to their neighbor, William Ridgeway, Ian had been incensed. The man had told him he was looking for an inexpensive but dependable and staid mount for his daughter. Ian had thought of the wounded gelding. He was a fine piece of horseflesh, and it was a shame to put him out to pasture simply because of the injury. Ian had told William about the horse, and they had struck a bargain.

Obviously his father did not share his view of the matter, for when the stable master had informed him of the sale, the earl had balked.

Ian continued through the rows of shrubs and flowers, his eyes peeled for any sign of his father. His agitation prevented him from appreciating the beauty of the garden. The earl maintained a veritable army of gardeners and groundskeepers to keep the formal beds of roses, lavender, tulips, lilies, bleeding heart and a myriad of other flowers and decorative shrubbery in perfect order.

Perfect order, that was what the older man demanded. And it must always be his own definition of what that meant. Lips tight, Ian moved on, determined to confront his father.

He was just passing through a particularly intricate pergola when he noted a woman working the soil in a glaringly empty flower bed nearby. He frowned thoughtfully as something about the bent figure gave him pause.

He stopped in his tracks and looked more closely.

A pert straw bonnet covered her head, but the golden tendrils that had escaped her bun drew the sun as if by magnetic attraction. His gaze slipped down over delicate shoulders, a slim back and narrow waist, then lower. Ian would know that slender backside in the faded blue gown anywhere.

It was Mary.

But what was she doing bent over the gardens in this heat? It was not her duty to work like a servant. Concern for her made him speak more brusquely than he meant to. "What are you doing here?"

Mary curled her fingers in the dirt as her stomach sank. Ian. And his tone was not pleasant.

She stood slowly, being fully conscious of the streaks of dirt on her hands and clothing. Her gaze came to rest on the front of his open-necked white shirt. He was so close, so very close, that when she looked higher she could see the faint stubble of dark hair on his cheeks, the disapproving tightness of his strong jaw.

Mary raised her chin and met his condemning gaze. Gracious, whatever was the matter with him? What could she possibly have done? She spoke with as much hauteur as she could manage. "What does it appear as if I'm doing?" It was he who had wronged her, not the other way around.

His scowl deepened. "It appears as if you are gardening. What I meant was why are you working here this way?"

She ran an unsteady hand over her blue skirt. "I am planting my mother's roses. The head gardener has said I might have this spot."

Mary could not even explain the desperation of her need to perform this task herself. How could she share any more of her inner thoughts with this man who had so easily deceived her? It was as if she would somehow make this one small place her own.

He seemed not even to hear her. "But you are working like a servant. Look at your hands, Mary. You aren't even wearing gloves."

Mary stiffened even more. Was he ashamed that she would get her hands dirty? She liked the feel of the damp earth on her fingers. It was one of the things she most enjoyed about gardening. Was that not a proper diversion for the wife of a future earl? Well, he'd known from the beginning she was interested in gardening.

Perhaps, she reminded herself, it was one of the reasons he had chosen her. She blushed as she realized that certainly it could be. He had hoped to disturb his father by marrying someone completely unsuitable. Obviously he had accomplished this feat more aptly than he had planned for she now was an embarrassment to him.

Mary felt the anger that she had been trying to ignore over the past three days rise up like a sweeping tide inside her. "How dare you." At his surprised expression she said the words again. "How dare you question me as to how would occupy my time. I have been left to my own devices other than sitting for hours having clothing fitted that I did not wish to own."

His lean jaw flexed. "That is not what I—"

She interrupted him without compunction. "Is not what you meant? What did you mean?" She then held up a hand. "On second thought, do not trouble yourself to answer that question. I can hardly find any curiosity in me about what you did mean. All I am interested in is that you have brought me here, then ignored me as if I was some... some...poor unwanted relation, whom you took in out of charity."

He leaned over her, his expression dark with growing anger. "Ignore you? I was not the one who walked away yesterday when I made an attempt to introduce you to the estate workers."

Her mouth fell open in shock. "You are certainly a one to accuse me of wrong after the way you've treated me." Mary stopped herself then, not wanting to go any further. She could not bear the indignity of having him know she was aware of just how little she was valued by him.

She met her husband's foreboding expression and glared up at him in defiance. He spoke slowly and with what was clearly an effort to control his own temper. "Mary, you are putting words into my mouth. At no time have I tried to treat you as an unwanted relation. You are my wife."

She turned away from him, the hurt of his reminder stabbing at her insides like a dull blade. If only he had meant her to be a wife to him. That had never been his intention from the beginning. Her voice was disappointingly ragged when she spoke. "Am I, Ian, am I your wife? I do not feel like a wife. I do not remember my mother well, but I do not recall her life being as mine is. She and my father talked and took long walks and..." She shook her head. "I am not a wife."

His immediate and amazed reply drew her gaze. "Of course you are my wife."

This seemingly earnest reply caught her off guard. Their
eyes held for a long, long moment. To her further surprise,
his looked dark and yearning. If only that wanting was real,
Mary thought as her breast ached with loneliness. In spite
of this, she felt that now-familiar sense of sensual awareness rise up inside her. No matter how angry or disen-
chanted she felt with Ian, she did not seem to be able to
control this wildly intoxicating attraction she felt for him.

She watched as his gaze sank to her mouth and his lids
became hooded. Her breath stilled and her lips parted.

Before she knew what was happening, Ian was reaching
for her. And Mary was melting into his embrace, her lips
turning upward to receive his kiss.

His sun-heated lips tasted slightly of salty sweat. Her
arms encircled his neck. How she had missed him, his hardness, his touch. A longing, warm and creamy like the rum
sauce one ate over Christmas pudding, slowly flowed down
through her to settle in her stomach.

His arms molded her to him as he whispered against her
lips, "Mary, it has been too long."

Her eyes flew open wide as reason came flooding back.
Too long, indeed, and who had insisted on that? It had been
Ian himself, and he'd only done so because he didn't want
her. Her face flamed. Calling on every ounce of will she
possessed, Mary raised her arms and pushed against the
solid wall of his chest. "Release me."

Obviously puzzled at her rebuff, Ian held her for a brief
moment longer, a moment in which she had to remind herself seemingly a thousand times that she must retain her
pride. Then he dropped his arms and stepped back, his eyes
darkly unreadable as she pushed her hair away from her
heated cheeks.

Then it hit her with a shame that was shattering. Ian had
kissed her because he had known how very much she

wished for him to do so. How could he not feel the way she looked at him, the yearning she could not control?

Angry with herself and with him, Mary turned her back to her husband. His voice was devoid of any emotion as he said, "Have no fear, this will not happen again." Each word fell on her battered pride with the weight of a boulder. She had no need of his telling her he was sorry for having kissed her. She remained silent, keeping the pain locked inside her, unwilling to let him see how lonely and unhappy she was.

The next thing she heard was the soft sound of Ian's footfalls on the grass as he left. Only then did she look out over the garden and realize that anyone could have come upon them. Though the arbor offered some privacy, it was by no means sufficient. The fact that they did not appear to have been observed offered very little comfort. Dear heaven, was she such a wanton as far as Ian was concerned that she would have him make love to her in a public place? The knowledge served only to make her embarrassment all the more complete.

Ian rode along the cliff tops, the wind whipping his white shirt against his body.

He was fraught with frustration and self-loathing. Her talk of her parents' marriage had driven home to him the fact that he could not give her the kind of life she deserved. How could he behave as a warm and loving husband with the guilt of his actions between them? Yet her mention of a more normal marriage had made Ian long for those things with an intensity that surprised him.

He had not been able to stop himself from kissing Mary. She was so beautiful, so honest, so proud. How could he not want to kiss her when she faced him that way? She was unlike any woman he had ever known, telling him openly that he had not treated her as she deserved. What drove it home all the more was the fact that it was the truth. He had neglected her and left her to her own devices.

He should not have touched her. Had no right to do so, had never had that right. If only he had not made love to her on their wedding night, she would not be in this untenable position.

But how could he be sorry for having taken her that night when he burned when the merest memory of that event passed through his mind? She had given of herself so completely, so unselfconsciously, that there was no longer room in his mind for the other women he had lain with.

Ian galloped on. He was unable to glean even a modicum of satisfaction from the fact that his father had acquiesced to his wishes in selling the gelding. What difference did it make that he had stood up to the older man and won, if his wife was disgusted by his very touch?

He was so caught up in his own misery that when he rounded a bend he very nearly missed seeing the two men who were arguing in the road. His stallion reared as he brought the animal to a halt just scant feet from them.

With irritation the two looked up from the loud discussion they were having. Their faces changed with dawning respect as they saw who it was. The taller of the two, whom he recognized as being a fisherman named Walter Middleton, pulled at his cap and said, "My lord."

The other man, seeming much less able to control the anger he felt toward his fellow, barely looked up as he did the same and muttered, "My lord."

Walter cleared his throat. "May I be so bold, my lord, as to say how happy we are to hear of your marriage. And that you've brought her home to the Hall."

Ian was washed by a fresh wave of regret and loneliness

at this mention of his marriage. He forced himself to reply politely. "I thank you for your kind words."

"Aye, and that goes for myself, as well—Nathan Long," the other man echoed. When Ian looked at him he saw that Nathan's dark blue gaze was filled with annoyance and remained fixed on his companion in spite of his obvious attempt at politeness.

Ian could not ignore these indications of strife. "What is the problem here?" he asked them.

Middleton looked to the other man. "I borrowed Nathan's boat and whilst we were out fishing the patch came loose from the side. He is now saying that I must pay for the repair."

"That's right, you are, Walter Middleton, and pay you will." Nathan hit his palm with an angry fist.

Walter looked to Ian with beseeching eyes. "I believe the patch was ready to fall off at any moment. It could be that was why he was so eager to loan it."

Nathan scowled. "It's lying you are, Middleton."

Walter focused his brown gaze on Ian. "Would you, my lord, I mean if it wouldn't be too much trouble, would you come down to the shore and have a look for yourself? I know you've been around a boat or two as a youngster."

Ian felt a strange sense of pleasure pass through him. None of the tenants had ever asked such a thing of him, although he had made various visits to Sinclair Hall over the years, even if they had been admittedly short-lived. "You would have to abide by my decision," he warned.

Both men nodded.

Ian nodded in return. "Very well, then. In the morning."

Ian left the scene feeling somewhat as if he had made some momentous advancement. Always before, the villagers had gone to his father. Now they were asking him to settle a dispute.

Walter had mentioned his marriage. Were the tenants now seeing him as a man and their future lord because of his marriage? It seemed that might be so, in spite of his father's lack of enthusiasm and clear desire to keep anything from changing.

Perhaps life could be different for him now?

A sardonic smile curved his lips then as he recalled Mary's rebuff after their kiss. Her initial response had not prepared him for the revulsion he had seen in her eyes.

Clearly she had no desire to have him in her presence, yet also as obvious was her sense of isolation. He knew that in Carlisle she had been much occupied with charity work, having taken the position her mother would have held. It was no wonder she was feeling somewhat desolate here. He would see to it that she was introduced to the community. He would treat her with the honor that was her due, no matter how difficult it became to keep his attraction to himself.

Ian approached Mary as she was leaving the breakfast room the next morning. As usual, he had not put in an appearance at the meal and she was more than slightly surprised to see him.

Her gaze flicked across his wide shoulders, which were encased in an impeccably fitted coat of dark blue, then down over lean hips in matching trousers and on to highly polished black riding boots. As usual, these items were all worn with casual elegance. Mary had to restrain a sigh. There was no denying it, he cut a dashing figure without even trying, which was part of why he was so compellingly attractive.

He spoke softly, drawing her attention back to his face, his dark eyes holding her own. "I want to ask you something, and I don't want you to say no immediately. Take a moment to think before you decide."

She only just stopped herself from smoothing an anxious hand over her pale green morning gown. Their last encounter had been admittedly devastating to her self-control. After the way he had behaved, kissing her when it was he who had said they should not be together, Mary wanted to walk away.

But the earnestness in his face stopped her. "I will listen."

He went on with what she might have thought was relief if she hadn't known that Ian had no reason to be that concerned about whether she listened to him or not. "I wish for you to accompany me to the village. I would like you to meet some of the people. They have begun to ask after you, and I am sure they are understandably curious about their future mistress."

Future mistress. Mary bit her lip. She did not feel like anyone's future anything. She had spent an entire meal trying not to see Barbara's surreptitiously disdainful glances. Ian's father, though no longer openly hostile, was little better, sitting at the head of the table in near silence for the whole of the meal. Every few minutes she would catch him watching her with a strangely assessing expression that made her want to lower her own gaze, but she forced herself to face him each time.

Mary had walked out of the dining room desiring a few moments of peace away from them. Although she knew she meant nothing to her husband, was he not offering her some time away from this dark, solemn house, its even more solemn occupants, its ghosts?

In spite of the fact that she would be spending the next few hours in the company of the one who most disturbed her, she found herself saying, "Yes. I would be very glad to be out meeting some of the people who live in the village.''

She was surprised at the seeming pleasure on his face before he quickly became more sober and went on, ''We will be riding, if that is agreeable to you?''

Mary nodded. ''Please give me just a few moments to change.'' She then turned and hurried up the steps, only by chance noticing the fact that Barbara was watching her from the doorway of the breakfast room. Her expression was so cold that Mary felt a chill run down her spine, before she quickly pushed the reaction aside. She was not going to let Ian's cousin spoil her outing.

Ian was waiting at the foot of the front stoop when she came down. He was holding the reins of his own favorite black stallion. A groom held the reins of a lovely chestnut mare.

The groom moved around to assist her in mounting, but Ian waved him away. His hands seemed to linger at her waist. Mary pointedly ignored the intimacy of his nearness, his touch. She wanted no reenactment of what had taken place in the gardens. The groom's watchful presence on the steps was obviously deterrent enough to control her wayward attraction to Ian, for she was able to keep a tight hold on her reactions.

Without looking into her husband's face, she settled herself in the sidesaddle, arranging the skirt of her butter yellow velvet riding habit with studied care. Yet she was infinitely aware of him as he went to his own mount. A moment later they were on their way. A heavy silence fell over them, and the sound of the horses' hooves on the tree-lined drive seemed unnaturally loud in her ears.

Ian seemed as uncomfortable as she felt. Mary could think of nothing to ease the tension. Nor, she told herself, did she have any desire to.

It was with no small feeling of relief that she saw a cart being pulled by a donkey approaching them. As they drew closer she saw that the man at the reins was an odd-looking fellow. He was dressed in grubby homespun fabric that had seen better days. Though his stomach was round and solid-looking, his arms and legs appeared thin. As he pulled his cart to a halt on the road before him, forcing them to stop as well, Mary also saw that his face was a deep shade of red, his nose bulbous and covered with broken veins. She did not need to smell the scent of gin that rose up to assault her nose even from atop her horse to see that this man was a drunkard.

He spoke to Ian without preamble. "My lord."

Ian nodded. "Kemp."

He took off his cap then and nodded respectfully toward Mary before turning back to Ian. "My lord, I was wondering if there was some work I could do up at the Hall. I've got my cart here." He pointed behind him with some pride.

Ian replied, not unkindly, "Have you spoken to the estate manager, Wally?"

The man nodded his gray head, frowning. "He says there's nothing for me." Then he turned pleading eyes to Ian, licking his lips, then running a hand across them. "But I've a sore need, my lord. I will give you good service for whatever I am paid."

Ian looked at him for a long, thoughtful moment. "All right, then. Go on up to the stables and tell Herman that I sent you. He'll tell you what to do."

"Thank you, my lord, you won't be sorry." Wally Kemp was already nudging his donkey out of the way to get past them. Without another word he was plodding down the track to the manor house.

Mary looked at Ian for a long moment. "That was very kind of you."

Ian glanced back over his shoulder and shrugged. "I'm not so sure of that. The poor old sot will just run to the tavern as soon as he gets a few coppers. We won't see him again until it's gone."

"Nonetheless, one can't help feeling sympathy for him in his trials," Mary returned quietly. She was surprised at this new side of Ian, and for some reason it disturbed her. Possibly because this level of sensitivity had not extended to herself.

He went on, unaware of her thoughts, his gaze on the distant blue sky. "Yes, I sympathize. He was once one of the finest fishermen in the village, well respected and prosperous. Then he lost his wife and children in a storm. I believe all he has left is that cart and donkey. It's a pity what losing the people you love can do to a man."

Mary had the distinct feeling that he was talking about more than Wally Kemp. "You are speaking of your father, are you not?"

He looked at her as if only then remembering her presence, the cool mask back in place. "I was speaking of Mr. Kemp, nothing more."

Mary raised her chin. It was a mistake for her to forget for even a moment that no matter how kind or approachable Ian might seem at any given moment, he would not allow her past that outer facade. Unable to speak at all for fear of saying too much, she started down the road in silence.

What were they to do, neither of them happy in this marriage and with no way to resolve it? For Mary suddenly realized that she felt alone and isolated for more reasons than her estrangement from Ian. She felt detached from her own self.

For the first time in her memory she had something on

her mind that she could not say aloud. It had been all she could do to keep from telling him that she knew he didn't want her when he kissed her in the garden. Only her anger at his remarks about the inappropriateness of her working there had driven it from her mind.

Even now, the force of her own sense of honesty prodded her to speak her mind, to have the truth out in the open instead of gnawing away inside her like a nest of termites. The depth of her hurt and her own responsibility in it were just too painful to risk revealing. So she rode on in silence, as he did.

They went some way and the silence stretched until Mary knew she had made a grievous error in agreeing to come with him. As she was about to turn and tell him she must go back, Ian spoke. She heard unexpected hesitancy in his tone and listened carefully to his words. "Mary, I have been thinking about what you said to me yesterday. I can't help realizing that you were speaking the truth when you said I have neglected you."

Flushing, she replied quickly, "I did not say you had neglected me." She had no wish to sound the complaining wife. Mary had even less wish for him to take her with him today out of guilt.

He answered with equal haste. "That is true. The words are my own."

Mary felt his gaze on her down-bent head and could not resist him. She looked up and over into his face, which was too handsome for her peace of mind. His eyes were dark with some undeniable emotion. She felt that familiar tug at her insides. Heavens, why could she not stop feeling these things when she was with him?

Self-preservation told her that she did not wish to speak with Ian about any of this, not now, not ever. Mary did not need his pity—or anything else from him, for that matter, she thought. She dragged her gaze from his. "I...there is no need for you to worry about me. I am faring quite well."

He was silent for a moment and she thought, hopefully, that he had decided to let the matter rest. He had not, for he began again, "Mary, I just want you to know that you are free to do whatever you please. You may garden, or visit with the tenants or any number of other things that will keep you happy and occupied. I do, in fact, plan to introduce you to some of the village women this very day. Whatever needs doing in that area you are free to decide, being much more expert with such works than any of the rest of us. Barbara seems not to have much time for such things."

As he continued to speak, Mary felt her heart drop. He wanted her to be the caretaker of those in need. It was what she had done all her life. Not that she resented the work she had done with the poor and needy—she had just hoped to be more than that to someone, someday.

Anger rose up to cover her pain, and she felt herself grow stiffer. Occupy herself, would she? That would certainly absolve him of any guilt in her unhappiness. Why, she felt like a mischievous child who was being given a task in order to keep her out of trouble. At the mention of the name Barbara, her control finally broke.

Mary knew that Ian had had feelings for his cousin, had likely only put them aside out of his own need to defy and upset his father. How could he, with any conscience, compare her to the woman that, if Barbara was to be believed, he really loved?

With an exhalation of outrage, Mary halted her horse and glared over at her husband. "How dare you? How dare you, sir?" she repeated in an unthinking rush. "You think that giving me something to busy myself with will make it all well. That it will absolve you of any involvement with me.''

All the pain of the past few days rose up to crash over her in a drowning wave as he faced her, his expression filled with shock. Shocked, was he? At her?

''What?'' he sputtered.

''You will not go on,'' she told him coldly. ''I have heard quite enough.''

''Mary,'' he growled, ''what has gotten into you?''

What had gotten into her? Suddenly she could no longer hold back, even for the sake of her pride. The hurt rushed forth in a gush of misery that could no longer be hidden. ''Ian, there is no need to go to such pains to occupy me. I would prefer it if you just went about your own devices and left me to my own. You may do so without worry. I know that you did not want me as your wife, and I would be grateful if you ceased in these efforts at pretending otherwise.''

He interrupted with a frown that was growing more irritated by the moment. ''Not want you...efforts at pretending otherwise. I do not understand.''

She halted him with a gasp of outrage at his continued evasion. ''I heard you say as much, Ian. The night you spoke to your father in the library at Sinclair Hall.'' At his confused expression, she went on, ''I wanted to talk to you and waited, but you did not come. I had gone looking for you. I felt we should talk about—'' she blushed, but forced herself to go on ''—about what you had said in the carriage. I felt that there was no need for... Well, after I heard what you had to say, I understood the true reason that you did not want to be with me.'' She raised her chin and faced him squarely. ''I did not intend to eavesdrop. But when I heard your father's voice I hesitated to go into the library, and then you were speaking...and I could not... Well, it was too late then, wasn't it?''

The confusion and regret in his eyes penetrated her misery. Mary stopped for a moment, wishing with all her heart that it was not true, that she could have misunderstood what she heard that night. If only things could be the way she had hoped they would be between herself and Ian.

The dawning horror on his face was proof enough that all of it was painfully true. She went on, having to say it all, to get the unbearable weight of it off her chest. "I heard what you said to him about marrying me to spite him."

He ran a hand over his face, obviously distressed, obviously trying to think of something to say. "But Mary, you were not meant to hear that."

"I'm sure I was not," she answered without intonation, her heart a heavy and aching thing in her breast.

"I did not mean...I can explain."

She looked away from him. "I really hope you will not. There is nothing you could say that would heal the hurt you have caused me. For even if you did not really want me or care about me, Ian, how could you tell your father? How could you expect me to face him with him knowing you valued me so little that you married me simply to upset him?''

Ian had no reply. He could not think of a single thing that could rectify what he had done. He felt a sweeping relief that she now knew, that this secret was no longer such a heavy weight upon his soul. At the same time, he realized it had brought Mary all the pain he had hoped to spare her. Even more unfortunately, he knew that Mary would never forgive him for this.

He suddenly understood that even from the beginning Mary had been more to him than a means to test his father's love. That issue had simply clouded the truth. Ian had respected and admired her since the first time they met. But she would never believe that now. He raised hopeless eyes to hers.

Mary sat there staring at him for what felt like aeons, her face set with resentment and disillusion. Ian knew her disdain was only what he deserved. He shook his head, wishing he could change what he had done. "I am so sorry. I have wronged you and there is nothing else to say."

She turned away and swung her horse around. "I hope you'll forgive me if I do not stay."

Ian called out, "Wait, where are you going?"

Briefly her eyes met his. "I want to be alone, if you don't mind."

He held up a hand. "I can't just let you go off alone like this."

Her jaw tightened. "You can and you will. I feel it is the least you can do under the circumstances. You have no right whatsoever to tell me what I may or may not do."

He said not another word, though his own jaw flexed as she prodded her mount away from him. For a moment Ian sat watching her trim back, which remained stiff and unyielding. Finally with a growl of frustration he swung away and urged his stallion to first a canter, then a gallop.

She was an obstinate and willful young woman. And he desired her more with each passing day, a fact that served only to fuel his ire.

Mary wiped the tears from her cheeks with the back of her hand. She had not wanted to tell Ian that she knew, but his persistence in treating her with such studied tolerance had driven her past the point of breaking.

Well, she told herself fiercely, there would be no more

need for pretense. Now both of them knew exactly where they stood.

She rode on, unheeding of where she was going as the road curved to the right and she realized that she could now see the sea off to her left and far down from her. The track appeared to follow the edge of the cliffs that rose at the back of the shore below. Slowly she became aware of the seagulls overhead screeching and diving in the sparsely clouded blue sky. The salty sea breeze was reviving, and soon her tears dried, though the ache in her chest eased very little.

As she continued, Mary became aware of a man kneeling at the edge of the cliff just a few paces from the road. He seemed very occupied with what he was looking at and did not even take note of her approach until she was directly upon him.

He swung around, his gray eyes troubled and relieved. "Thank God, someone has come."

Reacting immediately to the panic on his face, Mary drew her mount to halt and slipped to the ground. Without even thinking, she dropped the reins and moved toward him. "What is the matter?" Immediately she heard the sound of the mare's departure. Mary looked after her in consternation, but quickly turned back to the man, who was paying not the least bit of attention to her escaping mount.

He was peering back down over the edge. "It's my boy, little Tom. He's gone over the side."

With a gasp of horror, Mary rushed to his side, the mare forgotten. But the moment she looked out over the verge of the cliff an attack of horrendous vertigo seized her. Some hundred feet below, the rocky beach seemed to tilt and sway. Her stomach rolled as her head seemed to spin. She closed her eyes even as she heard the man say, "See him there? The poor mite has hurt his head and can't tie the rope I've brought around him.''

Mary took a deep breath, fighting the waves of dizziness. The situation was desperate. She could not allow this weakness to overcome her now. Carefully she opened her lids and looked—not out over the wide expanse of open space to the beach and ocean beyond, but straight down below her.

This method did help, for her eyes focused on the small boy without that sickening vertigo. He was lying on a narrow ledge about ten feet from where they crouched. She gasped aloud as she saw that not only was the boy hurt but he was quite young. He could not be above five or six at the most. "Heavens," she whispered, "how did he fall?"

The man shook his head. "The side of the cliff gave way here. One moment he was standing beside me and the next he was gone. We were looking for gull eggs. That's why I had my rope along. The boy knows how to tie a knot, but he can't do it unconscious." His voice caught. "I don't know what I'll do if he falls. How can I tell my wife?"

Even as he finished speaking, the child moaned and moved restlessly on the narrow ledge. Mary held her breath with fear until he settled back into deeper unconsciousness.

Something had to be done—and now.

If only she had not let her horse get away. They could have tied the rope around the man and used the horse to pull him and his child to safety. But that was not an option.

Since there was not even a remote possibility that Mary could hold the man's weight, let alone his coupled with the child's, she would have to be the one who went over the side. Just the mere realization of this made her swallow down the nausea that rose in her throat.

Standing before she could give herself any more time to

think, Mary said, "I will go. Tie the rope around my waist.
I can hold on to the boy and you can pull us both up."

He looked at her with eager agreement. "Yes, I can do
that. I'm strong as an ox."

Quickly he began to do as she had said. Mary was glad
that he seemed too happy at the thought of actually saving
his son's life to notice her fear. For she was not sure that
she was hiding it at all well in spite of her efforts. Her
knees felt as if they would collapse at any moment.

When the rope was tied, she stepped to the edge, wiping
her damp palms on her yellow riding skirt. She hesitated,
her gaze meeting the man's. For the first time he appeared
to sense some of her agitation, for he frowned in concern.
"Are you sure you wish to do this, miss?"

She smiled with forced confidence. "Oh, yes, quite
sure."

From below them little Tom moaned again. Mary
shrugged. "Well, let us hurry now, before it's too late."
She did not know if the urging was directed more at herself
or him.

The man did not have to be encouraged again. He braced
himself at the ready, the rope wrapped around his waist.
Mary turned her back to the seemingly endless open space
and swallowed, feeling her way backward until there was
no more solid ground beneath her heels.

With a last glance at the man's face, she nodded and slid
carefully over the edge. As she slipped into nothingness,
her body pulled the rope taut and she dangled helplessly
there in the void. Mary's stomach rolled as an indescribable
terror rose up from her belly to hold her in its taloned grip.
Again she had to close her eyes as she clutched desperately
at the rope.

God help her. She couldn't do it. She couldn't help them.
A hoarse sob escaped her. She would crawl on broken

crockery to go and fetch someone else to do this, but she could not.

Even as she opened her mouth to give voice to the panic gripping her, the little boy groaned again. This time the sound was louder and Mary knew that he was coming around. If he did so, he might surely fall to his death.

There was no time to fetch anyone else. She was his only hope.

Calling on a well of inner strength that she had not even known she possessed, Mary focused her mind to a fine point. She looked down, allowing herself to see the child and only the child, his milk white cheeks, his limp little limbs. All else—sound, touch, emotion, even the fear—was pushed to the farthest recesses of her mind.

The rope lowered. Slowly she came to rest on the ledge, and looked down into a pair of confused blue eyes just as they opened. Softly and with more confidence than she would have thought possible, Mary said, "Listen to me very carefully. You must not move. You've fallen, Tom. Lie still now for a moment until I am in a position to get hold of you. Then your father will pull us both to safety."

To her great relief, he seemed prepared to do exactly as she had said without question. He stared at her with those wide eyes. "Do you think you can do what I have asked?" She spoke only to keep him busy while she maneuvered herself to get hold of him.

He nodded. "Aye." To her surprise he asked with a child's curiosity, "Are you the young lord's new wife?"

She nodded in return. "Yes, I am." She was glad to see that he did not seem addled by the injury to his head. The child's astuteness in guessing her identity seemed proof of that. His father had made no remark on her identity, though she could not fault the poor man for being too distracted to care who she might be.

Chapter Nine

Fury scalded Ian's mind as he urged his horse to a gallop. But as he rode on, he realized that the anger he was feeling was directed toward himself, not Mary. Finally he began to acknowledge the hurt he felt at the disdain he had seen in her eyes. He had no one to blame but himself.

He could go to her, explain that he had married her to test his father, but tell her of his other reasons, as well. He could speak of his desire for her, his respect for her honesty and directness. But what right did he have to defend the wrong he had done to Mary?

He continued toward the village, fighting with all his might his inclination to go after his wife. He had no right to expect her to listen to his explanation. Yet the desire to go back to her did not leave him even as he bypassed the village and went directly to the docks where he was to meet the men. Forcing himself to concentrate on the matter at hand, Ian located the boat. To his amazement, the men were not there.

In fact, there was no one working in the dock area at all. There were no women cleaning fish, no men mending sails or nets, no children playing or searching for shellfish. No one.

Ian scowled and peered off down the beach, first to the left, then the right. He was rewarded with a sight that further surprised and intrigued him.

A group of villagers was running down the beach off in the distance. They were calling to one another and pointing on ahead of them. Wondering what might be happening, Ian turned his horse to ride after them.

The stallion covered the distance in no time, and Ian was preparing to call out to those just ahead of him when he saw that farther ahead of these folk a sizable crowd had gathered at a point where the beach grew narrower and more rocky. Some of them were gesturing to the cliffs above, but Ian could not see what they were looking at because of an outcropping of rock that blocked his vision.

Becoming more and more intrigued by the moment, Ian hurried on. But when he rounded the outcropping and saw what lay above them along the wall of the cliff his heart lurched. He could see the form of a woman dangling from a rope as she slid over the edge of the cliff. To his utter horror he realized it was Mary.

He did not want to believe the evidence of his eyes. But that butter yellow dress was unmistakable. An image of that dress tattered, of Mary cut and bleeding on the rocks, came to his mind and he groaned at the pain it brought him.

He also had a vivid memory of the fear of heights she had exhibited on the day he had found her on the steps of the bell tower in Carlisle. Her terror had been all too real.

What, then, could have induced her to do this?

Without pausing to consider whether he could reach her in time to be of aid, Ian swung the stallion around and headed back the way he had come, unheeding of the rock-strewn beach. He could not remain there on the shore and do nothing. The wind whipped his hair into his eyes and he paid it no attention. He trusted in the horse to find the way.

The ride seemed to take forever, and yet had no feeling of reality for him. It was only when he finally reached the place along the top of the cliff and found a man, a rope pulled taut around his waist, that Ian began to see, to hear, to think again.

He leapt to the ground and hurried to the other man's side. Looking down, he saw that the man had pulled Mary nearly back up to the top and that she was holding what appeared to be a child tightly against her.

Only now did he understand how Mary could have overcome her fear of heights. She had done so to rescue a child. This did not surprise him in the least.

Yet this realization did not lessen his certainty that she must be terrified. He knelt and reached for them as they hovered at the edge.

Ian barely heard the shout of triumph and joy that went up from the beach far below.

Mary seemed to have very little awareness of him when he put his arms around her as she held on with almost desperate determination to the precious burden in her arms. He pulled her up into his secure embrace, feeling his heart pound with relief and exultation. Only when he had carried both his wife and the child back a safe distance from the ledge did Ian even attempt to separate them. And it was only with the other man's assistance that he was able to do so.

Leaving the other man to see to the boy, Ian ran shaking hands over his wife, who lay still against him, her eyes closed. When he came to her hips he discovered with a jolt of dread a wet red streak. "Do you hurt somewhere?" he asked her, his voice harsher than he had intended in his fear for her.

She shook her head, her eyes glazed. "What?"

He lifted her face, looking directly into her eyes, trying to make her see him. "Mary, you are bleeding. Are you hurt?"

She looked up at him, her golden eyes only then at last taking on a semblance of recognition. "No, no, it must be young Tom's blood." She seemed to have completely forgotten her anger with him, and did not even question his presence.

Somewhat calmed by her finally seeming to have some awareness of what was happening around her, Ian was relieved that she accepted his presence, but was certain it had more to do with her anxiety over the little boy than that she was no longer angry with him. He pushed such selfish concerns aside. He determined to discover where the blood had originated, and glanced over at the man. "The child, is he bleeding?"

"No, my lord, just a bump on his head is all I can find." He held the child close.

A frown of worry creased Ian's brow as he looked down at the streak of blood, which he could now see was spreading quickly. Turning so that his body offered some modicum of privacy for his wife's modesty, Ian lifted her skirt and found the injury.

It was a jagged and badly bleeding cut right along the outside of her thigh. It looked to him as if it had probably been made by a tree root or some other such object. "It is you who are bleeding, Mary."

Mary waved a careless hand. "I am sure it is nothing. I cannot even feel it. You must see to little Tom. He will need the doctor." She tried to sit up, though he could see that the shock of what she had been through was still apparent on her pale face and in her haunted eyes.

Ian held her down with gentle insistence. "Lie still, Mary."

Her golden eyes focused on him in confusion. "Why will you not listen to me, Ian? We must see to little Tom."

He was surprised at the depth of tender emotion that rose in his chest at Mary's insistence on taking care of the little one even though she herself was hurt. His voice was gentle but resolute. "Your injury is quite serious, my dear. You can do no more. We must get you home."

He stood and lifted her into his arms just as a pony cart arrived on the road behind them. Two men jumped down and raced toward them.

"You see, he will be fine. Assistance has arrived." Ian held Mary so that she could get a clear view of the men as they placed the little one in the cart.

With a sigh she subsided back against him. Looking down at her, Ian saw that she had fainted.

Another unexpected wave of tenderness tugged at his heart. For some reason these fond feelings were nearly as devastating to his equilibrium as his earlier feelings of fear. He had no time to question why.

Holding her close against him as he rode for Sinclair Hall, Ian tried to think of nothing save getting her home and looked after. The demons in his mind would not be set aside. Guilt prodded him as they flooded him with images of the hurt and disillusion on her face when she'd told him she had overheard what he'd said to his father. Ian knew that such an offense would not easily be forgiven, possibly not at all. Though he could not blame Mary if she did hate him for what he had done, he wished in some small part of himself that it was not so.

Mary opened her eyes and surveyed the beautiful cor-niced ceiling with some bewilderment. Her last clear memory was of being held in Ian's arms. After that, things had become too muddled for sense, faces and voices mingling confusingly.

She had a vague recollection of being taken to her room, of being examined, then drinking some unpleasant-tasting substance. After that, the blur became darkness.

A soft knock sounded at the door, drawing her attention. Mary leaned up, then gasped as a jolt of pain radiated out from her thigh. She sighed and subsided back against the pillows. "Come in."

The door opened to reveal Ian. She felt a shiver of nervousness grip her even as she took note of his surprisingly disheveled appearance. An unaccustomed heavy shadow darkened the lower half of his face, and even as she watched he raised a hand to rake it through his already ruffled dark hair. She vaguely remembered Ian being there to help her over the edge of the cliff, of his being concerned about some injury to her leg. That injury must be the one that was causing her such discomfort now. But that did not explain his unkempt appearance nor his being here in her bedchamber. What, she wondered, could he have to say to her?

She watched, biting her lip as he moved across the carpet silently. Ian came to a halt at the foot of the bed. To her surprise he seemed somewhat uncomfortable, even hesitant. Finally he spoke. "Mary, it is good to see you awake. I came earlier, but you were still sleeping."

At his gentle reticence, Mary felt an unexpected tug of emotion she did not want to examine. But it eased the perturbation she felt toward him. She nodded and pushed a golden curl back from her forehead with an unsteady hand. A glance toward the windows showed her that the light peeking between the drawn drapes was bright. "It must be quite late. I am sorry for my lassitude. I don't know what is the matter with me. I only just awoke."

Ian shook his head. "There is no need to apologize. You have been through a very traumatic ordeal. That coupled with the laudanum the doctor gave you before stitching up your wound would make anyone sleepy."

She moved a questing hand down to her thigh beneath the covers. "Stitches? Why, is it so very bad, then?"

He nodded. "Serious enough to keep you immobile for some time. The doctor insists that you do not walk or put any weight on it for the next few weeks."

Mary shook her head. "Weeks, I cannot..."

His jaw tightened, and she couldn't help noting that with that shadow of beard he looked quite rakish and autocratic all at the same time. "You can, and you will."

Her own will rose up to combat his. "I will not lie abed for weeks." She told herself her opposition to him had nothing to do with the twinge of awareness she felt in her belly as his eyes met hers.

He raised a hand. "That you will not have to do. The doctor has said that once you begin to heal you may certainly get up." Just as Mary was enjoying the sense of relief that washed through her, he went on, "It is simply a matter of being transported from one spot to another. I myself will carry you anywhere you wish to go."

Mary's eyes flew wide in horror. "You will not." The last thing she wanted was to be thrown into such close contact with the man who had used her so vilely. Especially when his ignoble actions did not seem to make the least difference to her mutinous senses.

Ian frowned, clearly fighting his own temper. "I think there are some things that must be discussed, after what you revealed to me yesterday."

She turned away, her face set. "I do not wish to speak about any of it further."

Ian shrugged. "Nonetheless, you will listen to me."

Though she balked at his commanding tone, she was quite helpless to do anything but listen at the moment. She could give in to the childish impulse to place her hands over her ears, but that would serve only to give her husband more of an upper hand.

She remained silent as he went on, surprising her enough with what he said to make her look at him again. "I am very sorry for becoming angry with you yesterday. I had no right. I was simply reacting to my own guilt over what I had done. You were and, I suppose, continue to be within your own rights to be angry with me. I did not treat you fairly and there is nothing I can do that will change the fact. I can only hope to do better in the future. Have, in fact, tried to do so since realizing just how wrong I was on the morning after our wedding night."

Mary gasped, this catching her completely off guard and thus drawing a more open response than she wanted to give. "If that was the case, why did you withhold yourself from me? I am a clear embarrassment to you. You did not want me anymore." A deep blush stole over her face and neck as she realized how much she had revealed.

Ian looked at her in obvious shock. "Withhold myself? Not want you? Nothing could be further from the truth. I simply did not feel it would be right to touch you because I felt that if you knew the truth you would not want me."

Mary felt the heat of his eyes as they raked her, and pulled the covers more securely against her bosom. She did not want him to know how very wrong he had been, that even now, knowing all she did, her body responded to him with a force that surprised and appalled her. She raised her chin, determined to keep him from knowing the truth, for how could she give in to this unwanted desire with any sense of self-respect?

She spoke quietly. "I thank you for your apology. But under the circumstances it changes nothing. You are so angry with your father, and I think—" she looked at him then "—with yourself over your brother's death that you cannot give your heart to anyone, Ian."

The ensuing silence was deafening. At last he said, "Perhaps you are right, Mary. I do not know that I am capable of loving anyone. But I had hoped that we might...well, we are married...and I thought we might try to have some kind of relationship, learn to respect each other, make peace with one another."

Mary shook her head sadly, her heart heavy at hearing him admit what she had already known to be the truth, that he was not capable of loving. Even though she'd not expected any such emotion from her husband, she now knew that that was exactly what she did want, and desperately. Why this was so when she did not care for him, Mary refused to question.

She forced herself to concentrate on the other things he had said. "I did give you respect, Ian. It is you who did not return it. How could I ever trust you again?"

He flinched as if struck, then grew stiff and dark as this house of shadows. He did not face her as he bowed. "Very well, you are within your rights to feel that way. But I am your husband and that cannot be changed. We will try to behave as a married couple, if only to show some modicum of normalcy to people of this household and community. I owe them that as their future overlord. In view of that decision, I will be the one to aid you in getting about when the time comes. There will be no more discussion on the matter."

Mary's lips tightened, but before she could form a reply

he was gone, shutting the door behind him with finality. It was clear to her that Ian was determined to do just as he said. Though she wished there was some way around it, in her present state of helplessness there was really nothing she could do. Mary could only hope that when the time came he would see reason.

He simply could not expect her to allow him to carry her about, to hold her next to that hard, strong body, the memory of which haunted her dreams, day and night.

Three days later when the doctor said she might get out of bed, Mary was so grateful that she was willing to accept assistance from anyone in doing so. Well, nearly anyone.

When Ian came to her only minutes after Frances had finished helping her dress and do her hair, Mary forced herself to fight the flutter of awareness that raced down her backbone and made the fine hairs rise all along her neck. He was so very handsome in his snug-fitting buff riding breeches and white lawn shirt. It was obvious that he had just come from working with his horses, for his dark hair was wind tossed and his aristocratic countenance was lightly flushed as if by the sun.

Mary looked down at her hands where they lay tightly laced before her. She wanted to tell him that she could not allow this, but the expression of total immovability on his face told her it would be no use. She could either stay here in her room or allow Ian to take her down to the sitting room where Frances had prepared her a spot on the settee. One quick glance around the bedchamber, which, though beautiful, had begun to feel like something of a prison, decided her.

Surely she could manage this small inconvenience to escape for a few hours. She glanced over to where Frances hovered nearby. The maid had barely left her side since the

accident, and if not for her, Mary might indeed have fared
far worse over these days in bed. The maid's worried eyes
told Mary that she was not about to leave her side now.
Thus they would not be alone.

When Ian moved toward her, she squared her shoulders
and looked up at him in resignation. "Thank you for coming to help me."

He seemed slightly surprised for a moment, then
shrugged. His answer was delivered with cool politeness.
"As I have told you, I am happy to do so."

Mary pushed aside the disappointment she felt at his re-
moteness. It was, after all, what she desired. A nervous half
laugh escaped her as she glanced up at Ian when he came
closer to the bed. "Well, how shall we go about this?"

He bent over her without preamble and scooped her up
into his strong arms. "Just like this." Ian then moved
across the room with a purposeful stride as Frances raced
ahead of them.

Mary felt somewhat silly to have made such an issue of
his assisting her when Ian took her the whole way without
so much as even looking at her once. Apparently he was
doing this for just the reasons he had stated. That he wished
for them to appear like any other married couple.

Unfortunately Mary was the one who could not still the
flutters of her own pulse as the warmth of his hard chest
penetrated her violet morning gown. She held herself
stiffly, determined to keep him from knowing how she reacted to him.

It was only briefly, as he laid her on the settee, that his
onyx gaze met hers and she thought, just for the space of
a heartbeat, that she saw a dark, heavy sensuality in his
gaze. But he looked away immediately, directing his attention to Frances, his voice devoid of emotion as he asked,
"Is there anything else you need?" Mary told herself she

had been mistaken. What he had said about still desiring her had only been another effort to salve her pride.

Knowledge of this helped Mary to recover her composure as Frances replied, "No, thank you, my lord." Her awe of Ian was apparent in her tone and the roundness of her eyes. Mary saw this with some sense of irony. He affected members of the female sex without even trying.

Ian turned to her. "Is there anything else you would like, Mary?"

She bit her lip. "I would like something from the library. Frances does not read, thus cannot assist me." A fact that Mary intended to change when she was better.

Ian nodded. "Of course. I should have thought of that myself." He then added, "I am also certain Barbara would have been willing to do as much."

Mary looked down at the green-and-peach-patterned carpet. She had no intention of telling him that Barbara would be the last one she'd ask for help. The woman had been to see her for a brief period each day at precisely three-thirty, and had stayed exactly ten minutes. That ten minutes had been the longest of Mary's day, as they really had nothing of note to say to one another—that was, until yesterday.

Barbara had quite surprised her with a sarcastic remark about how tragic it was that she had hurt herself and put the whole populace into an uproar. From the expression in her dark gaze, Mary had had the uncomfortable feeling that the other woman would have been much happier if she had not returned from the ordeal at all.

Mary had quickly told herself that this was ridiculous. She was reading far more into the acerbic woman's remark.

Still, Mary had no wish to have more contact with Ian's cousin than was absolutely necessary, but could see no point in telling her husband this. She simply replied, "She is so busy with running the household. I have not felt right about inconveniencing her.''

Ian looked as if he would like to argue the point further, then obviously changed his mind, for he said, ''I will be back with some reading material shortly.''

When Ian had left, Mary looked around the attractive chamber. She had purposely asked to be taken to one of the rooms Ian's mother had redecorated. This was a pleasant apartment with its light colors, but the drawn drapes prevented it from being as cheery as she would like. Raising her chin, Mary turned to Frances. ''Please pull the drapes aside. I have no wish to sit here in the dark.''

Frances gave a start of surprise, but immediately moved to do as Mary had asked. The bright sunlight flooded the room from the tall windows and Mary felt her spirits rise with its entrance.

Thus it was without enthusiasm that she heard Barbara's incredulous and condemning voice from the doorway. ''What are you doing, Frances?''

Mary stiffened from her head to her toes. She spoke quietly to the maid. ''Frances, would you please go up to my room and fetch my shawl.'' The pretty maid looked at her mistress with concern. ''Are you sure, my lady?''

Mary was developing a real affection for the gentle-hearted maid, and with each day that passed was more certain she had made the right decision in taking her as her own personal servant. She knew that Ian's cousin was still resentful for having been overridden in that matter, and she would not allow Barbara to take her anger out on Frances now. ''I am quite sure. I don't want to take a chill now when I am doing so well.''

Mary said nothing more until Frances, frowning with concern, left the room.

Slowly she turned to face the other woman. "I do not wish to sit in the dark."

Barbara's dark brows rose high as she came into the room to stand near the settee. "How dare you countermand Cousin Malcolm's wishes?"

Before Mary could voice the stinging reply that hovered on the tip of her tongue, Malcolm Sinclair himself spoke up from behind the entrance. "Thank you for defending my position, Barbara, but I believe I will make an exception in this case. Mary may have the drapes drawn if she wishes."

The dark-haired woman faced him with surprise. "But..."

He raised an age-spotted hand. "But nothing. Mary is to have whatever she needs to recover from her ordeal. She has behaved with the kind of courage other members of this family should take heed of."

With her hands clenched before her, Barbara nodded. "As you wish, Cousin Malcolm. I did not mean to cause you displeasure. If you will excuse me, I must see to dinner." She left the room without a backward glance, her back as straight as those on the chairs in the formal dining room.

Mary's gaze returned to Malcolm Sinclair as he spoke softly, almost as if to himself. "I have not been in this room for many years." His dark eyes fell on the mantel clock, the furnishings, the carpets, with sadness.

Mary could not prevent the question that rose to her lips. "But why?"

The older man looked at her, and for a long moment she thought he might not reply. Then to her utter surprise he did so, speaking almost as if he could not prevent himself. "My wife decorated this room shortly before she died."

Mary wondered if coming into the chamber had broken

through the barrier of long-buried pains as he went on, "She died giving birth to Ian. Even then, I came here on occasion to remember our times together, but that was before our son Malcolm..." His face appeared gray and haggard with the sorrow of missing his lost loved ones.

Mary spoke softly. "There was an accident."

"Yes." He nodded. "On that day all the light and laughter went out of this house."

Mary flinched. Dear heaven, no wonder Ian was hurting, unable to forget the past. She found herself saying, "But what of Ian? He is your son. You had the responsibility of living on for him."

He shook his head as he looked at her, his back straight and inflexible. "He had caused the deaths of the two people I most loved in this world. I had nothing to give him."

A hoarse gasp sounded from the doorway, and Mary looked toward it. Ian stood there, his face as white as his lawn shirt. His gaze was fixed on his father, who also paled at seeing his son's reaction to his revelations.

Without a word, Ian moved forward and set the books carefully and quietly on the very table his father was leaning against. The two men exchanged one long look, then Ian was gone.

No wonder, Mary told herself as she continued to watch after her husband long after he was gone, he was not able to love. No love had been shown him. Malcolm Sinclair had allowed his grief to overshadow all else in his life, and though he now seemed sorry for it, how could such a wound be healed?

In spite of the division between herself and Ian, her heart ached for him, for the losses he had been forced to face alone. She turned to her father-in-law, driven to speak by sympathy for her husband, even when she knew her words would not be welcome. "Ian was a boy and he needed you. It is your choice to allow this to continue, my lord, or not."

To her utter amazement he did not reprimand her but shook his head. "I fear that was once the truth. But no longer. Ian is a man now and no longer needs or wants my attention. Too many years and too many hurts on both sides have preceded the current state of affairs." His voice hardened then. "I realize that you are only trying to help, and in deference to what you have just done to save one of our folk, I will allow you this one attempt at interference."

He moved toward the door and Mary kept her silence, knowing she had already pushed far beyond any right of hers. To her surprise, Malcolm Sinclair stopped briefly at the door, his gaze assessing as he looked back at her. "My wife was very like you, my dear. Brave and courageous and honest, but she died and left us dour men to our own devices. There is no salvaging us now."

Then he was gone, leaving Mary feeling cold and empty, though the sun continued to stream through the tall windows and the birds continued to dip and dive in the blue sky outside, casting their quickly moving shadows on the carpet.

Mary envied them their mobility, their freedom. If only it was so easy for her to fly away from her own troubles.

Chapter Ten

Ian raced the young white stallion across the pastureland. In the days since he'd heard his father admit that he blamed him not only for his brother's but also for his mother's death, Ian had driven himself to the point of exhaustion. It was the only way he could keep from being crushed by the pain that threatened to totally overwhelm him. On some remote level he knew that as a man he should have some sympathy for his father's sorrow, which was still so heart-rendingly deep after all these years. But it was difficult to keep this in his thoughts. He was too wrapped up in his own grief at his father's lack of care and the pain of not having known his mother at all.

The stallion reacted to his urgings for greater speed with enthusiasm. At any other time Ian would have taken both pleasure and pride in the fact that the animal was more than living up to the promise Ian had sensed in him. He was still training the beast, but felt if he continued to give such abundant time and attention to the stallion he would soon be able to trust the horse as he did Balthazar.

The only time he had left the horses in the past few days was to carry out his declaration to take Mary wherever she wished to go. Privately he had instructed the maid, Frances, to send for him no matter when. She seemed to take this as some sort of attempt at love play on his part, for she had smiled with approval. She had also faithfully complied. Ian was sure the maid could not be completely blind to the strain between himself and his wife.

Ian had been stung by Mary's rejection of his attempts to make peace with her. Yet the sympathy he had seen in her since he had inadvertently overheard his father telling her why he so resented his son had not been any more welcome. Sympathy was not what he wanted from her.

Ian was a man, with a man's desire. He did not need her compassion. Last evening he had been unable to withhold the sardonic response to those pitying glances. He'd been taking her to her room after dinner and had halted in the act of carrying her across her own threshold. "That is quite enough."

She had looked at him in surprise. "What?"

"I do not now, nor will I ever have a desire for you to look at me as if I was some wounded child and you my nurse."

She had flushed, looking down at the buttons of his shirt. "What makes you think I am doing that? I do not feel sorry for you, Ian Sinclair. You've got enough armor around your heart to protect you from everyone and everything. I wouldn't dream of inflicting any tender feelings upon you."

He'd known she was speaking out of anger, but he also knew his outburst had effectively done away with those tender feelings she spoke of. Ian had tried to convince himself he was glad. He had neither expected nor accepted that kind of compassion from anyone for many years. He was not about to show any sign of weakness. He owed no one that.

Mary's stony silence had greeted him this morning when he went to see of she wished to go down to the sitting room for the morning meal. She'd broken that silence only to tell him she was breakfasting in her own chamber.

He felt unexpectedly regretful for having hurt her again. But he simply could not expose the fragile inner parts of himself to anyone. Too many years had been spent securing them from pain.

Mary lay on the settee, her book forgotten on her lap. Her father-in-law had succeeded in persuading her to allow him to carry her down to the sitting room.

Yet nowhere could she escape from the unhappiness of her thoughts. Ian's words to her of the day before had proved again that he had no wish to allow anyone into his heart.

Mary looked up, grateful for the distraction, as Frances came into the room.

Frances approached her slowly. "Lady Mary, Emma Smith, the mother of young Tom, is here to see you."

Mary sat up straighter. Although she was not able to walk as yet, her movements did not cause her nearly as much pain as in the beginning. She smiled with pleasure at this news. "Please tell her to come in."

Grinning from ear to ear, Frances hurried from the room. The woman the maid returned with was dressed in home-spun clothing that was both clean and meticulously mended. The child that clung to her skirts was outfitted in the same tidy manner.

Frances announced with impressive formality, "Mrs. Emma Smith and young Tom Smith, my lady."

The little boy peeked around his mother's skirts, and Mary saw that he seemed none the worse for his mishap. His round cheeks were flushed with health and his eyes wide as he looked at both Mary and his surroundings with a child's open curiosity. Mary turned to his mother with a smile. "Mrs. Smith, it is so good of you to come."

Emma Smith dipped a respectful curtsy. "You are kind, my lady."

Mary indicated the chair near her. "Please do sit down."

Emma did so hesitantly, putting her arm around her son's shoulders as he leaned against the arm of the chair. Mary could hear the deference and slight nervousness in her tone as she said, "I came because I wanted to tell you myself, my lady, how very thankful I am for what you did for me and mine. My family, and the rest of the folk in the village, for that matter, are so very glad that Lord Ian had found himself such a kind and brave lady. We hope you will live a long and fruitful life together and soon have children of your own." She hugged her son just a bit tighter.

Mary blushed. "I did nothing that anyone else would not." She was embarrassed at the praise, but even more uncomfortable with the remark about her and Ian soon having children. The possibility seemed completely remote, considering the state of their relationship.

Mary pushed the unpleasant thought aside as Emma went on, "But you could have come to harm, my lady. You were, in fact, hurt."

Mary shrugged. "I am healing very well, thank you. No permanent harm was done me."

Before Emma could go on, Mary turned to Frances, who hovered nearby. "Frances, could you please ask the cook to prepare tea for us?"

Frances bobbed and nodded. "Yes, my lady."

As she left the room, Emma Smith stood. "There is no need to have us to tea, my lady. Young Tom and I only came to say thank-you."

Mary motioned her back down. "I feel under no obligation to do so. Please do sit. Quite honestly I am most glad of the company your presence affords. I have been anxious to meet the women of the village." She made a sweeping gesture to indicate her prone form. "Unfortunately I find myself bound to inactivity for a time. I would indeed be grateful if you would stay to tea."

Emma Smith looked at her with an expression of deepest sincerity in her eyes. "My lady, I should not. It would not be proper."

From the entrance to the room Malcolm Sinclair spoke up, drawing their gazes to him. "Indeed, Mrs. Smith, you must stay to tea. I myself insist." He came into the room and took the chair at the foot of the settee.

Mary was glad for her father-in-law's support in this matter. The older man had been different over the past few days, often coming in to sit with her and have his afternoon tea. He did not speak a great deal, but his mere presence made Mary wonder if he was coming to accept her.

Emma Smith stood and curtsied. "My lord."

Malcolm motioned her back to her seat. "Sit, sit." He looked to the child. "Is this the young man who caused so much excitement?"

The child's eyes were enormous as he looked over at the immaculately groomed and usually dour older gentleman. Mary was surprised at the gentle teasing in the earl's tone as he quirked a brow at the little boy.

They were interrupted as Frances appeared leading a footman with a heavily laden tray. She motioned for him to put it on the low table in front of the settee.

Mary said, "Thank you, Frances," then nodded to the footman. "And you, Charles."

She then moved to pour out the tea. By now she knew that Malcolm took his with milk and three sugars. He reached for the cup with a nod of thanks.

Next came Emma, then a cup for the little one, which

Mary mixed half tea and half milk. She saw the avid interest in his eyes as he studied the cakes. She reached for one of the delicate china plates as he looked at his mother. "Might he have one?" Mary asked.

Emma nodded. "But only one."

The little fellow did not look pleased, but he said not a word of protest. The more Mary saw of this woman and her child the more impressed she became. The woman was raising her offspring with some manners. It would be good to continue this new acquaintance and make others from the village. Mary would indeed be glad to be up and about. Perhaps taking up her old duties in this new place would offer some satisfaction. Perhaps, she told herself, being of use to someone would at the very least offer some distraction from her unhappiness over her marriage.

When Mary heard the voice of the man who was so much in her thoughts she started, rattling the china cup and saucer she held. She looked up to see that Ian had come into the room and was standing just behind Emma Smith's chair. Her preoccupation with pouring out must have kept her from noting his arrival.

She knew she should not be surprised at his presence. He had taken to coming to fetch her and carry her up to her room for a rest in the afternoons. The fact that she had refused to have him take her down to breakfast this morning would not deter Ian from his chosen course. His cold assurances that he did not need any sympathy from her or anyone else had stung. Having guests had extended the afternoon ceremony on this particular day.

He met her startled gaze with what seemed for a moment to be chagrin and sadness, but the accustomed sardonic mask soon covered any hint of emotion. He shrugged. "Might I join you?"

Mary recovered herself quickly, realizing he was only

disappointed at being delayed in returning to the stables. He did continue to believe he must tote her about, no matter how much their relationship deteriorated. "Of course."

"Lord Sinclair." Emma Smith stood and curtsied.

"Please sit," Ian told her, his face remaining impassive. "It is good to see the boy well. Clearly he is none the worse for wear."

Emma perched on the edge of her chair, obviously feeling more out of place by the moment. It was equally obvious that she felt the need to overcome it and speak to her overlord's son from the heart as she said, "My lord, I came to the Hall to see your lady. I wanted her and all of you to know how very glad we are that she has come here. If not for her…"

She paused for a moment, not able to go on, and Mary halted her. "There is no need for this."

Ian looked at Mary, his expression completely unreadable. "Your appreciation does you great credit, Mrs. Smith, but should not be directed toward me. My wife acted from her own conscience, not from any prompting of mine." Mary wanted to squirm under that close regard, but she did not.

She was glad of the task of picking up another cup, for it saved her from having to look into those dark, enigmatic eyes for another moment. She prepared his tea, having now come to know how he took it. It was exactly the same way as his father, with milk and three spoons of sugar. She doubted that either of the men had noted this similarity between them. She also doubted that the two of them would wish to acknowledge having anything in common.

They studiously kept from looking at one another as Ian found a place on the small settee across from her. The tension between them was palpable.

And then, as if there was not already enough to keep her

nerves stretched to the breaking point, Mary heard Barbara's voice. "Well, what have we here? A tea party."

She looked up to see the other woman's disapproving gaze on Emma Smith, then her little boy. As if sensing Mary's attention on her, Barbara raised her gaze to Mary's, her brows arched with disdain.

Mary turned away, sending a sweeping glance over the other occupants of the sitting room. Again it seemed she was the only one to notice the woman's displeasure.

Barbara moved to seat herself beside Ian. Avoiding looking in that direction, Mary began to make polite conversation with Emma Smith, asking questions about the other women in the village and trying delicately to ascertain if there was any area where she might be of use to the people of the community. It did not take long to learn that there was much to be done.

Despite her very genuine interest in Emma and what she had to say, Mary could not help the fact that most of her attention was centered upon Barbara and Ian where they sat on the love seat. They appeared lost in what seemed a very compelling conversation. Only once did she allow herself to glance their way, caring not at all for the intensity on their faces as they bent their dark heads so close together.

That was until Ian glanced up and met her gaze. He looked from her to Emma with an expression she could not even begin to fathom. Barbara followed the path of his gaze and scowled, leaning even closer as she spoke to him, and Ian nodded. Mary felt outrage rise up inside her. Could he not see his cousin for the snob she was? Ian himself did not appear to harbor such an elitist attitude. How could he love a woman like Barbara?

Mary would never be able to feel herself so above those around her, even if she became the wife of a duke. If this type of woman appealed to him, it was very unlikely that he would ever have come to care for her, even if she had wanted him to.

Mary's heart thudded with disappointment and disillusion. When Emma Smith stood only a few moments later and said she must be going, Mary made no effort to dissuade her. Malcolm Sinclair himself showed her and her little boy to the door, leaving Mary, Ian and Barbara alone.

Mary carefully avoided the superiority of Barbara's gaze. She concentrated instead on her teacup, though she could not bring herself to drink. Just a moment later she started as she felt a warm hand take the cup from her fingers.

She looked up to see Ian standing over her, his face wearing that accustomed mask. "Would you care to go up now? Pardon me if I am mistaken, but it appears as though you could use a rest."

Mary nodded without saying a word. She did feel tired and drained. She wanted to go up to her room, to have some time to herself. Even if it meant being taken by her husband. Ian would not linger. He wanted no more part of her than she did him.

Mary's easy manner with the boy and his mother had moved Ian more than he would ever wish to say. They were simple folk, yet she treated them with the same deference she would have shown Victoria and her children had they come to call.

He had been so preoccupied with her, the sound of her voice, the tilt of her golden head, the sweetness of her smile when she spoke to young Tom, that he had hardly been aware of anything his cousin had said to him. He could only sit there and feel an outsider in the face of her relaxed camaraderie with the others.

He had found himself wishing that he, too, could expect to be on the receiving end of Mary's sweet good humor

But that was not likely to happen, ever. And he would do well to accept that. When he rejected her sympathy, he himself had made certain she would not be over kind to him.

Just being in the same room with his father, knowing that the older man blamed him for his mother's death, was difficult. Ian had told himself her death was not his fault, that there was no need for him to take that upon himself with all his other sins. He could not let the tight control he had over his emotions slip. He would not let himself be open to the kind of hurt he had experienced as a boy of seventeen. Never again would he go through that kind of rejection. To allow himself to give in to the warmth and comfort in Mary's eyes would make him too vulnerable.

When Emma Smith had risen to leave, Ian had immediately been aware of the tired droop of his wife's shoulders. Without a word to Barbara he had left her side to go to Mary.

Her ready acquiescence did surprise him somewhat. Especially after her refusal to have him touch her that morning. Ian chose not to question this. He simply leaned down and scooped her up into his arms.

As he made his way to the stairs that would take him to the upper floor, he tried not to think about how warm and delicate she felt, tried not to acknowledge the way his mouth went dry at the soft brush of hair against his face, nor the way his lower body tightened when the firm curve of her breast pressed against his chest.

Ian swallowed, knowing he must do something to distract himself from these unwanted thoughts. He spoke hurriedly, glad that his cool tone did not betray him. "How are you feeling?"

She answered with what he felt was an equal lack of emotion, which for some reason irritated him. "I am actually much better every day. There is really no need for everyone to coddle me so. I think I should be able to get around on my own soon.''

Because of his irritation Ian answered with more heat than he intended, drawing her gaze. ''Dr. Evan says you should not put any weight on your leg for several more days, at least.''

''I fear he, all of you, are being overcautious,'' she replied stiffly.

''We shall see,'' he told her. At that moment Ian felt a cool scraping sensation along his left leg. He frowned as it passed down his leg and into his riding boot. They had now reached the stairs, and as he placed his foot on the bottom step, a stabbing in his ankle brought him up short.

Ian's frown deepened even as he met Mary's questioning eyes. ''Is something wrong?'' she asked, her brows arched high.

Quickly he shook his head, his mind searching for a possible cause for his discomfort, which only increased as he took the next rise. Then it came to him. Earlier he had picked up a horseshoe nail from the floor of the stables. He had placed it in his pocket, not wanting any of the horses to inadvertently tread upon it. The sharp metal must have worked a hole in his pocket and slipped down to rest inside his boot.

Ian glanced down at Mary and saw that her lips were pursed with what he could only describe as proud disdain. A rush of anger overtook him. What had he done to upset her now, other than to be concerned for her? There was no way he would ever admit to having a nail in his boot. She would only find some way to hold that against him, as well, would surely use the incident as an excuse to avoid having him carry her. He was not about to relinquish this task to anyone else, no matter how eager she seemed for him to do so.

Clenching his jaw on the pain in his ankle, Ian continued up the stairs. He would see her to her room without giving away his discomfort.

Mary watched his averted profile for a long moment, realizing that she would get nowhere by arguing with this man. He had shown that he would do as he willed no matter what. There was absolutely nothing to be gained in discussing anything with him, and his tight, pained expression told her quite clearly that he was displeased with her.

Unfortunately, Mary's irritation with her husband did little to keep her uncooperative imagination from straying to things it should not. His large, warm hands seemed to burn through the fabric of her gown where they held her bottom and her back. Her breast was pressed firmly to the hard wall of his chest. And she could not keep her gaze from straying to the smooth column of his throat and down, where the open neck of his shirt gave her a heady view of that equally smooth chest.

With each step, Ian's carriage became stiffer, his jaw more tightly clenched. But that did not stop the inevitable response of her hardening nipple where it pressed against him. Angry with herself and her husband, Mary crossed her arms over her swelling breasts, wishing she had even the slightest bit of control over her reactions to this irritating, yet undeniably compelling man.

His lips remained tight and sweat beaded on his brow, but he neither spoke nor even glanced at her, seeming lost in some dark thoughts of his own. Mary told herself she should be glad he was oblivious to her, but somehow she was not.

When, at long last they reached her room, she saw that Frances had turned down the coverlet on the bed. Eagerly

Mary's gaze searched the chamber for the comforting presence of the maid. To her chagrin, Frances was not present.

As he laid her on the cool sheets, Ian paused for a long moment and she looked up into his face, which seemed a pained mask. Mary turned away. Whatever was the matter with him Mary could not guess, and she was too hurt and angry to try.

Without even a word, Ian jerked away and turned to go. His rigid back and deliberate stiff-legged stride were like a slap in the face, dismissing her, telling her, oh so clearly, that she was just a task to perform before moving on to another.

In that moment Mary's sense of outrage nearly blinded her. How dare he continue to treat her this way?

Through the haze of her frustration she heard the opening and closing of first her own door, then Ian's. For several long moments she lay there on the bed, her breath coming more quickly with each remembered slight. Finally, and without the least bit of consideration of her injured leg, Mary found herself standing, albeit somewhat unsteadily.

Ian had made it clear that he would have none of her compassion. Well, she intended to make it equally clear that she was not going to accept his disdain.

Uncaring as to the wisdom of her actions, Mary moved toward the connecting door between their rooms. She was not pleased that the twinges of pain in her thigh kept her from doing so as quickly as she would have liked. But she did at last gain the portal and took the knob in her hand, meaning to rattle it and demand entry.

To her utter amazement the door swung open at her twisting of the handle. It swung open to reveal a most surprising sight. Ian was sitting on the dressing stool at the foot of his four-poster bed. He was, even as she watched, in the act of turning over the riding boot, which he held in his hand. As his shocked gaze flew to her, a small dark object, which appeared to be metal, fell out onto the light carpet.

To Mary's further amazement Ian flushed, his gaze going from her to the object, then back to her. "Mary, what are you doing here? Can't a man have a moment's peace?" Why was he acting so strangely? She frowned as she looked more closely and saw that it appeared to be a nail of some kind.

At the same moment Ian seemed to realize that she should not be standing there. He scowled as he said, "Why are you walking? You know you are not to."

She ignored the last part as realization slowly dawned. Ian's set face, his stiff, deliberate steps. Heavens, he'd had a nail in his boot and been too proud to say it. What a foolish man he was.

She could no longer hold in her frustration. "Ian, are you mad? Why did you not tell me you had something in your shoe?"

He stood, his lean jaw flexing, his boot still in his hand. If the situation had been the least bit less tense Mary would have laughed, for he did have the look of a schoolboy caught hiding broken crockery. But even as he strode toward her with one foot covered by only his stocking, her husband's air of dangerous grace was not to be denied.

He came to a halt before her, that schoolboy chagrin even more apparent as he raised his chin. When he spoke, it was clear that emitting the words cost him dearly. "I know how you feel about my carrying you about. But, damn it, Mary, I will continue to do it. I thought you would try to use any sign of weakness as an excuse to avoid me."

Mary could no longer hold it in. Her own uncertainty over what he meant by the words and the tension of the past minutes bubbled up inside her. She placed her hand over her mouth to still the sound, knowing that it would only irritate him further, but the laughter escaped in a choking gasp.

Ian's frown blackened to coal. "Laugh at me, will you, when I've just carried you all that way with a nail digging into my ankle?"

Mary shook her head, unable to stifle the sounds of her mirth even though her anger rippled up with it as she replied, "'Tis no one's fault but your own, Ian. Since when has what I wanted meant anything to you? I have told you on several occasions that I do not require your services to cart me about, and still you insist on doing so. I was wrong when I told you how much I needed someone right after we met." She blushed, then continued more firmly, "I need no one to take care of me. But that doesn't seem to matter to you, Ian. You always do exactly as you please."

It was obvious that her sarcasm cut deep, for his hands clenched and unclenched at his sides. The expression on her husband's face did not bode well for her.

"Always do exactly as I please, do I?" he growled, bending to pull on his boot in one graceful motion, then standing tall before her. "Well, if I'm to be accused, I may at least reap the benefits." Before she could react in any way, he reached for her and Mary found his mouth covering hers.

Heat shot through her, and Mary gasped against his mouth, finding herself returning the fierce pressure. Ian's fingers tangled in her hair and she gloried in the hard length of his body against hers. He made no effort to shield her from the depth of his response, his desire pressed to her quivering stomach.

"Mary," he said huskily, making the hairs rise along her arms and on the back of her neck. He continued to rain hot kisses over her forehead and brow. "Do you need me now?"

"I...oh, don't ask me that," she replied, then bit her lower lip, being not at all pleased at the breathless quality of her voice. Nothing could be gained by what they were doing. The Lord in his heaven only knew how much she needed this man, but for all the wrong reasons. Nothing had been resolved between them, and seemed as if it never would be.

But with his hot mouth on her skin it was so hard to think, to form the words that would explain what she was thinking. Why, oh, why was she so susceptible to this man?

"You are so very beautiful."

Her heart thudded in her chest. "Ian, please." She could not let this happen.

"Please, what?" he whispered, leaning ever closer, so close that his warm breath brushed her face.

"Please..."

"Do this..." He brushed those lips over her temple. "And this..." Now on her cheekbone. "And..." He reached up, drawing her gown from one shoulder, his lips slipping down to caress that tender curve, and she shivered.

She held her hand up to her chest to stop him from drawing the gown any lower. He raised his head in question. "What is it, Mary?" His mouth hovered over hers, so close, so very close, and her heartbeat grew so loud that she was sure he could hear it.

She could hardly speak. "We should not do this. So much has happened that has not been set right."

He looked at her eyes, her mouth. "Why can we not start again?"

The words were more temptation than she could ever allow him to know. But she forced herself to remember how he had hurt her, how she had hurt herself by believing in him.

Desperately Mary shook her head. "I cannot, Ian."

His jaw tightened. "Why, Mary, why can't we start again? Am I so despicable, so evil a man that you can never find it within yourself to forgive me?"

She shook her head again, not wanting to tell him the real truth. That she did not trust herself, that she had so badly wished for someone to look after her that she had married a man who only appeared to care for her. That her judgment had been so far from accurate that she could not trust it again. And nothing her husband had said since had made her think he had changed inside. "No, Ian, that is not it. If it will make you rest any easier, I want you to know that I forgive you for marrying me as you did. I see that there is so much bad blood between you and your father that you were consumed by your anger."

He looked as if he wanted to deny her words, but he did not. Instead he nodded. "Yes, there is much bad blood between us, and it did blind me to reason. I was a fool, a boy." He reached for her hand. "But now I would be a man, a husband to you."

Mary did not know how to reply. How very desperately she did want what he was saying, for him to be her husband, for them to have a life together. But it could not be, could it? Ian had seen the truth of his actions, but that had not taught him how to love. Could she allow herself to trust in her own feelings, to care for this man after the terrible error in judgment she had made?

She knew her own reactions to Ian were incredibly powerful. In spite of how very much she had wished to hate him after learning that he had married her to spite his father, she'd been unable to do so. That very fact kept her from giving in to the passion in his gaze. She looked away, recalling Victoria's warning to her that long-ago day in Carlisle. She'd said that Ian could not love, but that he would make Mary care for him. Well, the first part had proved true, and Mary was determined to keep the latter from becoming fact. "I cannot do as you ask."

He stiffened, stepping back, his expression remote as the stars. "So be it. 'Lord Sin' I am to you, and 'Lord Sin' I will remain." He bowed with cold courtesy and scooped her up into his arms. Quickly he carried her through the connecting door and deposited her on her own bed. He stepped back with another stiff bow. "If you will excuse me, Mary." Instead of going back to his own room, he then moved to exit through her chamber.

The hurt in him was apparent and sympathy stabbed her, but Mary did not tell him or attempt to retract what she had said. Ian would never thank her for doing so.

Besides, the fear of being hurt by him was too strong. So overcome by the churning emotions inside her was Mary that when Ian opened her door to reveal Barbara in the corridor she could not react. The other woman took in the two of them, her gaze raking Mary on the bed before Ian hurriedly stepped out to stand beside her and close the door. Mary raised her hand to pull her gown up over her, until now, forgotten bare shoulder. She feared the other woman had completely misread what she had seen.

Mary was not about to apprise her of the truth, feeling it was very likely that Ian would do so. For it would not be a great surprise to Mary if he should turn to his cousin for solace. Ian was not a man to live without passion.

Chapter Eleven

Mary spent the next day in her room. She did not wish to face either Ian or his cousin.

Thoughts of what had been said by both herself and Ian the previous day, remembering the way he had kissed her and her reaction to that kiss kept her a prisoner. She knew now that Ian wanted her. He had been clear enough on that scale, and he knew that she wanted him. But he had said nothing of love, of trust, and would never do so.

Should she have been so quick to refuse what he did offer? It could not have been easy for a man like Ian, so careful of his feelings, to ask her to try again with him. Could she allow herself to relax her guard, to believe in him again after the way he had hurt her? Theirs had never been a love match, that she had known from the start, so she expected no such declarations from her husband. Mary would have, in fact, been suspicious of them.

It seemed impossible to take another chance with her pride. It was the one thing she had.

Or perhaps, a soft voice within her whispered, the lonely price of pride was too great. Perhaps she had acted too hastily in refusing Ian's suggestion that they begin anew.

It was late in the morning when Mary became so restless

that she could no longer sit in the chair by the window. None of her tormented thoughts offered even a hint of comfort. Gingerly she stood. The fact that she had suffered so little from the walking she had done the previous night emboldened her to try again. There was a definite soreness in her thigh, but it was certainly not unbearable. Carefully she made her way to the other side of the room where her writing desk sat. There she penned a letter to Victoria, though it was of necessity quite short, for Mary could not tell her friend of her troubles.

When she was finished she made her way with equal care back to the window.

When Frances returned to the room from seeing to her mistress's laundry, Mary gave her the missive to post. The maid never questioned how the writing of it had been accomplished, obviously believing that someone else had been of assistance. Mary did not dissuade her.

Later that night Mary lay awake in her bed. She rose, being ever mindful that Ian might very well be on the other side of the door that separated their rooms.

She moved back and forth across the floor a few times, taking care not to put too much pressure on her leg. It had come to her that she was far too dependent on others with this injury plaguing her. Once she was up and about on her own again, she might then be in a better frame of mind to think clearly about her relationship with Ian.

She passed the next day in much the same fashion, still taking care not to allow anyone to know that she was exercising her leg. She knew that the doctor had forbidden it, but her steady improvement encouraged her.

Ian did not make any attempt to see her. She began to wonder if he had forgotten the things he had said to her about starting anew, or worse yet, that he might not have meant them. She became even more determined to recover from her injury and restore what small amount of autonomy that was hers.

That night Mary found herself slowly pacing the confines of her chamber. Biting her lip, she realized the bedroom was just too short a span to test her endurance. The house was quiet at this late hour. She could, without much fear of meeting another soul, go down to the long gallery at the end of the hall.

So nervous was she of being found out that she kept her ears and eyes peeled for any sign that someone else might be about. Ironically enough, she was not sure that she would hear any warning sounds above her own quickened breathing. After walking only two lengths of that hallway, Mary was quite ready to find her own bed. But having succeeded in doing so much, Mary realized she would soon be ready to tell the others that she was walking again.

Once the house was quiet the next night, she set out to repeat the exercise.

The hallway, as on the previous night, was dark except for the light shed by her candle. Mary did not want to light any of the wall sconces and thus risk discovery.

Last night she had managed to traverse the long hallway twice. On this night she would double that. After the lack of mishap on the previous evening, Mary was much less nervous this night. As she made her way carefully down the hall, she noted the portraits of Ian's ancestors, which seemed to stare down at her from either side. Yet far from being intimidated by them, Mary felt as if they approved of her efforts. These folk had been the masters of this land for generations. Surely they would applaud her own resolve to be strong and independent.

They would understand why she found it so very difficult to put her happiness and well-being into the hands of one who had already hurt her. Namely Ian. Quickly she brushed this worrisome and painful thought away.

It was on the third pass down the hall that Mary began to get an odd sensation that something was not quite right. Raising the candle high, she looked about, but saw nothing revealed in the circle of light. The far end of the hall lay in heavy darkness, and the feeling persisted as she tried to penetrate the gloom. Telling herself not to be foolish, Mary reached up to wipe the dampness from her brow with the sleeve of her nightdress. She was simply growing tired, that was all.

She was determined to follow through with the goal she had set herself. Gaining back her mobility was of the utmost importance.

Setting her jaw with resolution, she continued on her way. At the end of the hallway was a set of stairs that led down to the kitchen. The family never used this narrow flight, as it was designed for the servants, who could go about their tasks with less intrusion.

Directly across from this stairway was a tall window with a long velvet drape that obscured a little-used window seat. It was there that Mary knew she would have to rest for a moment.

As she moved down the hall, the feeling of apprehension grew. "I'm just getting tired," she whispered with forced confidence.

As she reached the staircase, Mary paused for a moment gripping the balustrade before turning to find the window seat. She glanced back the way she had come. It was quite a distance, but surely with a rest she could manage. Under no circumstances was she prepared to call for assistance, even if she had to crawl back to her room.

She took a deep breath and released the railing.

It was at that moment that she felt the fingers of a

splayed hand dig into her back, but before she could even think about what was happening she was being shoved. With a cry of shock Mary fell forward, the candle dropping from her hand. Desperately she grabbed for anything within reach.

Her groping fingers closed around that balustrade, stopping her forward rush. Another unexpected cry escaped her lips as her healing wound was brought into painful contact with the railing. In an instinctive reaction she brought up the other hand to hold on with it, as well.

Gingerly she moved to ease herself up into a sitting position, and halted with a sharp intake of breath. She was unable to restrain a moan of anguish. Mary closed her eyes as the pain radiated downward and up into her hip. She waited for several long seconds as the ripples subsided somewhat.

When the pain eased a bit, she was able to gain a sitting position. Only then did Mary think to look behind her, but encountered only darkness. The candle must have gone out when it fell, which she supposed was fortunate in one way, as she had no wish to have set fire to Sinclair Hall. But she could see nothing that might give her a clue as to who had pushed her.

It was then that Mary saw a flicker of light approaching down the length of the hall, and knew a moment of panic. But immediately the presence of the light told her this was surely no foe. She must have awakened the household with her cries. Shame washed over her, even as she, unwillingly, was grateful that someone was coming to assist her.

The light came closer, and she soon realized that the bearer was Malcolm Sinclair. She realized her excursion must have brought her nearer his rooms. He rushed toward her, his face haggard with concern as he saw her there.

Before he could do more than gasp, "My God, Mary,"

the sound of Ian's agitated voice coming toward them drew her gaze back down the hall. A candelabra in his hand, he appeared in the opening to the corridor, Barbara at his side. The other woman was wearing a diaphanous night rail and her dark hair hung in wild disarray about her shoulders. Even in the candlelight her cheeks looked flushed, her eyes luminous.

Even in her present state of distress, Mary could not deny her own surprise. She would not have thought Barbara could be so desirable looking. Elegant and cool was the way she would have described her until now. It was almost as if she had just been... Mary looked to Ian and saw his own tousled hair, the haphazard state of his obviously hastily donned night robe, which had been pulled only halfway across his firmly muscled bare chest. She turned away, not wishing to think the thoughts that were churning in her mind.

She tried not to look at the man and woman as they rushed forward at seeing her there.

Mary did not meet Ian's gaze as he knelt at her side, but she could hear the horror in his voice. "Mary, what has happened?"

She looked at Malcolm, finding it much easier to meet his gaze. "I was exercising my leg...."

She paused for a moment as the two men gasped in both shock and exasperation. "Please don't lecture me now. I know that the doctor said I must not, but I assure you I have been doing so for several days and have been faring quite well." She faced them with a raised chin.

Ian spoke with what sounded like anger. "Obviously not as well as you would have us think. You've fallen and hurt yourself."

She looked directly at him then, her eyes narrowed. "I did not fall. I was pushed."

There was a long silence. Then all three of the others spoke at once.

"But that is impossible."

"Who would dare do such a thing?"

"You must be mistaken."

Mary looked at each in turn, a growing anger churning inside her. She had been pushed, yet none of them was even willing to listen.

Not even Ian. The ache in her chest was nearly unbearable as she faced him again. "I assure you, I was pushed. Yet, since no one believes me, there is really no point in discussing the matter."

He blanched, but did not waver in his stance. "Mary, you must understand how very difficult it is to think that someone in this house might wish to harm you. Why, the servants and the townsfolk fair worship the ground you walk upon."

Barbara spoke gently, drawing Mary's attention. "We saw no one, and came here directly upon your cries. How could anyone have gotten past us?" Her eyes were narrowed and her lips were pressed together tightly despite her seeming kindness of tone.

What the woman said was undoubtedly true. Mary herself had been blocking the stairway to the lower levels when she fell. Anyone leaving the scene from the other direction should have been seen as the others approached.

It made no sense.

But Mary did know that someone had pushed her. How they had gotten away should certainly be secondary to that fact.

Barbara spoke again, in that same reasoning tone. "Your leg must have given out, thus causing you to fall."

Ian nodded his head. "That must be what occurred."

Malcolm nodded, too, though his expression was filled with sympathy. "There is no other explanation, my dear."

Mary glanced at Barbara, to see that she seemed overly pleased with the fact that both men took her explanation as fact. She even laid a possessive hand on Ian's arm as his father went on speaking. "You simply overtired yourself. It would be easy to think such a thing had happened if you had pushed yourself beyond your physical limits. You are far too hard on yourself." Looking into those reasoning eyes, Mary could not find it in herself to be angry with Malcolm. He was very worried about her.

But Ian, and Barbara. They were another matter.

Mary refused to allow herself to think that her anger with them had anything to do with the fact that they had arrived on the scene together, both of them disheveled. Surely Ian would not carry on an affair with his cousin beneath Mary's own nose. Yet even as the thought rose like a festering wound inside her, Mary reminded herself that Ian was not a man who would long live without female companionship.

"And now—" Ian interrupted her thoughts "—I think it best if Mary goes to bed. I want to take a look at her wound."

She folded her arms across her chest. "There is absolutely no need for that. It is fine." The leg was not hurting so very badly now that the initial pain of falling had subsided.

Ian ignored her assurances. "As I said, I will take Mary back to her room and look at the injury. We will discuss this in the morning should anyone feel the need to do so further."

At his words, Mary's mouth twisted with chagrin, then determination. He was bent on doing things his way and she would not argue with him here in front of the others, but she was not about to let Ian look at her thigh.

Barbara appeared slightly less pleased with herself now as she turned solicitous eyes up to Ian. "Would you like me to come along and have a look at the injury, too?" He shook his head and swung away from his cousin. Mary did not think he noted the way her brows curled in a frown of displeasure.

Yet only a moment later when Ian drew her up into his arms, Mary's interest in Barbara evaporated like a drop of dew in the sunlight. Immediately she became aware of the feel of those strong arms, that hard body against hers.

As he moved down the corridor toward her chamber, Mary was washed by a rising sense of outrage. God, how she hated him, hated herself. No matter what he did, which might even include sharing the bed of another woman in the same household with his wife, she could not stop herself from responding to the feel of him, the warm male smell of him.

Ian felt the tension in Mary's slim body as he carried her.

In the days since he had asked Mary if she would be willing to start afresh, Ian had done more thinking than he would have wished. He had not planned to ask her that, had not known he was going to do so until the words were out. He had been overcome by his desire for her, the need to be with her.

Her immediate rejection of his attempt at reconciliation had hurt more than he would have thought possible. The strength of his reaction had made him realize that Mary had come to mean more to him than he would have expected.

In the course of the past days Ian had come to know he wanted to have a relationship with his wife for more reasons than just respect or even because of desire—that need he could satisfy elsewhere if he wished. She was bright, kind and undeniably brave. Those things he had known.

But somehow in spite of his determination to keep anyone's opinion of him from mattering, hers did. For some reason he wanted her to approve of him, of the changes he had made.

The rigidity of her body told him very clearly that she did not. Though he knew he had no right to expect it of her, he could not stop the ache in his chest.

Feeling as if his heart had suddenly taken on the weight of a heavy stone, Ian opened the door of Mary's room and closed it carefully behind them. He then took her across the floor and laid her on the bed with too deliberate care.

Only as Ian looked down into her stormy golden eyes did she speak. "You may certainly go now. I do not require your examination. I will ask Frances to look at the wound in the morning." When he did not reply she leaned up on her elbows to glare at him, her golden hair flowing about her.

Her vehemence was like a slap in the face. He straightened with a groan of frustration. "What is wrong now? What have I done to make you so angry with me? My God, Mary, it is all I can do to keep myself from you. I want you so badly I think of nothing else night and day. Just now before I heard you cry out I was pacing that room—" he pointed toward their adjoining door "—and wishing I had the right to come in here to you. That you would not send me away if I was to do so. And every time I come near, you reject me."

Mary felt the blood rush to her face. He had not been with Barbara. He had been thinking of her, wanting her. In spite of all the other problems assailing them, her heart sang at his admission. But she forced herself to think, to respond with some reason to what he had said. "Reject you, Ian? Do not accuse me of rejecting you. I have never done that."

He bent low over her. "Have you not?" Even in the heat

of her outrage she was indescribably beautiful, her breasts
rising and falling beneath the thin fabric of her nightdress.
Even as he watched her nipples hardened.

With a gasp she moved to cover them with her arms, but
it was too late. Her body had given her away. She wanted
him, as he wanted her. Unable to stop himself, Ian pressed
his mouth to hers.

With a groan of despair Mary reached up to push him
away. But her arms seemed to have a will of their own, for
they closed around his neck.

He responded by putting his own arms around her, drawing her closer still and deepening the kiss. She melded to
him, unable to think about anything but the heat that spread
from his long body into her own as he eased himself down
beside her. Her legs opened to allow him to fit more fully
against her pliant form.

He raised his body and slid one hand down her side to
her hips. "Lovely, so very lovely, Mary." Slowly and with
infinite patience he ran that same hand over her quivering
belly, then up across one breast, circling slowly around the
turgid tip.

Heat rippled through her body in waves, moving outward
over every part of her from his hand. Her breast felt full
and aching with the longing for him to touch that eager
point. And still he did not, moving to the other breast to
tease and caress it in the same vein as its sister.

She could barely breathe. Every nerve, every part of her
was centered on the tips of her breasts. And so it was with
a cry of sheer ecstasy that she felt his mouth close around
one nipple even while his thumb found the other. A honey-
warm desire flowed through her to the tips of her fingers
and toes. Her lower belly spasmed and clenched as she
pressed herself to him.

It was only when she begged him, gasping, "Oh, please, Ian, please," that he leaned back with a husky laugh.

"Oh, Mary, I had not remembered what a complete delight you really are, how easily you respond to me."

She looked up at him through heavy lids. Sweet heaven, how he made her want him. And from somewhere inside her came the desire to see Ian as helpless with passion as she herself felt.

Though she had but one night's experience to guide her, Mary knew she would do well to think on what drove her own body to such need. Surely a man was not so very different from a woman.

Deliberately Mary reached down and tugged at the front of his robe, pulling it open to press her lips to his warm flesh. How many times had Ian carried her from one place to another? How many times had she imagined herself doing just these very things, kissing him, running eager fingers over the smooth hardness of his muscular chest?

With unwavering insistence, she rose next to him and pushed him down where she had been. Ian looked at her in question and she shook her head. "Shh, Ian. I will have my way."

He subsided then, looking up at her with heavy lids as she bent to ply his own small male nipples with her tongue. She was rewarded for her efforts by the sharp catch of his breath and the closing of his eyes. His hands tangled in her hair. "Mary, Mary."

A strange feeling of power filled her and she wanted to do more, to make him quiver with passion as he had her. Her head moved lower. Her tongue flicked out to wet his navel, as he had hers on their wedding night, and his stomach muscles spasmed. His response made her own body ache with longing.

But when she dipped her head lower to nuzzle the dark

hair above the joining of his thighs, he stopped her. "No, sweet." His eyes met hers with a heat that was scorching. "You are not ready for that...yet."

He then pulled her up above him, drawing her along the length of his body to press his mouth to hers. She opened her lips, taking his hot tongue into her mouth, feeling the pulsing of her blood in her veins, reveling in the feel of him beneath her. His hands smoothed the length of her, then clasped her to him, holding her hips to his lean ones. She felt the evidence of his arousal firm and ready against her lower belly.

Mary could wait no more. Opening her legs, she slipped over him before he could move to stop her. Mary arched at the sheer ecstasy of having him fill that moist and throbbing void.

Ian pulled his mouth from hers with a gasp of pleasure and surprise. She smiled down into his eyes. "Do not tell me I am not ready for this, my lord husband. For I have done it."

He grasped her bottom in his palms and pushed himself deep inside her. Mary felt herself opening to him, accepting him into the deepest, most secret places of her body and soul. He filled those lonely recesses that had been empty too long. Only joined as she was to Ian was she whole in this way, connected to the source of her completeness.

The sensations built to a pinpoint of incredible pleasure, making her breath come in sobbing gasps. She threw back her head, rocking against him at the absolute rapture of it, drowning in the pleasure of the waves of indescribable delight that rose to close over her.

Even then as she sighed her rapture aloud she felt him stiffen beneath her and call her name. "Mary."

Chapter Twelve

Mary woke slowly, her body responding with heavy languor to her mind's instructions to raise her arms. Then as she asked herself what had caused that languor, her eyes flew open wide. In the next instant she was sitting straight up in bed, her gaze going immediately to the bare pillow on the other side of her bed.

Ian.

Dear heaven, he had made love to her. Immediately she corrected herself even as the heat rose to her face— *they* had made love. No woman could have been more eager or more forthcoming in a man's embrace than she herself had been. A fact that did nothing to soothe her. She raised her suddenly chilled hands to her hot cheeks.

What had she done?

Mary was not prepared to trust in Ian, to believe in him as a husband. The power of her reaction to his lovemaking told her she could not let this happen again. There had been something far beyond mere physical pleasure in their coming together and it frightened her. Ian was not a man she could allow herself to care deeply for. Nothing he had done had shown her that she could do so. How could she allow herself to behave as if they had a normal marriage, as if there was some basis for trust and respect between them?

She could not.

A knock sounded at the door and Mary called out "Just one moment" as she searched frantically beside the bed for her discarded nightdress. Settling herself back on the pillows with as much calm as she could call forth, she added, "Please, enter."

It was Barbara. She smiled with what appeared to Mary's eyes to be forced solicitude.

Mary tried to conjure a smile of welcome, but felt she did little better than Barbara had. Ian's cousin came into the room and closed the door. "I hope I'm not disturbing you, Mary."

She answered hurriedly, "Oh, no, of course not. Good morning."

Moving closer to the bed, Barbara folded her hands before her. "I trust you are feeling better this morning."

Mary nodded, looking down at her own hands. "Yes, I am, thank you." She only wished the other woman would say what she had come for and go.

Instead Barbara took the seat beside the bed and said, "My, you have no idea what a turn you gave us when you screamed like that in the dead of night. Ian's countenance went completely white."

Mary's startled gaze flew to the other woman's face, though she quickly tried to hide her shock even as she asked, "You and Ian were together?"

Barbara blushed, then nodded her head with obvious reluctance. She replied, "I...yes, we were together. I don't know why I should not admit that. We were...going over some of the household accounts." Mary could see that the other woman was thinking desperately even as she spoke. Ian's cousin finished with an uneasy laugh. "We were perfectly innocent of any wrongdoing. Although I know you are aware of the true state of Ian's and my feelings for each other, you may rest assured that he has broken no vow to you."

Mary watched her for a long moment. Barbara was just too wide-eyed, her smile too fixed. Could she be lying about how far their relationship had gone? Had Ian lied? The thought left a cold ache inside her. Her decision to keep her heart safe from her husband seemed all the more sound. But Mary was not about to let Barbara know how upset she was over this. She replied softly, "You have no need to tell me this. I did not accuse you of any wrong."

Barbara answered soothingly, "Of course you did not. I just did not wish for you to think..." She trailed off meaningfully. "I was especially concerned after your impression that someone had pushed you last night, however impossible that might be. You have stayed to your room over the last few days. I thought you might have been unwell and I feared it might have made you overwrought and imaginative."

Mary frowned. "I am not overwrought, nor imaginative. Someone did push me."

Barbara placed a hand on the dark blue silk that covered her bosom. "I have upset you. You must forgive me. I did only come to see if you were all right after your mishap."

"I am fine." She met the other woman's gaze levelly.

Ian's cousin stood. "I...well, that is most fortunate. I will not stay and overtire you."

"Thank you for your concern." Mary did not even bother to try to dissuade her from leaving, though she was not in the least bit tired. With thinned lips she watched the other woman go.

The moment the door was closed, she threw back the covers and sat up on the edge of the bed. The hurt she had

experienced since Barbara's disclosure that she had been
with Ian the previous night emerged in a growl of outrage.

Ian must have lied to her. He had told her that he was
alone in his room, thinking of her. Yet why would he do
so if, as Barbara had insisted, they had nothing to hide?
Mary had not liked the odd way the other woman had behaved over the whole matter. It had been as if she was
holding something back in spite of her assurances that all
was perfectly innocent. And what had Ian been doing helping her with accounts in the middle of the night dressed in
nothing but his robe? As Mary recalled quite clearly, he'd
worn not a stitch beneath it.

She leapt up and had taken several steps toward the huge
oak wardrobe before realizing that she was walking with
no more than a slight limp and no discomfort. She had told
Barbara the truth when she'd said she was fine. Her leg
seemed none the worse for her mishap and certainly had
not been any deterrent to the activities she and her husband
had engaged in the previous night.

Again Mary was assaulted by anger and hurt. Ian had
lied about being with Barbara. Did he think that because
she was not of noble birth as his cousin was that she
counted for nothing, that he could use her without compunction? Her chest ached with regret and sorrow.

She pushed the hurt away. It only reminded her anew of
how foolish she was, how very much all of this was her
own fault. If she had not wanted so desperately to have
something that belonged to her, to have someone care about
her above all else, she could be living quite comfortably
with Victoria. The void inside her would not be filled, but
neither was it now. It only seemed to yawn wider and wider
with each slight from her husband.

Ian took the stairs two at a time. He had woken early
and realized that he was with Mary, in her bed. As he

looked at her sleeping face he'd been overcome by a feeling of tenderness that had nothing to do with the passion they had shared. Just being near her like this made him feel warm, complete.

He'd wanted to wake her to tell her how contented he was, but she'd been sleeping so deeply. Her ordeal of the night before had likely left her exhausted. It would be selfish of him to wake her.

He'd decided instead to go out and take the white stallion for a turn around the pastureland. By the time he returned, his wife might be awake.

The stallion had not gotten his accustomed length of time. Ian had cut the ride short, unable to wait to see Mary again.

As he raced up the wide staircase, he wondered what might be her reply to a suggestion that they spend the remainder of the day in bed. Ian's lips curved upward at the thought that his passionate little wife might feign shock, forcing him to the task of kissing her into agreement. He paused for a moment at her door, wondering if he should knock. He did not hear any voices coming from inside.

He shook his head. No, he'd just slip inside, being quiet in case she was still sleeping. Carefully Ian opened the door, his eager gaze going toward the bed. It was vacant, the covers thrown back.

His gaze moved quickly over the room and came almost immediately to Mary's face where she stood beside the open wardrobe. Mary's scowling face.

He paused for a moment in surprise. This was not the reception he had envisioned.

"Get out," she cried before he could say a word or even assess the situation.

"What?" He could not digest this reaction so quickly.

She put her hands on her slender hips, and raised that pert nose of hers high. "I said, sir, that I want you to leave."

He stepped into the room and closed the door behind him as an unexpected pain rose inside him. He swallowed the lump of sadness in his throat, letting anger take him over. Was he not owed some clarification for her apparent anger? If she thought he would just go with his tail between his legs, no explanation given, Mary could certainly think again.

She watched, gasping with outrage, as he closed the door. "How dare you? I do not want you here."

His lips thinned to a forbidding line. "And I will not go without an explanation of some kind. What has gotten into you?"

"What has gotten into me?" She tossed her long golden hair back over her shoulder. "I am not the one who has lied to you since the beginning."

He grew very still. "Mary, I have tried to show my regret at the way I treated you. I wish to heaven I could take back what I did to you, but I cannot. All I can do is be honest now and in the future."

A cold light burned in her golden eyes as she scoffed, "Do you mean to tell me that you have been honest with me?"

Would they go over these same grievances endlessly? Ian knew she had a right to be upset with him, but they could never hope to move forward if they could not put it behind them. He threw up his hand in exasperation. "Yes, I believe I have. I thought all that was behind us. I have admitted to how wrong I was. Can you not find it within you to forgive me for more than a few hours?" His eyes bored into hers as she looked up at him. Ian could see the sheen of tears she was trying desperately to hide.

She turned her back on him and he moved closer to her as she said, "I would be willing to forgive you that and try again to have a life with you if you were able to be honest with me from that moment. But you have not been."

Ian felt more confused than he had ever been in his life. What was she talking about? "Mary." He tried to keep his tone even despite his bafflement. "Please tell me what is wrong. The last words that passed between us were anything but angry."

She faced him, her cheeks flushed, her gaze uncertain. Then she again turned her back to him. "I cannot, Ian, for you will only deny it. And there are other issues that would not be solved even if that insurmountable problem did not exist."

Realizing that he was not going to get more from her on the first subject, Ian tried to follow this new train of thought. "And what might those problems be?"

She did not look at him. "I will never be your equal in your eyes. I will always be the vicar's daughter and you the earl's son. It was there the day you came upon me working in the gardens after we first arrived here. Surely a more nobly bred woman would not soil her own hands like some peasant."

How could he even begin to tell her that her accusation could not be further from the truth? He felt nothing but the highest admiration for her nobleness of character and strength, as he knew his father did. As far as working in the garden was concerned, he had simply reacted out of the guilt of having neglected her, as he had told her then. He could see, though, that she was in too agitated a state to heed him and a further explanation of this would have to wait until a more opportune moment.

He stopped only inches from her back, wanting to reach out and smooth his hand over that tangle of golden hair.

Even now in his anger he could not keep back the feelings of tenderness that he felt for her. If only he understood what was hurting her. "Mary, I have not lied to you."

She swung around to face him, seeming somewhat taken aback to find him so near. He watched in grudging admiration as she stood her ground, answering as if merely saying the words was painful. "You have lied to me. You told me last night that you were in your room thinking of me. I have since learned that that was not true."

He shook his head, feeling more confused than ever. "What are you talking about?"

She raised her chin as her gaze focused on the distant wall. "You were not alone in your room last night."

He ground his fist into his palm. "This is completely ridiculous. From whom did you get this ludicrous tale?"

She refused to look at him still. "You know that as well as I, Ian—in fact, better. I will not lower myself to go over the sordid details."

He stood for a long moment in silent frustration. "Why can you not just take my word?"

She did face him then, her eyes glistening like wet amber. "And why should I, Ian, when you do not trust in me and what I say? Last night you did not believe me when I said I was pushed down those stairs."

He tried to reason with her. In his mind the two situations were not at all the same. "Is this some test, Mary? Is agreeing with you on this matter how I make you understand that I respect you? Am I to believe that you were pushed down those stairs when you have been at Sinclair Hall only a short time, and in that time have already come to be more loved and admired by all the folk who live here than I have been in my whole life? Including my father." He could not completely keep the hint of melancholy from his voice.

"And how would this attacker have gotten past myself, Barbara and my father as we went to you?"

She closed her eyes. "I cannot explain that. But I know what happened."

He watched her for a long moment, his heart so heavy he thought it might surely cease to beat. "How can I possibly measure up to such a testing, Mary?"

Mary faced him. "Then tell me something of yourself, Ian. You expect so much faith on my part, show me yours. Tell me of your secrets."

"What secrets?" he asked her too softly.

"You know. You told me yourself that your father believed wrongly about your brother's death. What did happen that day?"

Ian felt anger rise inside him, anger at his father, his brother, at himself and, yes, at Mary, too. Why must she dredge up this ancient pain? Well, tell her he would, though it would solve nothing. His cold gaze met his wife's determined one. "My father believes I was driving the carriage when it overturned. I was not. I had been prodding him to let me drive the new phaeton, and my father knew it, but Malcolm did not give in. My brother himself took that corner too quickly, a mistake that cost him his life."

Her eyes grew round with shock. "And you have let your father go on thinking it was you."

He shrugged without emotion. "He chose for himself. I was unconscious for several days. When I awoke my father had assumed the worst. I was judged guilty without even a trial."

"You must tell him the truth. He would want to know that he has wronged you so dreadfully."

Ian shook his head. "I cannot...will not." The pain rose to engulf him in a throbbing ache as he went on, "You, Mary, you say you want to be believed in. Why would I want any less? You want me to trust in you when no one had trusted in me."

She stared at him with sad golden eyes, biting her lip.

Ian shook his head. There was no way around this impasse. She would not believe in him because of what he had done to hurt her in the beginning of their relationship, and she would use every excuse to keep herself from doing so.

Without saying another word, Ian turned and left the room. As he had thought, telling her about his brother had changed nothing.

Ian threw himself into the business of the estates. His realization that his father's resentment of him went even deeper than his brother's death made him understand that he would never gain acceptance there. He could no longer wait for his father to welcome him but found the areas where he could be of value around the estates.

Mary spoke to him only when it was necessary. And none of what he accomplished felt as if it meant a thing.

Thinking about Mary and what she had said to him had occupied nearly all Ian's waking hours no matter what else he did. The fact that she had alluded to his lying to her again was surely connected to the fact that she had not forgiven him for being deceptive in his courtship of her. Thus he felt he could do nothing to resolve this issue, as he had not lied to her since. What he dwelled on most was her assertion that he felt she was beneath him.

He began to wonder if proving this was not true might somehow break the impasse between them. If he could make her see that he valued her and felt nothing but pride in her and the things she did, she might begin to see that he was not as untrustworthy and dishonorable as she imagined.

He realized that the reason his perceived disapproval of her gardening was so hurtful to her was that it meant so much to her. Perhaps he could do something about this.

One morning his father stopped him as he was on his way out for his early-morning ride. Ian never let himself think about the fact that riding each morning meant he need not take his morning meal with the family. It also meant he had no need to face his wife's hurt silence.

"I wondered if you'd come into the library with me for a moment, Ian?" Malcolm requested in a noncommittal tone.

Ian hesitated. He did not wish to have a confrontation with his father, not when it was all he could do to go through each day with a modicum of normalcy, given the state of affairs between them.

Malcolm looked at him directly. "As I said, it will only take a moment."

Ian shrugged. "Certainly."

He followed his father into the room and watched as he went around the enormous walnut desk and sat down. Wondering what was coming, he sat in the red leather chair that was pulled up near it.

Malcolm began immediately. "It has come to my attention that you have taken it upon yourself to make certain changes with the way things are done around the estate."

Ian stiffened. He did not wish to have a confrontation with his father—those days when he had deliberately set out to antagonize the older man were long past for him now. Yet neither did he wish to stop the work he was doing. For the first time in his life Ian felt as if he belonged at Sinclair Hall, that he had something to give. He faced his father levelly. "Yes, I have."

Malcolm picked up a sheet of paper from the cluttered

desk. "I was wondering if you would be willing to add one more task to your plate."

Ian sat up even straighter. Was he hearing correctly? Was the taciturn Malcolm Sinclair actually asking for his assistance? Never would he have thought this day would come.

Malcolm went on, "It has come to my attention that Squire Wensley has decided to sell a goodly portion of his land. It is, according to reports, a most desired piece of property. I myself have another matter to attend in the village this morning. I was wondering if you might be willing to go and negotiate with the squire in the hope that we might acquire this land."

Incredulous, Ian spoke slowly. "What would you like me to offer?"

His father answered with deliberate casualness. "Whatever you feel is appropriate. I have reason to believe your decision will be a dependable one."

For a moment Ian couldn't speak. It wasn't precisely what he had wished for from his father, which was a demonstration of some affection. But surely this request was an indication that Malcolm had some confidence in his son and his abilities. But why now, especially if he really believed the things he had said to Mary that day in the sitting room?

Malcolm prodded. "Well?"

Ian answered softly, trying to gauge his own confused feelings. "Yes, of course. I will see to it this morning. The groom can exercise my horse."

The elder Sinclair nodded with satisfaction.

Ian felt a sudden stab of resentment. "Why now, Father, after all these years?"

The older man did not meet his intent gaze. "Marrying Mary has made you a man, Ian. Even I can see that."

Though he had braced himself, the older man's reasoning

hurt. "Then this newfound acceptance is brought on by your regard for my wife?"

Malcolm looked at him then, the words coming with an obvious effort. "Not entirely. There are things... Suffice it to say that I have not always said and done what I should have."

This was certainly not an apology or a declaration of love, but it was much more than he had ever expected his father to say. Ian did not allow the hope that rose inside him to reach too high.

A short time later Ian went to his chamber and changed into something more suitable for calling on the squire. As he changed he caught himself glancing several times at the connecting door between his room and Mary's. Unexpectedly he found himself wishing he could share the news of this positive development between himself and his father. Her presence had made a difference to his relationship with the earl—the older man had admitted as much. He pushed aside the disappointment that arose at knowing this was not possible.

It was some minutes later, as he was crossing the foyer to go out to the waiting carriage, that he met his cousin Barbara. She was dressed in one of the dark silk gowns she preferred and was in the act of putting on a light wrap the same color of gray as her extremely conservative bonnet.

She greeted him effusively. "Oh, Ian, how very fortunate I am to meet you. That is, if the carriage outside is for your use."

He nodded politely. "It is."

She smiled, putting her hand on his arm. "I was wondering if you could drop me by the market. There are some things I need to purchase. That is, if it would not be too much trouble?"

He looked toward the door, which the butler was opening. He had heard Frances telling the housekeeper a few moments before that Mary had gone for a walk. Despite their estrangement, he could not help wondering if he would catch a glimpse of her as he was leaving. He both dreaded and longed for a sight of her, the dread coming solely from knowing that she would not be glad of seeing him.

"Ian?" Barbara said softly.

Distractedly he turned to her. "It would be no trouble. I would be happy to take you. Please." He waved a hand toward the door.

With a smile, Barbara preceded him out onto the stoop.

It was a fine day, the sun shining in a clear blue sky, but as he helped his cousin into the carriage, Ian's eyes searched the grounds in front of the house for a glimpse of Mary. No matter how fine the weather, or that his relationship with the earl seemed to be improving, he did not feel whole.

He did not know why this was exactly. All he knew was that it was connected to Mary. He told himself that it was because they were married and his life could never be truly settled as long as there was such tension between them. But that did not quite seem to explain the depth of his unhappiness.

It was as he moved around the carriage to take his own place in the driver's seat that Ian thought he saw her. Or rather thought he saw a flash of lavender skirts in the trees to his right. His eyes strained, but he could see nothing moving in the stand of elm and oak, aside from the swaying of the branches in the gentle breeze.

With a sigh he flicked the reins over the horses' backs. He had a difficult time concentrating on what his cousin was saying as she took up a sociable line of conversation.

But he did try to make some reply in the appropriate pauses and she seemed not to notice how his attention wandered.

As he listened to Barbara chatting on about the household, he suddenly wondered how long she would stay at Sinclair Hall. Surely she must be missing her own family, and they her. He now realized that she must have come to Sinclair Hall on the expectation that he and she would marry, and he felt a stab of regret at the thought that he might have hurt her. He only wished he had had more concern for the feelings of others before he had made so very many mistakes. He resolved to treat his cousin kindly. He found himself once again wishing Mary would notice and approve of his newfound sensitivity.

Mary did not want to believe the evidence of her own eyes, but there were Barbara and Ian going off in the carriage together. Over the course of the past four days she'd wondered more than once that she might be making a grave error in thinking Ian had played her false again. His sharing the truth of his brother's death had made her wonder if there was some way to breach the walls of his self-protection. But the very desperate need she felt to break through his reserve kept her from doing so. She did not want to be hurt again.

Yet what if Ian was telling the truth? He'd seemed so genuinely surprised at her accusation that he had lied to her. What if it was Barbara who had misled her? More times than she cared to admit, Mary had stopped herself from going to her husband and telling him exactly what his cousin had said. Her pride would not allow her. She felt that she was so attracted to Ian, wanted to be with him so badly, that she would believe anything he said, no matter that it was not the real truth. The feelings of completeness his lovemaking had awakened in her seemed to have a will of their own, making her want to accept any excuse he might offer, do anything to be back in his arms again.

Mary could not give in to this need. She was battling desperately to convince herself that the desire she felt to be loved and cared for by Ian was a weakness she could not accept in herself. Her lack of strength was what had brought her to this disastrous situation to begin with.

Now, seeing Ian and Barbara in the carriage together, when Ian had not so much as approached her for four days, Mary was glad she had not gone to him. He would surely have only succeeded in convincing her that she should take him back to her bed.

Though what he wanted with her when he could have Barbara, who had come right out and said she loved him, Mary did not know. The one thing she did know was that she would not allow herself to love him. To love Ian would consume her.

Over the course of the next days, Mary remained out of her husband's path. When he was at Sinclair Hall he was either with his horses or with the men who were working on that strange stone structure at the far end of the gardens. Those workers kept themselves completely separated from the household, except one man whom Mary noticed watching her and scribbling something on a sheet of paper. When she made to approach him and see what he was about, he quickly departed the garden. Though this left her infinitely curious, Mary made no other attempt to approach the men or the structure for fear that she might meet her husband.

Her determination to stay away from Ian was made only more steadfast because she knew he was often in the company of Barbara. It was as if in being found out he now felt he could flaunt his association with his cousin, squiring her here and there about the estate.

For her part, Barbara made no attempt to hide her relationship with Mary's husband. She was quite open in relating their outings to the village or the shore—with Malcolm or anyone else who would listen.

It was during just such a cheery discourse on how beautiful the morning had been when Barbara and Ian had driven over to Mittendon, which was the neighboring village, that Mary could hear no more. She rose from her seat by the sitting-room window, leaving her afternoon tea unfinished, and headed for the door.

Both Barbara and Malcolm looked up from where they were having their tea. Her father-in-law spoke not unkindly. "Are you off then, Mary? You haven't finished your tea."

In spite of feeling Barbara's curious gaze upon her, Mary paused and offered him a slight smile. The old curmudgeon had been as good to her of late as she felt he knew how to be. "I am going for a walk before the ladies from the church arrive to discuss the bazaar to benefit the local widows." On Emma Smith's second tentative visit to the Hall, Mary had made known her interest in contributing to villagers' well-being. Her offer had been greeted with happy enthusiasm.

Malcolm looked up at the window through which streamed cheery golden sunlight. "It is a fine afternoon. Do enjoy your walk."

Mary followed the direction of his eyes with some satisfaction despite her unhappiness. The curtains were always open during the day now, and the difference in the house was vast. No longer did it feel so forbidding, though the colors were still dark. Now they looked rich and deep with the light of day shining upon them. That was one battle she had won, although it had been on the earl's say-so.

Mary left the house feeling less pleased with her small successes than one might think.

None of it seemed to matter, when she and Ian had not exchanged more than the most necessary of phrases for weeks. And even that had been only in passing. Ian was well occupied with his new activities. Too busy for anything but Barbara.

Mary shook her head. This was not something she wanted to dwell on today. She was making something of a life of her own here, and if it did not include her husband, all the better. She had determined that she would not allow herself the weakness of leaning on anyone.

She went out through the solarium to the terrace at the back of the house. Slowly she walked down the stairs, turning her face up to the sun as she went, wanting to feel the heat of it warm the coldness inside her.

Victoria would be aghast at this lack of regard for her complexion, and Mary smiled sad nostalgia. Surely Victoria's child would be coming soon, she thought, wishing she could be with her.

According to her last letter, her friend was quite ready for the event to take place. She had expressed regret that Mary would not be with her for her confinement. Reading that, Mary had even thought of going to Victoria, had felt the pangs of their separation with great sadness. But she could not go to Carlisle. Victoria knew her far too well. There would be no hiding the truth of her own unhappy circumstances, as she could in her letters.

No, best that she stay here and endure the results of the choice she had made. In all honesty she had to admit that if it was not for her unhappy relationship with Ian, Mary might have been quite contented at Sinclair Hall.

Sighing, she wandered on through the garden, then stopped as her eyes came to rest on Ian's mysterious round wall. Not even the earl seemed to know what the purpose of it was, but he spoke of the structure with indulgent cu riosity. He appeared to have come to some acceptance of his son as a man in the past weeks. For the sake of both men she was grateful. She realized Ian was right in thinking his father should care for him in spite of not knowing the truth of what had happened to his elder son. She only hoped it would come about.

She pushed these unhappy thoughts away.

Looking at the noncommunicative length of wall, Mary searched for any sign of activity. She could see none, which was somewhat odd. Over the past weeks the work on it had gone on from early morning until late evening each day. Yet she had to admit that such diligence had obviously had its reward. The project appeared to be nearly if not completely finished, at least from the outside.

Mary moved toward the structure, drawn there almost against her will. As she approached, she saw that the wall was larger than it had looked from the distances from which she had previously viewed it. On closer inspection, it did somewhat resemble any number of medieval towers she had seen, though it was not nearly as tall.

Slowly she circled the wall, finding that it had only one heavy oak door, with a keyhole. Odder still, she told herself, pausing before it with a puzzled frown. Almost as if it had a will of its own, her hand reached out toward the closed portal....

Then even as she hesitated, the dratted thing opened and out stepped her husband. It had been so long since they were this close to one another without some other person around to act as a buffer. Her wayward heart fluttered as her gaze took in his wide chest in a light blue shirt and open dark blue vest, his lean flanks in a pair of matching dark blue trousers.

Why, she wondered, could he not be less pleasing to the eyes and senses?

Ian stopped still when he saw her there, a frown marring his brow. "Mary." Abruptly he pulled the door closed behind him. His onyx eyes went immediately to her face. She saw that his tan had darkened from exposure to the sun and that, if anything, this only added to that sensual air that was so much a part of him.

He spoke too hurriedly, too bluntly. "What are you doing here?" Mary felt his avid, pulse-quickening gaze move over her. Why did his expression seem so at odds with the impatience of his tone?

It was hard to know how to react to him. Even though they could not be man and wife in the truest sense of the word because of the problems between them, she wished it did not have to be so very painful just to see him.

She spoke with a regret so deep it shocked her, especially as she had no wish to give way to her own principles and accept Ian on the terms he was willing to offer. "I was only taking a walk. I did not mean to cause you any irritation. I will be on my way."

She turned to go, her throat tight.

Ian held out his hand. "No, wait, please, don't leave."

He couldn't let her go. The shock he'd felt at seeing her was not nearly as great as his pleasure. He'd felt as if he'd opened that door and found a golden ray of sunshine standing right before him.

When Mary hesitated, he moved away from the door to stand beside her. "Walk with me."

She glanced at him, then away. "I don't know if that's such a very good idea." Her gaze focused on the stand of trees in the distance. Dejection assaulted him at realizing that she would look anywhere but at him.

"Can we not even walk together?" he asked sadly. "I promise you I mean you no harm of any kind."

"I do not know that we have anything to say to one

another, Ian.'' Mary glanced at him briefly again. "I wish it was not so, but it is."

With a quick inhalation of breath Ian cursed softly. "Damn, but you are a headstrong woman." Suddenly he knew he could take no more of this silence. Arguing would be preferable to this cold emptiness he felt at not even knowing how to defend himself. "There are things that need saying. And they need saying now." He reached out and took her hand in his warm one.

She scowled, pulling away abruptly. "I will talk to you, but you will not force me."

Without further ado Ian led her across the grounds. He told himself not to react to her disregard but to concentrate on what he was trying to accomplish here. Ian wanted to talk with his wife and he did not wish to be overheard. Without thinking, he headed for the wooded area some distance across the grounds.

Mary was silent, walking along at his side until he stopped just inside the sheltering privacy of the trees. "Mary," he began, "I don't quite know how we came to this impasse, but I wish with all my heart that we could overcome it. I had hoped that time would make a difference. It has not. Tell me, then, if there is something I can do."

She met his eyes, hers growing more stormy by the moment, her lips clamped in stubborn insurrection. Seeing this, Ian felt sure there would be no hope of resolving this situation. Thus he could not but be surprised when she finally spoke. "Ian, it is not easy for me to say this to you. I have tried to understand how difficult it must be for you to be near her and deny your feelings. I realize you were not in love with me, that you loved her all along, but I can't—"

He stopped her with an amazed exhalation. "Love who, what are you taking about?"

She looked at him closely, frowning pensively as if the sheer depth of his amazement had reached some confused place in her mind. "Your cousin. Barbara."

He shook his head, still not understanding where any of this had come from. "I do not love Barbara. If I had done so, I would have married her."

Mary shook her head in obvious bewilderment. "But she said... You are having an affair with her, are you not?" She blushed to the roots of her hair.

He began to laugh. "Having an affair! With Barbara! Good God, Mary, if I was going to have an affair, which I have no desire to do," he rushed on, "I would not do so with my cousin. She is...well...not appealing to me in that way, has never been."

She raised an accusing finger. "But you have been going everywhere with her. And the night I was pushed on the stairs you were with her in your robe with nothing under..." Her blush deepened.

Ian shook his head emphatically. "I was not with her. How did you get such an idea? And as far as taking her everywhere, I have been about the lands a great deal and have only given her a ride now and then to where she was going. I have not been with her." He paused, then added, "I repeat, Mary, how did you get the mad notion that I was with her the night you...fell?"

He could tell she had heard his hesitation over the word but obviously felt it was not important enough to argue in the face of what was being discussed. "She told me so herself," Mary informed him.

Ian ran a hand through his hair. "She told you that we had *been* together?"

She hesitated. "No. She told me that you had been helping her with some of the household accounts."

He nodded. "That much is true. I had been helping her.

But that was earlier in the evening and I was certainly fully dressed, as I have been any other time I have been with her. Surely there was some misunderstanding.'' He looked at her then, his eyes darkening with barely restrained desire. ''God, Mary, to think that this has been keeping us apart. I have needed you so.''

''But...'' She stared into his eyes for a long moment, then turned away. Mary put her hand to her forehead as if trying to make sense of it all, as if she did not want to see the passion in him.

''Oh, Mary,'' he whispered huskily. ''Are we going to let this misunderstanding stand between us? I have not ever touched Barbara in any way that was not proper.''

Her hand slipped from her forehead and their eyes met and held. A stillness seemed to descend upon the forest around them. It was as if even nature understood the electric quality of this moment between man and woman.

Her gaze went to his mouth and she wet her own lips with the tip of her pink tongue. Ian felt the familiar tightening in his body that he had always known when he was with her.

Her creamy cheeks, which were framed by wayward golden curls, were flushed with agitation and, he suspected, her own determinedly concealed yearning. As he watched, her heavily lashed lids came down to hood eyes that had darkened to amber. Even in her confusion and distress she was so beautiful. So very desirable, and he had wanted so desperately to hold her again.

As if she was not able to resist the force of his gaze, Mary's lashes fluttered and she met his eyes. Softly she uttered his name on a breath. ''Ian.''

He reached for her then, pulling her close into his arms.

Mary melted against him, her body molding itself to his. She fit into the circle of his arms as if she'd been made to be there. Her head filled the hollow of his shoulder with equal perfection.

When his mouth found hers, she kissed him with fervor to match his own and he felt the need inside him grow to an ache. Her hand tangled in the hair at the base of his skull as she slanted her mouth and opened it beneath his. Her tongue flicked out to collide with his in feverish desire.

How fortunate he had been to find this woman.

Ian ran his hands down her sides to cup her delightfully rounded bottom, drawing her womanliness up against the hard pulsing of his manhood. She gasped and held more tightly to him, kissed him all the more wildly.

He drew back, looking down into her swirling golden gaze. "Mary, I need you so badly."

"And I you." She sighed, kissing him again.

He gasped with shock and pleasure as her hand slid down between them and she brushed her palm with gentle but firm pressure over him. He pulled her back to him, whispering against her ear, "I can't answer for what might happen if you do things like that."

She tilted her head sideways to allow him better access to that delicate flesh. "So do not try. Why do you wait? Can we not go to my room, my bed?" She pressed him again.

With a groan of sweet agony, Ian went down on his knees, pulling her down before him. "What need have we of a room or a bed?" His dark eyes mirrored his intent as their gazes held.

Chapter Thirteen

Could Mary complete this most intimate of acts, here, now, with nothing but the lacy branches of the overhanging trees to shield them from both God and man?

Could she not?

"Oh, Ian." She reached her arms around his neck and kissed him again.

When he laid her back on the softness of the carpet of moss and tender grass, she went gladly, pulling him down with her. She raised her head, kissing him deeply even as her fingers made surprisingly nimble work of his buttons. Soon his smooth, hard chest was exposed to her hands and she ran them over him eagerly.

Ian lost no time in vanquishing the barrier of her own fastening and she soon found her aching breasts bared to his gaze, which was warmer even than the sunlight that filtered through the branches to bathe her quivering flesh. Mary arched as his hands closed on her, his fingertips finding her already erect nipples.

A current of molten honey seemed to flow down into the core of her to settle at the joining of her thighs. Without even knowing that she did so, Mary opened her legs, fitting herself more fully beneath him. Her gown had ridden up

on her hips as they caressed one another and Mary gasped
with need when the sweet pressure of his body came into
such direct contact with the most intimate part of her. It
only added to that aching pleasure.

She reached down between their bodies and tugged at
the fastening of his trousers. She discovered that fingers
that had only short moments ago been so dexterous now
trembled too much to be of any use. "Ian, help me," she
murmured desperately.

Ian's hand moved down, and she soon felt the length of
him spring free against her hand. The mere touch of that
smooth hardness made the honey flow anew. Briefly he
leaned away to remove both his pants and her own bloom-
ers. Bared now to him, Mary drew him back down. She
opened herself to him, desperate to end the sweet torment
that raged inside her, crying out with rapture as he slipped
into her, filled her. Made her complete.

And then she could hear nothing but the sound of Ian's
own shallow breathing as he leaned over her, his breath hot
on her ear and throat. His response only heightened hers,
and she lost herself as the rapturous tension grew to an
apex of unbearable ecstasy that broke on the edge of eternity, and dissolved into bliss.

Mary lay beneath the pleasurable weight of her husband's body, feeling the incredible pulsing inside her ebb,
then subside. Even after the delight had passed away, her
body retained a certain mystical lightness.

She opened her eyes to see Ian's face above hers, his
dark eyes tender. A feeling of deep sadness filled her at
that expression. Even in her lack of experience she realized
what a skilled lover he was, so tender and considerate, as
he had been the first time they were together.

Yet she knew it did not mean anything beyond that. Ian
might in fact have been faithful to her, but he would never

love her. His heart was locked away inside him, battered by his father's rejection of him at a time when he was young and in need of comfort himself. It had not come, and Ian had sought that comfort in the beds of the many women he had lain with.

He could not love her. But heaven help her, Mary realized that no matter how she had fought it, she had fallen in love with him. She loved the way he raked his hand through his dark hair when he was disturbed about something. She loved the gentle way he had with his horses, his almost parental pride in them. She loved his perseverance in taking up his rightful duties in the running of the estate no matter how his father felt about him. She loved the schoolboy chagrin he sometimes exhibited. But most of all she loved the way he made her feel when he was with her like this, holding her in his arms.

How this had happened she did not know. Mary had always believed that love came from mutual respect and care, as it had for her parents, as it did for Victoria and Jedidiah. Ian neither cared for nor respected her.

He still refused to even contemplate the possibility that she could be right about being pushed. He had jumped to the immediate conclusion that it was Mary who had misunderstood what Barbara had said when she'd told Mary they were together on that night. Surely if he cared about her at all he would at least be willing to consider the fact that she was not in error.

These thoughts tortured her mind even as she realized that none of this stopped her from wanting to be with Ian like this. Mary felt powerless in the grip of the overwhelming feelings of love she had for this man. Ian had said they could begin anew, simply attempt to come to a more peaceable understanding, but she could not. She wanted more, still felt that longing to be cared for and loved. Thus she had no one to blame but herself for her present state of unhappiness.

So it was in silence that she regarded him when he reached out and traced a gentle finger over her lower lip. "So beautiful, Mary."

She closed her eyes, angry at herself for the swell of desire that rose up at even this small caress. And so soon after he had loved her with a thoroughness that should have left her sated.

She opened her lids at Ian's next words. "You don't know how very sorry I am to say this, but there is something I must tell you. It is especially difficult now, after we have reconciled."

She stiffened. Mary felt little interest in hearing something that would most likely be unpleasant, if his tone was anything to judge by. She looked up into the canopy of branches over her head.

He went on. "I have to go away for two days."

Her gaze centered on his face once more. "Away?"

Ian nodded, moving his hand down to stroke the exposed curve of her breast. "Yes, to attend an important matter of business." He grew still as he looked back into her eyes. "I assure you, Mary, that it is a duty I cannot shirk. My father has finally begun to seek my assistance in the running of the estates. I must carry out my responsibilities no matter how difficult that may be with more…appealing activities to distract me."

So that was what she was, an appealing activity. A lump rose in her throat and tears stung the backs of her eyes, but she did not shed them. His cavalier attitude was even more difficult to accept coming as it did immediately after her own realization that she loved him.

He watched, his gaze full of regret. "I assure you, Mary, I wish I did not have to go."

She continued to look at him for a long moment. Clearly Ian had sensed but misread the cause of her distress. She felt no resentment of him as to his duty to his father and the estates. He had waited so very long for the earl to begin to accept him in any way.

"I understand why you must go," she replied, even as she realized that Ian had known all along that he was leaving.

He leaned over and kissed her, and Mary felt herself respond in spite of the ache in her heart. When Ian pulled away, he said, "Unfortunately, the carriage is waiting for me even now. I was on my way to prepare myself for the journey when I met you." He paused, shaking his head with regret. "You do know, Mary, that I had no idea that we would end up here, together like this. I simply wanted to talk to you. I knew we could not go on as we were for a moment longer."

She sat up and began to pull her clothing together. "I believe you did not plan this, Ian." Her voice sounded distant even in her own ears. Even if he had not planned it, he had callously taken her here without bothering to mention until the deed was done that he was leaving.

He put his hands over hers, willing her to meet his eyes. "Wait, Mary. I must make you understand before we leave this place that I would rather stay here with you than anything."

She refused to look at him. Mary had nothing to say. As she moved to button the gaping front of her gown, he halted her. "Allow me."

She stepped back from him. "No."

Ian turned away, his lips set grimly.

Mary could think of nothing to say as she walked back to the house on shaking legs. Ian seemed no more inclined to talk, appearing to be lost in some unhappy thoughts of his own.

She felt empty and unable to decipher her own feelings. Everything had happened too quickly. One moment she had been so upset with Ian that she'd finally told him of her suspicions about him and his cousin. The next thing she knew she was tumbling about on the grass like a...like a harlot. He had certainly withheld the fact that he was indulging in a moment of light sport, but she had not tried to halt him. Her cheeks flamed as she recalled just how eager she had been.

Was she never to gain any command of her reaction to this man?

Perhaps, Mary realized, it would be best if Ian were gone for a few days. She would then have time to think, to understand her own emotions. Surely she must do that if she was to know any sense of autonomy in this relationship.

They went back to the house through the gardens, just as she had come a short hour ago. How much had changed in that time. Yet how much had stayed the same.

As they entered the door that opened into the solarium, Ian paused and looked down at her, his gaze assessing. "I am sorry you are so angry with me, Mary. Again I assure you I cannot delay this journey, much as I might wish to."

She focused on the top button of his shirt, deliberately keeping herself from dwelling on the image of her own fingers undoing that button only minutes ago. "Why would I be angry with you, my lord? You have only behaved as you always do."

With a growl of frustration he pulled her into his arms, his lips descending to her. Despite everything, Mary felt her own mouth cling to his. Only when her already weak knees threatened to give out did he draw back. "You drive me to distraction, Mary Sinclair. Think about that while I am gone.''

Forcefully Mary pulled away, and as she did so her gaze came to rest on Barbara, who had obviously just entered from the main corridor. She stood for a long moment watching them, her face white with shock and some other emotion that made Mary shudder. The dark-haired woman then swung around and hurried away.

Ian raised his head to see what Mary was looking at. ''What is it?''

Mary shook her head, not meeting his gaze. ''Nothing.'' She realized she would not have told him even if she wasn't angry.

There was little to be gained in talking about having seen his cousin there. He would not understand why her presence had chilled Mary so. She did not know herself. But for the first time Mary realized that Barbara might indeed be a formidable enemy.

To tell her husband would be an utter waste of words. He clearly saw his cousin in a completely different light than Mary did. His assurance that she had misunderstood Barbara's innuendo that they were lovers was proof enough of that.

Two days later Mary looked over at her father-in-law where he sat at the head of the table. The two of them were eating alone, as Barbara seemed to have gone to the village.

''This beef is so tough. I'm sure they've cut up one of the carriage seats to get it,'' he muttered as he chewed with a scowl.

Mary hid a smile behind her napkin and reached for the bell. When the maid emerged through the door to the kitchens, Mary directed, ''Please, bring in the pheasant.''

Malcolm nodded in agreement. ''You're a bright girl,

Mary.'' He frowned darkly at the maid. "And tell cook
we'll have no more meat from that cow. She can donate
the remainder to the widows or orphans fund, or some such
cause.''

Mary smiled again as the girl curtsied and took their
plates, then made a hasty retreat. The maid was clearly
intimidated by her master. It was quite unfortunate really,
she told herself, for the earl's bark was most assuredly
worse than his bite. He simply liked to have things done
his way.

The more she knew him, the more she realized how very
unnecessary the feud between Ian and his father had been.
It was quite awful that Malcolm had treated Ian so badly
in the pain of his grief, so badly that Ian had left home and
gone to live with his grandmother in London. Ian was not
likely to forget the isolation of those years, but judging by
his actions of late, it seemed he was willing to forgive his
parent.

Unfortunately, Ian's improved relationship with his father had not opened his heart as she had hoped.

His having used her so thoughtlessly the day he was
leaving made that obvious. In the two days she had come
no closer to understanding what to do about her own feelings in regard to him and their marriage. In her braver hours
she told herself that she must confront him, tell him that
she wanted all of his trust, his respect. And yes, his love.

That he had remained faithful to her, she now believed.
But Mary was certain that had more to do with his desire
to change his life than that he had any care for her. Ian was
attracted to her, wanted her, but no more than he would
any other woman who took his fancy.

As if from a distance, Mary heard the earl say her name.
"Mary.''

She looked up in some confusion and embarrassment to

be caught feeling sorry for herself. It was clear from her father-in-law's expression that he had been speaking to her for some time.

His words confirmed her suspicions. "Mary, girl, where have you been?"

She shook her head. "I'm sorry, Father. Did you want something?"

He flicked a glance to her right. "Not I."

She looked around to see the butler standing beside her chair. He was holding out a folded sheet of paper that had been sealed with hot wax. A blush rose up to stain her cheeks. "Oh, forgive me for not hearing you. I was thinking."

Malcolm interrupted impatiently, "Well, take it, gel. He says it's from Ian."

Looking at the note with widened eyes, Mary hesitated, then reached for the missive before the earl could say anything more.

Ian was due back this very afternoon. Why ever would he send her a letter?

"Thank you," she told the servant.

"That will be all, Winslow," Malcolm informed him. The butler bowed and left the dining room. The elder Sinclair then turned to Mary. "Well, get on with it, then. Let's see what he has to say."

Mary blushed again as she realized why she felt such a reluctance to open the note in front of Ian's father. Slowly, trying her best not to show how hesitant she was, Mary used her knife to pull up the wax.

"Well?" Malcolm prodded as she began to read.

Mary let out a deep breath of relief and, though she didn't wish to acknowledge it, disappointment. The message was quite short and contained nothing that could not be read aloud. She did so. "'My dear Mary, I have returned from Workham some hours sooner than I had thought to. I request your attendance at the docks in the village. There is something that I wish to show you. Please do come.'" It was signed simply Ian.

She looked up at her father-in-law, who was frowning. "Most odd of the boy. Perhaps he has brought you something."

Mary shrugged. "I cannot think of what it might be." It was rather a cryptic request, Mary thought. And how very like the overconfident Ian. But even as she felt her irritation with him rise, her gaze strayed back to those last three gentler words.

Malcolm raised craggy gray brows. "Nor can I myself, but you must certainly go."

Mary bit her lip, staring down at the note with uncertainty. Her immediate reaction was an unequivocal no. But that *Please do come* would not be ignored.

"Mary."

She looked up and found Malcolm watching her with an expression of sadness and concern. He spoke more gently than she had heard him since her injury. "I know that Ian is not an easy man to love, any more than I was. But when he does give his heart, as I did to my Laura, it will be forever. He cares for you, deeply—he just doesn't know how much. You may, in fact, be the one person he will ever love." The pain in his eyes was obvious.

She could not prevent herself from speaking, though she feared it would make no difference, and Malcolm Sinclair had warned her not to interfere again. She had to try. "Father, I know that I am being overbold to say this, but I feel that now is the time that I must do so. Ian loves you." Mary could not bring herself to tell him that he was very mistaken in thinking Ian cared for her.

He made a grunting noise in his throat.

She went on before he could otherwise interrupt her. "No, it is true. I know that Ian's brother was killed and that you were very angry with him when it happened. There are things that you do not know, but that I have no right, nor desire, to tell you. And the reason I will not tell you is that in this area I believe my husband is right. The circumstances of the accident are not as important as the fact that Ian is your son. He was a boy. He lost Malcolm as you did and he needed your comfort and attention. Those things did not come. Although I know you are making an effort now, forgiveness takes time."

Malcolm turned away, his jaw set. "He will never forgive me—how could he?" Mary had to look away from the ragged agony on his face.

Mary knew she must answer carefully. Somehow she felt that she was also fighting for her own relationship. Perhaps the softening of his father's hard stance had begun to influence her husband. Was this last, gently rendered sentence a sign that he was changing?

It was not love, of course. Mary realized Ian would likely never be able to give that, especially after the way they had begun their marriage. But maybe the wall he had built around his heart would yield enough to make him show her some feelings besides the passion that seemed the one thing he was able to give.

Thus it was that she found the courage to go on, though she knew her intrusion was not welcome. "I feel your assessment of Ian is not correct. I believe he would welcome any sign of affection you might give."

When he only stared back at her, his expression unreadable, Mary rose. "And now if you will excuse me, sir, I will heed your advice and go to my husband."

It was only a short time later that Mary was riding down the road toward the village. She did not let herself contemplate what would happen now. She was still amazed at her own temerity in speaking to Ian's father as she had.

She was also amazed at her own decision to give her relationship with Ian another chance. For once she resolved not to worry herself over what she could not change. Nor whether or not she was doing the right thing.

All was not resolved, but perhaps those three words, *Please do come,* were a start.

The day was fine, the sun warm on her shoulders. Giving way to decorum, Mary had donned a stylish hat with her riding habit. She found that she had a sudden inexplicable desire to prevent any more freckles from joining the three faint ones on her nose—she could certainly rid herself of those by using a preparation of lemon.

She urged her mount to a faster pace. She would speak to Frances about it this very evening.

It was as she was riding through an area where the trees grew thick on either side of the road that Mary felt a sharp pain at the back of her skull. As a wave of sudden nausea assaulted her, Mary swayed on the mare and gripped the reins in desperation.

"What...?" she cried out.

Another, even more agonizing shaft of pain raced down her spine hard on the heels of the first, and she felt herself falling....

Slowly Mary became aware of a throbbing in her head that blocked out all other sounds. Even the act of raising her hand to feel the lump along the back of her skull added to the intensity of her suffering and she moaned, drawing in upon herself. But even curled into a ball there was no escape from the pain.

Feeling hands upon her legs and feet, Mary opened her eyes. For a moment she feared that she had been blinded.

Then she realized it was dark and she was looking up into the sky.

A smell came to her next, one that made her nose wrinkle and her already churning stomach retch. It was the stench of gin. Mary only just managed to swallow down the acrid bile that rose in her throat.

She then felt herself being dragged across what felt like sand. Putting out a weak hand, she managed to scrape up a bit and saw that she was right. It was then that Mary realized she could hear the sound of waves lapping at something. Possibly the side of a boat or dock.

Panic gripped her. God above, what was happening?

The last thing she remembered she'd been on her way to meet Ian.

It was clear that she had not gotten there. The motion of being dragged ceased and her legs fell to the earth. There was the sound of shuffling and scraping. Mary raised her head, ignoring the pain as best she could while she tried to see who was there.

The crescent moon offered little illumination, and it seemed as though this was made worse by cloud cover. There was an almost ominous heaviness in the air, but Mary had no time to dwell on this impression as she took in her immediate surroundings. She could make out nothing more than the vague outline of a small boat against the night sky. Then, confusingly, the sky blurred. Mary squinted, trying to understand what was going on, then gasped as a face leaned over hers.

She squinted in the gloom. The bloated, gray-stubbled face that leaned over hers seemed somehow familiar. "Who...who are you, and what is going on?" Quickly she subsided, as speaking aloud made the pain thunder through her skull.

He seemed to grimace, just before taking a long swig

from the bottle he carried. He wiped the back of his mouth on his ragged sleeve and said, "Now, you just hold you gob. I don't want no trouble out o' you."

Mary peered up at him. Surely it was Wally Kemp, the man she'd been told was the town drunkard, the man Ian had given work to at Sinclair Hall. As he raised the bottle again she became even more certain she was right. "I know you," she whispered, fearing that to speak any more loudly would only add to the agony in her head and prevent her from thinking as clearly as she needed to.

He stumbled back a pace and his voice emerged with hoarse intensity. "You don't know nothin' about me. You hear that?"

Mary could hear agitation in his voice. He was disturbed at the idea of being recognized. She attempted to play on that fear. "My husband will see you in gaol for this."

He took another long pull. "Not if there isn't anyone to tell what I done."

Mary stilled. What did he mean?

Realization hit her with the force of a cannonball ripping through the hull of a ship. God above, he meant to murder her. There was no other way he could even hope to prevent her from telling Ian.

"You can't mean to kill me," she blurted out. "I've done nothing to you or anyone else."

He lifted the bottle and drained it, then tossed it to the sand. "Aye, I do mean to do just that. And what you've done I don't care a fig about one way or another. I got me enough gold to keep me in gin for quite some time. And that's all I need to know."

She gasped in horror. The man had obviously consumed too much alcohol to care what he divulged at this point. Or possibly, and this seemed more likely judging from what he had said, he had simply decided it didn't matter how much she knew, for she wouldn't be around to tell anyone.

Whichever was the case, Mary knew she was in grave danger. In desperation she rolled over onto her stomach, with an iron will ignoring the renewed waves of nausea that swelled through her. Escape was surely her only hope.

But he was upon her immediately, catching her feet in a surprisingly strong hold.

Frantically Mary kicked at him, thrashing wildly from side to side. But she was unable to loosen Kemp's hold on her.

Finally she did succeed in freeing one foot. Mary knew a thrill of satisfaction when she felt the heel of her riding boot connect with what might have been his bloated middle.

Wally Kemp grunted, releasing her just before she heard a noise that sounded like a heavy body hitting the earth. Not pausing to see if she was right, Mary scrambled away from him, clawing her way through the sand.

Not knowing exactly where she was only hindered her cause, but she was aware that along some stretches of beach there were enormous boulders lining the inward side of the shore. If she could only make her way across the beach she might be able to find some rocks to hide amongst. Hope soared inside her as she gained her knees without having to gulp down bile.

In the next moment her heart plummeted when she felt her attacker's foot on her back. Roughly he pushed her down into the sand. It rasped her face, and she had to close her eyes to protect them.

His arms closed around her waist from behind, then she was being lifted and carried back down the beach. Instantly she began to fight, kicking and hitting every part of him she could reach.

Her struggles subsided when she felt a hard cuff to the side of her head. Again the waves of sickness engulfed her. She realized that she would have to choose her time carefully. If he continued to hit her in the head she might become too ill to escape again.

He carried her to the side of the boat and dropped her inside. It was a small boat and stank of rotting fish and wet wood. A few inches of cold seawater lay in the bottom, and she tried to sit up enough to keep it from soaking her skirts. She had no desire to become wet and chilled. It was obvious that Kemp was taking her somewhere and she needed to do whatever she could to keep her wits about her.

As her kidnapper climbed into the boat, he raised an oar and told her menacingly, "Don't try anything else, or I'll be letting you have it with this."

When she made no effort to reply he sat and began to row them out to sea, being careful the whole while to keep her fully in his sight. As they moved through the water, Mary became aware of the fact that the wind was picking up. She drew her knees up close to her body and wrapped her arms around them, shivering with apprehension as she felt the sea beneath them turn choppy.

Within a shockingly short space of time, it had risen quite fiercely. It had in fact begun to blow so briskly that it would have been difficult to maintain a conversation with Wally had he been so inclined.

On one level this frustrated her. She wished, in the event that he was able to carry out the unthinkable, that she could have gained the name of her enemy before she died. For that was surely what she had if someone had gone to the trouble of paying this reprobate to kill her. The knowledge that someone wanted her dead was shocking in the extreme. Even her certainty that someone had indeed pushed her that night in the hallway at Sinclair Hall had not equaled this horrific evidence that someone wished her grave ill.

Mary knew her only hope was escape, but in the next few minutes she saw no way to accomplish this. Jumping over the side and taking her chances with the sea seemed foolish. To go into that churning water would be to invite death.

To her surprise it was only a short time later that Wally Kemp ceased in his silent rowing and drew in the oars. She then cringed back against the side of the boat as he slid along the seat toward her. "What are you doing?" she cried as he reached for her.

"What I was paid to do." He grabbed her arms before the numbing horror of what he meant to do released her from her immobility.

"Please." She fought against him. She then closed her eyes on the pain as his fist hit the side of her already aching head and she realized her pleadings were falling on deaf ears. Wally Kemp cared only about the money he had been promised.

She opened her lids and looked into his eyes without flinching as she said, "At least tell me who has paid you to do this. That much I have a right to know."

Silent, he produced a length of rope from the bottom of the boat. It was wet and cold, but Mary did not react as she willed him to tell her. When her hands were securely bound, he stood and pulled her roughly to her feet.

"Can't you answer me?" she asked him one last time as he picked her up in his arms.

He stood there staring down at her for a long moment. She faced him directly, not asking for mercy, only the information she felt was her right.

To her great surprise he said, "What harm can there be

in telling you now? You will be gone from this world soon
enough. It was—''

At that moment a wave, decidedly bigger than the rest
rocked the boat beneath them like a cork in boiling water
A drunken Wally staggered, her weight throwing him even
further off balance.

The next thing she knew Mary was hitting the icy-cold
water. It closed over her head and drowned out the sound
of the wind and waves.

She'd not had time to take a breath before she went in
and her lungs were already beginning to ache. Fighting her
way desperately to the surface, which was made doubly
difficult by the complication that her hands were bound
Mary at long last broke out into the night. She gulped in
ragged breath of air and stinging salt water as the waves
foamed and broke all around her.

There was no sign of the boat, nor of Wally Kemp. He
must have been capsized and he thrown into the ocean a
Mary had been. But where was he, and would he in his
sodden state still think he must finish her off in the hope
of getting back to shore and gaining his fee?

Another wave crashed over her head, pushing Mary under. Again she fought her way to the surface and sucked
in air. She realized Wally Kemp was the least of her wor-
ries.

There was little chance of her surviving this ordeal a
best. And if she did not get her hands untied, none. She
could not swim this way—she could barely keep her head
above water.

Raising her hands to her mouth, she began to pull at the
knot her captor had tied.

She soon found, to her overwhelming relief, that the rope
he had used was not very strong. The fibers had swelled

and softened from lying in the salt water on the bottom of the boat.

In a gratifyingly short time the rope parted and she was free. After this small but regenerating bit of good fortune Mary's hopes rose fractionally. It was not much, but enough to give her the courage to set out toward the shore. Or at least what she hoped was the shore. In the stormy darkness it was impossible to tell.

Trusting that God would somehow guide her, she started off.

She had no idea how much time had passed when her feet touched bottom. She'd made it, thank God above, she'd made it. Dragging her debilitated body forward, Mary managed to get to the edge of the sea. She then fell forward on the beach, half in, half out of the chilly water.

With a sob that was a mixture of relief, exhaustion and accomplishment, she slipped into unconsciousness.

Chapter Fourteen

Ian leapt from his horse and ran up the steps and into Sinclair Hall. He had meant to be home much earlier in the day, had in fact endured with ill humor the delays that had kept him in Workham.

As the interminable hours had passed he'd found himself thinking of her smile, the sweetness of her nature, the gleam of sunlight in her hair with even more yearning than he did the desire they shared.

Why this was so, Ian did not know. He knew only that each delay of his return to her was frustrating to the point of madness.

When he entered the house, he was surprised to hear voices coming from the sitting room. He had thought the household would have long ago found their beds.

On the chance that Mary might be one of the occupants of the sitting room, Ian went to the open doorway. What he saw surprised him. His father was pacing the length of the room as he spoke with heat to the butler and several of the other male servants while Barbara sat pale and silent on the edge of a chair. "If there is no sign of her in the woods and no one has seen her in the village, then we must branch out. She is somewhere."

A prickling chill ran from the base of Ian's skull down his back. "Who is somewhere, Father?" Even as he said the words a terrible fear gripped his chest.

The older man looked up at him in abject relief. "Oh, son, thank God you've come home."

Ian barely registered the fact that his father had called him son for the first time in his memory. "What has happened?"

Malcolm came toward him, his face set with anxiety. "It's Mary. She did not come home and we've reason to believe there may be foul play involved."

There was a loud rushing in his ears and Ian's knees threatened to give out on him. He fought the urge to sink down, to give in to the despair that engulfed him. "But how? Who?" It made no sense. Mary had no enemies.

Malcolm raked a hand through his thick hair. "That I do not know, son, but I will tell you what we do know. Mary and I were having lunch this afternoon when a note arrived. It was from you, Ian."

Ian frowned. "I sent no note."

His father nodded. "I have since come to realize as much. I suspect whoever has done this knew that she would come without delay if you sent for her." He paused, his lips tight before going on. "I encouraged her to go, son. I had no idea until her horse came back without her that anything might be wrong. It was then I sent someone out to see if she was well and we discovered that not only was she not with you at the docks, but that you were not there, either. This seemed a clear indication that you had not sent the note. Since then we have searched the woods and village, with no sign of her."

Ian felt as if the blood had drained from his body, leaving ice in its place. Then somehow he was sitting, his father standing over him in concern. "Son, are you all right?"

He nodded, but could not summon a reply. His mind was churning with questions about who or why anyone could have done this horrible thing.

He recalled how adamant Mary had been that someone had pushed her that night on the stairs. Ian had been so certain that she was mistaken. To even imagine that someone would wish to hurt her was impossible. She had made nothing but admirers since coming here.

He felt a hand on his arm and looked up at Barbara. She seemed pale and withdrawn, the skin tight over the line of her jaw and cheekbones. "Oh, Ian, we are so worried." For some reason her touch on his arm felt too intimate, and Ian stood. He barely noted the blush that rose in his cousin's pale cheeks.

He was grateful for her concern, but he could not think of her right now, or why her touch left him feeling uncomfortable. "I must go out and look myself." He raised his gaze to his father's. "I cannot simply sit here and wait for word."

Malcolm nodded. "I understand. Have no worry. I will manage things here, and if someone else is able to learn anything I will send a messenger out to inform you." For a moment the elder man laid a reassuring hand on his shoulder.

Ian felt a tightening in his throat as he reached up to place his own hand over it. For one brief instant the two men shared a silent communication, united in their fear and worry over Mary.

Afraid this unexpected emotional support from his father might unman him, Ian hurried from the room.

In the stables he realized that he could not take Balthazar out, as the animal had already endured a long, hard ride that evening. He strode to the white stallion's stall. The horse was still a bit green, but Ian felt his stamina would sustain him well over the next hours.

In minutes the pair were racing over the track toward the village. The wind whipped at his hair and blew his dark cloak back from his shoulders but he paid it little heed. Ian was aware of little besides his need to find his wife. His father had said the woods and the village had been searched. The next obvious area seemed to be the shoreline.

He raised desperate eyes to heaven. "Dear Father," he prayed, "in your mercy, give me some sign. Please help me to find her."

It was as they were skirting the edge of the village that Ian saw someone coming down the road ahead of him with what appeared to be a child. The taller figure carried a lantern that lit the area around them. Ian could see the wind whipping at their clothing as both clearly struggled against the gale.

Ian slowed his mount only a few feet from them.

Emma Smith looked up from the hood of her homespun wool cloak and cried out in obvious joy. The child must surely be little Tom, he realized.

Before Ian could utter a query about why they would be out in such weather, Emma rushed in. "Oh, my lord Ian, I am so glad to see you. I was on my way up to the manor house. My Tom is away helping his father or I would have let him come, as he'd surely be much faster. I heard as how your wife, God bless her, is missing. And I told the men that I had not seen her, which was true. It was only a short while ago that little Tom here woke from his nap and told me that *he* had seen her."

Ian leapt from his horse to kneel in front of the child, thus putting their gazes on a level. "You have seen my wife?" He tried his best to keep his tone and expression even in spite of the thundering of his pulse.

Little Tom nodded, his blue eyes wide. "I did see the lady. She was sleeping in the back of old Wally Kemp's cart. She had a blanket over her but I seen her pretty hair."

Sleeping. Ian experienced a chill of fear. Dear heaven, he prayed Mary was not hurt. He pushed down his reaction. He must not think of her hurt or... He must only concentrate on finding her.

Ian spoke with deliberate care. "Did you see where they were going?" The little boy turned and pointed toward the track that led to the beach behind him. "They was going down there, Lord Ian."

Unable to restrain himself in the rush of hope that washed through him, Ian hugged the boy. "Thank you, little Tom. You've been a great help to me."

"And you, Mrs. Smith." He mounted in one fluid motion. As he turned his horse to go, he paused briefly. "Please go to Walter Middleton's house in the village and ask him to take word to my father. Don't go all that way yourself with your little one."

With that he was gone.

The steep decline soon leveled as Ian reached the shore. But the wind was even sharper here, and the sting of salt water that had been churned up by the wind made seeing in the dark all the more difficult.

Ian had no idea how Wally Kemp had come to be involved in some scheme against his wife. Wally clearly cared for little beyond his daily intake of gin.

It seemed the more he knew the less sense it all made. For all that little Tom Smith meant well, he might be wrong about having seen Mary in the back of the cart. After all, he was a child and by his own admission had seen nothing more than what he thought was golden hair.

Yet Ian had nothing else to go by. And he had been

praying for a sign. Surely this information meant something.

Ian rode on, battered by the wind and abrading sand. Time passed—he had no idea how much, but it felt like hours—and still there was no sign of Mary.

Even his faint hopes began to flag. Yet he went forward. The one thing he was grateful for was that the stallion did indeed show stamina. It seemed as fresh as when they had begun, dancing restively each time he paused to examine any object or shadow that caught his attention in the darkness.

In the end it was the stallion who discovered her. Ian could hear nothing above the howling of the wind, and his eyes watered constantly as he fought to keep the sand from blinding him.

When the stallion halted suddenly in his progress down the beach, Ian dug impatient heels into his sides. Still the horse would not move, lowering its head to sniff at something on the ground.

Forcing himself not to allow the hope that soared up inside him to take a firm hold, Ian slid to the ground. They had wandered much closer to the sea line than he had thought and he slipped into a couple of inches of cold water.

Ignoring this, he dropped the reins and moved forward to feel in front of them. His fingers closed over wet fabric. Further investigation told him that it was a portion of a silk skirt. He then frantically moved on to skin. Ian paused as he brushed against a smooth cheek, anxiety gripping his throat at feeling its icy chill, even as he realized that this was indeed Mary.

"Don't let her be dead. Please don't let her be dead." The words were a litany in his mind and he didn't realize he was repeating them out loud until his own hoarse voice sounded in his ears. He held his face to her mouth but could detect no breath with the elements in such an uproar around them.

His shaking hands moved over her too-still form to her chest. Ian ripped at the wet fabric of her gown as he felt desperately for her heart. At last he was able to locate the right spot, joy flooding him as he felt a slow but steady beat.

He cried out with exultation, gathering his wife's still body into his arms. He had no time to question the sheer limitless depths of his joy, for at that moment a particularly nasty gust of wind shrilled over them.

The stallion, now riderless, squealed in fear and reared, his hooves flashing. Throwing his own body over Mary's, Ian fully expected the weight of the terrified animal to come down upon his back. It was with relief that he heard the stallion's hooves hit the sand several inches from them and then the sound of him thundering down the beach.

His relief that they had not been pummeled by the sharp hooves was dampened by the fact that they were now out here in the elements without any way to get home. He stood and scooped his wife up into his arms.

A soft moan escaped her and he cradled her head against his shoulder. "It's all right, Mary. I'll take care of you," Ian soothed, even though he knew she could not hear him.

He searched the gloom for some landmark that might tell him where he was, and saw nothing. At the back of his mind was the thought that he had noticed something as he had come this way, a wide outcropping of rock that swung down from the cliff face far above and covered approximately half the shore in that area.

Ian had roamed this length of beach for hours as a boy. If he was not mistaken, there was a fisherman's hut snuggled close to that outcropping. And he suspected it had been built right there for protection from the elements on nights such as this.

With a determined sigh, he started down the beach the way he had come. If there was any justice at all for mortal men, the hut would still be there.

Sometime later Ian was pushing open the door of that shack with a feeling of accomplishment. He felt his way in the dark until he found the narrow bed, and carefully laid Mary on it. He then began to search for something to make a light. It seemed to him that a lantern had been kept here in the past.

Again his memory had served him correctly.

After a bit more fumbling in the dark, Ian found the lantern and flint. He soon had the thing lit, and raised it high as he moved back to the bed.

He could not help noting that the shack seemed much smaller than it had when he was a boy. The bed, nothing more than a bunk, really, would not be long enough for him to stretch out in now, and the stove was barely the size of a cooking pot.

Ian removed his cape and covered Mary with it, then moved to light a fire in the stove from the stack of wood. The wood was as dry as it could be in this damp environment and was coaxed into a serviceable blaze fairly quickly.

Ian then swung around and took his wife up onto his lap. She was coming around somewhat, for her hand fluttered in her irritation at the disturbance. Ian felt an unexpected wave of tenderness sweep over him and kissed the pale cold fingers. He swallowed down the strange lump in his throat and hurriedly began to remove her sodden garments.

He knew he had to get her warm. Hypothermia had been the death of more than one strong man in his memory.

When she was nude, Ian felt another wave of overwhelming sweetness grip him. Her form was wan and slight
in the lantern light. With a sudden need to protect her vulnerability from even his own eyes, Ian hurriedly covered
her with the tattered blanket from the end of the bunk.

As Mary's body began to warm slightly, she started to
shiver violently, moaning and tossing her head. Realizing
that he had nothing more to cover her with, Ian stripped
out of his own wet clothing and lay down beside her, his
feet dangling over the end of the bunk. He took her quaking
form in his arms and held her, willing the heat from his
own strong body into hers.

He held her like that through the next awful hours, leaving her only to put more wood into the stove. Finally Mary
stilled and seemed to slip into a more normal slumber. Ian
heaved a sigh of relief and at last allowed his muscles,
which were stiff with strain and anxiety, to relax.

He closed his eyes, and ran a gentle hand over the tangle
of her hair. He was overcome at the realization that she was
safe and secure in his arms, and wave after wave of tenderness swelled out from his bursting heart.

Never again, he told himself, just before exhaustion
claimed him, would he be parted from her. Never again
would anyone harm her.

Mary became aware of herself slowly. There was a dull
aching in her head, but it felt distant, hardly part of herself.
But that pain reminded her of something and she scowled
trying to recall what it was.

Her lids flew open wide. Wally Kemp. He'd taken her
and tried to drown her in the sea, but the boat had overturned. The last things she clearly remembered were desperately swimming for her life, then the rise of relief she'd
felt as she had come to shore.

After that there was little besides the vague and surreal sensation of being carried close to a familiar strong body...thinking she heard Ian's voice...knowing she must be hallucinating, because Ian did not even know she'd been kidnapped.

He had made love to her and left her, left her as if she was nothing.

All these thoughts passed through Mary's mind in a heartbeat, even as her eyes focused on the low ceiling of rough-hewn boards. Where was she? In the next moment she realized that she was not alone. Curled against her back was a warm, firm body. An arm circled her waist, the hand resting just beneath her bare left breast.... Her eyes opened wider.... Bare. Good gracious, she was naked.

Before she could move, a deep male voice spoke her name. "Mary."

Ian? She rolled to face him, unable to believe her own ears.

It was her husband. He was lying there, his dark eyes filled with concern as he looked up into her face. "Are you all right?"

She rubbed a confused hand over her forehead. "I...yes, I think so. My head does not hurt as badly as it did. But...what happened? How did I...you get here? The last thing I remember..."

He sat up, lifting the blanket that had slipped down from her shoulders in her surprise, to cover her before speaking. Mary wondered at this, but was concentrating too hard on the questions in her mind to give the gesture more than cursory notice.

Ian shrugged. "I cannot answer all. I was hoping you could supply the answers to my own questions. What I can tell you is that I found you unconscious on the beach. My horse bolted, so I brought you here. I had known about this cabin since I was a small boy. Luckily it was still standing."

Mary frowned in concentration. "The last thing I recall was reaching the beach. When Wally Kemp attempted to throw me over the side of his boat, it overturned and both of us were dumped into the sea."

She saw the way he blanched. "He meant to dump you into the sea."

Mary nodded, going on quickly, "Ian, someone—I don't know who—had paid him to kill me."

He paled even further. "Dear God. To *kill* you, Mary? But why? How?" His lips thinned and his eyes became hard as granite. "Who?"

Mary shivered, even knowing that look of cold hatred was not directed at her. Though the object of his ire had tried to harm her, she felt a sense of pity for them should Ian ever learn their identity. It was with this thought in mind that she answered him. "I do not know who is responsible. Wally fell overboard before he could tell me. He was very drunk, is likely drowned and now shall never give up that secret."

Ian stood and began pacing the tiny cabin. "Damn. His drunkenness has robbed me of the pleasure of killing the bastard."

Mary could only wonder at the depth of Ian's vehemence. She clutched the blanket more closely about her shoulders as Ian swung back to face her when she said, "I would likely not be here if he had not drowned."

Ian stopped suddenly, coming back to her. "Forgive me, Mary. I am talking like a madman. I am overcome by my relief that you are all right. If only I had listened when you said someone had tried to harm you before, this might not have happened at all. I only hope you will forgive me.

There is just such a sense of unreality about the whole thing.''

She nodded. ''I believe I understand some of what you are feeling myself. It all does seem so unreal now, as if I imagined the events of last night.''

Mary was not sure Ian's believing her when she said someone had tried to harm her would have prevented the kidnapping. But she did think it would have made her feel less isolated and alone when Wally took her, feelings that had not gone away even now.

She did not wish to acknowledge just how desperately she had longed for him through that long ordeal, wished things were different so she might tell him of her feelings. Ian's coming for her had not changed the fact that he did not love her. She had been rescued from the arms of death to be brought back to the hollow reality of her life.

His voice interrupted her tormented thoughts. ''God, if only we knew who had engineered this plot. How can we possibly protect you from any further attempts without having some knowledge of who is at the bottom of it?''

Mary shrugged. ''That I cannot answer for you.''

He went on, seemingly lost in his own thoughts. ''The fact that this evil coward was able to pay Wally Kemp to harm you might mean that he was also able to get to one of the house servants. That would explain how you were nearly pushed down the stairs that night. It also means you might be in further danger to return.''

Mary shook her head. ''I do not think so, else the person responsible would not have gone to Mr. Kemp to see the matter done. I cannot believe any of the house servants would harm me.''

''Then whom?'' Ian shook his head.

Mary looked at Ian, saying nothing for a long moment, frowning as a sudden thought came to her. ''There was a man, Ian, in the gardens one day. He did nothing but write on a sheet of paper and look at me...but..."

Ian shook his head, not meeting her gaze. "That workman meant you no harm, Mary. He is in my employ."

She could see by the look on his face that he would say no more about this. Mary gave a mental shrug. She would not pry into Ian's affairs.

With this possible suspect set to rest, there was only one other person Mary could even remotely believe might harm her, and she had no real evidence for suspecting her. She squared her shoulders, drawing Ian's gaze. "You are not going to like what I am about to say. But say it I must. There is only one other person who I can imagine might—"

He interrupted her. "Who, Mary? You must tell me."

She took a deep breath. "I think it might be...your cousin."

Ian blanched, dropping down on the end of the bunk. "Barbara? Mary, whatever would make you think such a thing? It just doesn't seem possible. She is such a placid and cowed creature. Has she said something, done something?"

She shook her head, scowling. "Nothing I can really put my finger on. It is just a feeling I have." Oh, what was the use? She could never convince him, did not quite understand why she thought this herself.

He raised his hands in a reasoning gesture. "I cannot accuse her."

Ian's stomach churned as he looked at his wife's set face. He could never make up for not having believed Mary before, though he would do just about anything to do so. Again he recalled the odd feeling he'd had when his cousin had touched his arm the previous afternoon. There had been something...something...almost like possessiveness in that touch. But as he had just said to Mary, he could not accuse her of attempted murder because of it.

Ian knew how terrified Mary must have been. She had confided her need to be protected and cared for. He had failed to live up to that need. Regretfully he said, "I am so sorry, Mary. I should have protected you, kept you safe."

She looked at him then, her golden eyes strangely distant. "I am a woman now. I do not expect you to be able to right all wrongs. I simply want..." She shook her head.

He waited, but she refused to go on. Ian felt his stomach sink. If she did not need him to care for and protect her, then why would she need him at all? An unexplainable stab of pain rippled through his belly.

He'd never deserved her. And he couldn't seem to do anything that would render him worthy of her. Was Mary right in saying that his heart was firmly locked inside him? He could feel that offending organ aching and swollen in his chest right now.

Looking at her now, with her golden hair tumbled about her shoulders, her amber eyes wide with hurt and disillusion, Ian could not deny the desire he felt. Yet there was another feeling that rose up to completely submerge the other. It was the same overwhelming protectiveness that he had felt as he held her last night. The sensation was something Ian had never experienced before and didn't quite know how to deal with.

Looking at Mary, knowing how he had wronged her time after time, refused to listen when she said someone had tried to harm her, Ian knew that mere words would not suffice to convey his emotions. And even if he was able to do so, would she care? Though the unspoken question made his throat tighten with pain, Ian knew the answer would likely be no.

Why would she care? He'd given her no reason to trust and believe in him.

Ian turned away. Somehow, some way he would show Mary that he did care, that although he had made mistakes and would make mistakes in the future, he was worthy of whatever care she might be able to give him. Ian realized that he had forever ruined any chance that Mary might actually learn to love him. But perhaps he could erase some of the mistrust and disillusion from her lovely eyes.

The first thing he would do was get her home. So thinking, he went across the room and reached for her gown, where it hung close the fire. The garment was drier than he had expected and he turned to hold it out to his wife. "If you want to get dressed, I'll just step out—"

He halted as the sound of voices outside interrupted him. Ian went to the door and jerked it open. A group of men from the village stood there.

One of the men, whom he recognized as Emma Smith's husband, Tom, hurried toward him. "Lord Ian, are you well? Your horse was found this morning."

Ian nodded. "I am well." He gestured behind him, though he stood in such a way as to block their view. "As is my wife."

"Praise God," he heard several of them murmur. Again he marveled that she was so beloved by the people after so short a time. Only he had been blind to just how special she was.

Ian could only hope that he had not come to his senses too late.

Chapter Fifteen

Ian watched his cousin as she came into the library and sat down. Ian himself was seated behind his father's enormous desk. He looked down at the letter of credit he had just signed, and back to his cousin.

Realization that he must ask her to leave Sinclair Hall had been followed by the understanding that he owed Barbara something for any disappointment she might have felt at his not marrying her. Ian now knew he had deceived himself about many things, including his feelings for Mary, and his cousin's expectations. Ian had been blind not to see that she, along with his father, had hoped to someday become more than his father's companion and glorified housekeeper. London gossip had it that her family was not in the best of financial positions. He only hoped that she took the gesture in the spirit with which it was given.

She spoke demurely, her hands folded in the lap of her gray silk gown. "You wanted to see me, Cousin Ian?" As always, she was the picture of docile womanhood. It seemed impossible that she could ever even think of harming anyone.

But even if this was so, Ian knew she could no longer

remain at Sinclair Hall. Mary was his wife and her feelings on this matter had to be taken into account.

He nodded, coming directly to the point. "I did. I want you to know, Barbara, that your presence here has been a great help and comfort to my father. I now feel that we can no longer impose upon your or your family's goodwill by keeping you here with us."

Her eyes were wide with shock. "But Cousin Malcolm needs me. I cannot leave. My family understands perfectly. They would not wish for me to—"

He raised a hand, effectively halting her. "Mary will be taking over the duties of running the household. It has been very good of you to stay on here while she settled in, but I can assure you that you are free to go back to your home now." He handed her the note. "I hope you will accept this small token of gratitude for all you have done."

Her eyes widened further as she looked down at the amount. "It is very generous of you, but..." She frowned at him. "Your father will not wish for me to—"

"I have spoken to my father on this matter. He, too, feels that we have imposed upon you more than we had a right to."

Barbara stared down at her hands. "Ian, don't send me away. I..." She faced him again, her dark eyes filled with desperation. "How *can* you send me away? You must know how I feel about you."

Guilt made him speak gently. "I did not know."

She leaned forward, beseeching him. "But how could you not? I waited here for you, did all that was asked of me without complaint or regret. How can I go back to my family now when my life is here? I need to be with you."

Ian ran a hand through his hair. "How did this happen? Did I ever say or do anything to make you think that I..."

If I did I am very sorry, for you are my cousin, and only that.''

She shook her head, her dark eyes damp with unshed tears. "No...not anything that...but I thought...everyone thought...understood that we would marry someday. I was willing to wait for you, Ian.''

"I regret that you have been hurt in this, Barbara, but no one ever asked me.'' He stood. "Under the circumstances I can see that the only fair course is for you to go. I am married and contented in that.''

A hint of anger crept into her voice. "How could you be? She is not a proper...''

Irritation prickled at this criticism of his wife. "You know nothing of my wife. She has been hurt in all this, as well.'' He would not further shame her by revealing the details of their difficulties to his cousin. Ian moved to the door as he said, "I will see that the carriage is ready for you in the morning.''

He left the room before she could say anything else she would only be sorry for. Though he still could not imagine Barbara doing anyone harm, he was now even more sure that his decision to ask her to return to her own home had been the only one possible. He had not known of her feelings for him and had had no right to put either her or Mary through the embarrassment he had.

He squared his shoulders. This was just one more blunder he must take upon his conscience.

As Ian spoke from the entrance of the conservatory, Mary looked up from the letter she was writing to Victoria. "I trust you slept well.'' The words were said with a stiff formality that for some reason sent a tiny stab of regret through her heart.

She nodded, trying not to see how very handsome he

looked in close-fitting fawn riding breeches and a dark green coat. "I did."

Ian's father, who had not left her side the whole day, rose from where he had sat close by reading *The Post*. "If the two of you will excuse me, I have a few matters to attend."

Mary knew he was going only so as to leave the two of them alone, but she did not remark on it. "I will see you at luncheon," she told him gently.

"Yes, you will." He nodded to Ian as he passed him on his way to the door, his eyes gentle. "Son."

Ian replied softly, his pleasure in the word communicating itself to Mary, though he said only, "Father." She was glad to see that they seemed to have come to some level of acceptance toward one another. In spite of her own problems with Ian, she wished him well in his relationship with the earl.

When the older man was gone, Mary looked to her husband. "There was no need to post a guard at my door, Ian."

He replied with that same stiff formality. "I will take no more chances with your safety until we discover who is at the bottom of this." Since they had been brought to Sinclair Hall by the village men the previous day, he had been so very courteous toward her—too courteous, too protective.

Mary knew he felt guilty and responsible for the fact that she had nearly been killed. She knew only sadness at his single-minded determination to keep her from physical harm, for there seemed to be no emotion connected to it. When they'd first met she'd thought that she'd wanted, needed, someone to look after her. Now she had come to understand that was not enough in itself. What she needed was her husband's love—the one thing he could not give her.

She watched as Ian raked an agitated hand through his

thick, dark hair. Mary realized that something was wrong. Without looking away from him, she set her letter aside. "What is it? What has happened?"

Ian came closer to her, his eyes dark with some emotion she could not gauge. "Wally Kemp's body has washed up on the shore."

Mary took a deep breath. So he was dead. Even as she felt a swift stab of sympathy that she would have for any creature, however despicable, to have died in that storm, it was overridden by relief. He would not be back to harm her again. She had not realized until this very moment how much she'd feared his doing so.

Ian spoke with concern. "I must go to see if any clue can be found on the body. You will be all right while I am gone?"

She nodded. "Of course." Mary looked down at her hands. "There is no need for you to spend every moment with me. I am capable of seeing to myself. You are not responsible for me."

He scowled as she glanced his way. "I don't feel responsible.... I feel..." She looked at him more fully, wondering what it was he had been about to say.

But he did not enlighten her. "Very well, then, Mary. You do not need anyone. I am quite clear on that." He paused then, almost as if he could not help himself, and added, "You will be cautious until I return."

She sighed. "Yes." What had happened was beginning to seem more like a horrific nightmare than a reality. She had even begun to doubt her own suspicions of Barbara, for the woman had been pale and quiet when Mary and Ian had returned to the hall. Not by sign or word had she shown Mary any hint of ill will, though their meeting had admittedly been brief.

The line of his lean jaw was tight as Ian replied, "I know

you prefer not to have to rely on anyone but yourself, Mary. But try to be patient until we are able to find out who means you harm.''

She said nothing, only stared into those enigmatic dark eyes. If only he knew how much she wished to rely upon him, not because he was acting out of duty, but out of love.

He bowed stiffly. ''I will return as quickly as possible.''

Hours passed and still Ian did not return.

She remained in the sitting room with Ian's father long after the dinner hour had come and gone. Barbara had dined with them, but had said very little, seeming lost in her own thoughts, which if her demeanor was anything to judge by were not happy. Again she was nothing more than polite and diffident toward Mary in spite of her preoccupation. She had excused herself immediately after the meal.

Looking over at her father-in-law where he sat close to the fire, Mary became aware of the fact that the older man's shoulders had begun to slump and his head to nod. She realized how selfish she was being. The earl would not go to bed and leave her here alone.

She stood. ''I am going up to bed now, Father. I trust you will do the same.''

The relief in his eyes was obvious, though he tried to hide it. ''That is a good idea. You have been through a great deal and need your rest.''

Mary went up and found Frances waiting for her. The maid helped her to get ready for bed, then seemed reluctant to leave when Mary told her to find her own bed. She looked at the maid fondly. ''Really, Frances, there is no need to worry. I am quite safe here in my own room.''

The girl looked at her, her eyes damp. ''I would not want anything to happen to you, my lady. You...I...''

On impulse Mary gave her a quick hug. "I feel the same way about you. Now, please go to bed."

Once the maid was gone, Mary was alone with her own fearful thoughts. Ian had been most adamant in saying he would not be long. What if the person responsible for her own kidnapping had harmed Ian? Anxiety gripped Mary in a tight hold, though she told herself that Ian was simply delayed, that he would not fall easy victim, as she had.

Yet the words did not reassure her. She was sitting staring out the window into the darkness when a knock sounded at her door.

Thinking that it might be Ian, Mary hurriedly answered. To her utter surprise it was Barbara. Mary felt herself tense, even as the other woman rushed into the room wearing a long cloak, her usual reserved demeanor replaced by wild anxiety.

Mary stood. "What is it? What has happened?"

Barbara moved closer to her, wringing her long-fingered, pale hands. "It's Ian, he's been hurt."

Mary gasped. "Hurt? But how?"

"His horse slipped along the cliffs."

Mary grasped the other woman's hands in a viselike grip. "He is not...?" Her one brush with those cliffs had left her with a great fear of them. Just to think of Ian falling...

Barbara shook her head, her own eyes filled with obvious pain. "No, but it does not look good. And though it pains me to admit this, it is you he is asking for."

Mary closed her eyes on the flowering agony in her breast. "I must go to him. Where is he?"

"He is in the stables. I will accompany you," Barbara told her.

"Why was he not brought into the house, his father told?"

Barbara looked at her impatiently. "His father is there.

It was he who sent me to fetch you. Ian, the injury is…well, we did not wish to take the chance of moving him further before you—'' Her voice broke off on a sob.

Mary looked at the other woman for long moment. She did not trust Barbara, but what reason did she have for this? The other woman had done nothing to raise suspicion in the past day. The superior glances she had once cast toward Mary had been replaced by a quiet diffidence.

Yet Mary knew that, even if there was a chance Barbara wished her harm, she could not remain here. What if Ian really was hurt, asking for her? The thought was too much to bear. Mary's love for him would not allow her to take the chance of denying him her presence. There was no more time to think. She must go, or not.

Mary knew she could not do anything but go.

Besides, what harm could Barbara do her at Sinclair Hall? The stable hands slept in their own rooms at the far end of the building. They would surely hear her if she called out to them.

"Very well, let us waste no more time." Mary moved to take her own cape from the wardrobe. She would not take the time to change from her diaphanous white night rail and robe.

There was a lit lantern on the hall table where Barbara must have set it when she knocked upon Mary's door. Ian's cousin took it up and Mary allowed her to assume the lead, as she knew where they were to go. They met no one in the house. The night was thick as old ink, and a heaviness descended on Mary as they hurried across the courtyard at the back of the house. She told herself that it was only her fear for Ian that made her so anxious. Yet the sensation that something was dreadfully wrong only got more intense as they went.

Continuously she cast assessing glances toward the other

woman, but Barbara did not even look at her, seemingly bent on getting to Ian. This did not make Mary relax her guard. She did not mean to be caught unaware.

The dark-haired woman opened the oak door at the side of the stone building and stood back for Mary to enter. Even as she moved forward Mary frowned. "Why can we not hear anyone? See any lights?"

Barbara replied, "They are on the other side."

Mary stepped inside then swung around to face the other woman, who was close behind her. "Where are they, Barbara? Where is Ian?"

Mary's eyes searched the area around her, but she saw nothing in the light of the lantern besides two saddled horses. Her heart leapt into her throat as she realized that Barbara had indeed lied. Even as she turned to run, Barbara quickly reached into the pocket of her cloak and drew out a pistol. She then reached out with uncharacteristic speed and grabbed Mary's arm with her other hand.

"Help!" Mary screamed.

Barbara smiled coldly. "No one will hear you. I have given them something to make them sleep more deeply—not enough to arouse any suspicion in the morning, but the men will not awaken to the sound of your voice from this distance."

Ian's cousin spoke evenly, her voice chilling in its lack of emotion. "You and I are going for a little ride." Barbara began to pull her toward the saddled mounts. Mary was shocked at the strength of the taller woman's long fingers when she tried to shake them off, and failed.

"Dear God," she gasped, "do not do this!" The other woman did not heed her, but continued to drag her forward with that shocking strength that Mary was sure could only have been born of madness.

This time when she spoke there was a terrifying depth

of animosity in her voice. The sheer vehemence of her reply made her insanity all the more obvious. "I will not allow you to take Ian from me!"

Mary tried reason. "I did not take Ian from you."

Barbara did not look at her. "Did you not? He has asked me to leave Sinclair Hall because of you."

This revelation so shocked Mary that for a moment she could not reply. The other woman seemed to sense this, for she stopped and said, "You did not know?"

Mary shook her head. "No."

This appeared only to add to her rage, for she yanked roughly on Mary's arm as she continued, "It matters not at all. Once you are gone, Ian will realize how much he needs me."

"He will not. He will guess that you have done this."

"No, he won't, for I have given him no cause to think that I would harm you. I am leaving at first light. By the time someone discovers that you are gone, they will not connect me in any way."

Mary could not argue this. She knew Ian had never believed his cousin could do anyone harm. Mary herself had even begun to doubt her own perceptions of the woman.

Despair made her throat tight.

Then from somewhere inside her Mary felt a growing rage. Too many people had hurt her over the past months. The only one who could stop her from being a victim to the whims of others was herself.

And she meant to bring a halt to it right now. She had done nothing to this woman. From within her rose a depth of strength that surprised her even more than Barbara's. Setting her heels, Mary braced backward, bringing their progress to an abrupt halt and throwing the other woman off balance, thus gaining her release.

Barbara waved the gun. "Get on the horse."

Filled with righteous anger, Mary cried out, "How dare you do this to me? I did not take Ian from you."

The other woman screamed out in rage, "You did. If you had not come, he would have married me." She sobbed with the depth of her fury. "You come here, a nothing, a country vicar's daughter, and soon have the whole countryside dancing to your every whim. I, who have been obedient and patient, waiting for him to see me, to recognize my worth, was overlooked by him in all these years. I am despised for doing as I was told, for knowing my own place in the social order, for expecting the servants and country folk to know theirs. I obeyed Cousin Malcolm's every command, subjugated my will to show that I was willing to be a dutiful wife. Yet I was happy to do so in order for Ian to notice me, to have him marry and care for me."

Mary could not help the pity that rose inside her. "You should not have gone against your own principles. No one could expect that of you."

She did not seem to understand, for Barbara cried, "I was happy to do it if it meant Ian would marry me."

Mary realized that the other woman did not even understand what she was saying. She had completely given herself away, but that had been her decision and no one else's. Mary could not allow herself to feel the regret that she and Ian had not been able to have the kind of relationship she had hoped for. She concentrated instead on her attacker. "You had the right to choose, Barbara. It was in your hands."

Barbara only cried out more violently, waving the pistol, "That is so easy for you to say, Miss High-and-Mighty. You will be the wife of an earl. If Ian will not have me I must go home and face my family with nothing to show for the effort they have put forward on my behalf. I've had all my father could spare to afford me the wardrobe to come here so that I might make the right impression. The moneys Ian has given me to assuage his guilt are nothing compared to the wealth I would have known as the wife of the future Earl of Dryden. They, my parents and sisters, were depending upon me to provide for them.''

Mary had wondered if something like this was the case. Again she felt that swell of sympathy, but knew she could not allow it to make her let down her guard. This woman had tried to kill her, still wished to do so. However pitiful, she was potentially dangerous. She had to know just how far the other woman had been willing to go. "So it was you who hired Wally Kemp to throw me into the sea." Just the memory of that horrific night caused Mary to shiver. But she did her best not to let Barbara see the depth of her reaction.

Luckily the other woman was too caught up in what she felt was the injustice of the situation to care about Mary's feelings. "That utter fool. After you refused to fall down the steps I felt I had to find an ally. Unfortunately the drunken sot was not able to see it through." Mary could see her eyes narrow even in the darkness. "Which means that I am left to finish this off myself. Tonight you will meet your unfortunate end on the cliffs. It is the only way."

Mary took a step backward. "It will do you no good to kill me. Ian has asked you to go home."

Barbara's cold smile was obvious in her voice. "When news of your death becomes known I will return to Sinclair Hall to offer whatever help I can to him and his father. The death of their beloved wife and daughter will leave them devastated. Ian will need me to take care of things while he recovers."

Mary did not argue with the madwoman about Ian being devastated at the death of his beloved wife. That he loved her could not be further from the truth. But Barbara's assumption that Ian cared for her made her wonder if she could somehow use this to her advantage. The fact that Ian had asked his cousin to leave Sinclair Hall, though Mary did not know why, might aid her in trying to bluff her way out of this. "Ian will suspect you have had something to do with it."

Barbara seemed to hesitate, but only for a moment. "You are wrong."

Shaking her head, Mary said, "I told him that I thought you might be involved. We had no proof that you were. That was why he chose to send you home instead of accusing you. Even if he did not suspect you, you will not escape detection. I will not get on that horse, and someone will surely hear if you shoot me."

Ian's cousin threw up her arms in absolute fury. "You may be telling the truth and you may be lying. But even if it is true, I don't care. Do you hear me? I'm past caring about anything. Even if it is true and Ian won't have me, he won't have you, either. If what you say is true, my life is ruined. So must yours be." She waved the gun wildly. "Now, get on the horse or I will shoot you right here and take whatever comes."

Barbara was far beyond the reach of reason. Mary realized that her only hope was to get the gun.

And then even as she fought down the rising hopelessness inside, an idea came to her. Mary did not know if it would work, if she would be able to lull the other woman into a false sense of security by pretending to go along with her plan. Mary only knew that if she was able to do so it would be the greatest feat of prevarication she had ever heard of.

Thus thinking, she allowed her shoulders to slump with defeat.

Moving as if reluctantly toward the horses, Mary purposely passed as closely as she could to Barbara, being ever mindful of the gun in her hands. Silently she prayed that an opportunity would present itself. And it did, when one of the horses snorted, drawing Barbara's attention for the briefest moment.

But moment enough.

Mary leapt toward Barbara, grabbing for the gun. Barbara reacted immediately, tightening her grip. With determination, knowing this was likely her only chance to save herself, Mary refused to let go.

They grappled over the weapon, and Barbara stumbled backward in the hay. Then suddenly the gun came free in Mary's fingers, even as she watched the lantern fall from the other woman's grip.

It fell to the floor, oil spilling out as the flame leapt to consume it—and the dry hay. Mary moved to stamp on the flames, but it was too late and she had to back away as the fire licked at the fragile material of her night rail.

The horses screamed in fear as the flames spread toward where they were tied. Mary rushed to them, her fingers shaking as she undid the knots that held them captive.

As she turned to run toward the doors to open them, Mary saw Barbara there ahead of her. Tears were running down her face as she sobbed out, "Ian's horses, his horses. We have to save them, they mean everything to him. He will never forgive me if they are killed." Her need to kill Mary seemed to be forgotten in her obsession to save Ian his hurt.

Mary knew it was true that Ian would never get over the loss of his beloved horses. But as the other animals in the vast stable began to smell the fire and react in panic, she realized the two of them could not save them all.

Praying that Barbara was right in thinking she had not drugged the stable hands heavily, Mary ran to where she knew their rooms were at the very far end of the building. The horses at this end had not yet smelled the flames, but seemed restive. Desperately Mary banged on the doors, calling out for help. It took a long moment, but finally a groggy-looking Lester appeared in a doorway.

Mary wasted no time on preamble. "There is a fire in the stables. We must wake the others and get the horses out. Now."

His eyes widened with horror even as he rushed to help her. Soon the other four stable hands had emerged from their rooms. Though they did not appear as alert as Mary would have liked, they all hurried to empty the stables.

The fire had now spread at the far end of the building and Mary ran back to see that no animals remained there. All the doors had now been opened so the horses could be blindfolded and lead from their stalls, but the increased air flow only fed the flames.

Her lungs began to feel tight with each indrawn breath, and she knew she would soon have to make her own escape. Mary heard a hoarse whinny and looked toward it. Through the smoke, fire and heat waves she saw a figure in a long cape fumbling at the door of a stall. Ian's white stallion reared and thrashed in its fear.

Mary rushed forward. Quickly she pushed Barbara's fingers aside and easily undid the latch. She wondered at the other woman's clumsiness even as she ducked when the stallion leapt over them where they knelt on the floor. She could only pray that he would somehow find freedom.

Raising her head, Mary saw that Barbara was now lying upon her back. She did not get up when Mary called her name. Obviously Ian's cousin had been overcome by the smoke, which was now so thick that it was difficult to see more than a few inches in front of her. She had been in the area where the fire had started from the very beginning.

Mary crawled to her side, but could not wake her. She knew she could not allow the other woman to die here, no matter what she had done. She moved to take her arms, determined to drag her toward the door.

Barbara opened her eyes, her gaze dazed as it rested on Mary. A hoarse whisper escaped her. "Dear God, Mary, you would save me?" A tear rolled down her dirty cheek. "Forgive me." Then her head fell back as she lost consciousness again.

Mary drew in a ragged, scorching breath and coughed harshly as the heat seared her already aching lungs, but she did not drop her burden. Perhaps there was some good in this woman that would now show itself.

Chapter Sixteen

Ian had been gone much longer than he had planned. His examination of Wally Kemp's body had produced no evidence that would help in his search for whomever had hired the bastard.

Concern for Mary had prodded at his mind at every moment and he would have returned to Sinclair Hall immediately if it had not been for the fact that word had arrived that the man's boat had been spotted drifting in the sea some distance from shore. Thinking this might indeed be just what he needed to lead him to some clue, Ian had boarded one of the fishing boats and gone out to investigate.

Unfortunately nothing had turned up.

As he rode home, Ian noticed an odd light up ahead in the distance, a bright rosy glow against the night sky. A fire! And it looked to be at Sinclair Hall.

Ian spurred Balthazar to a gallop, not heeding the darkness of the road ahead of them. His mind was a panicked blur as he raced down the drive and rounded the house, following the dreaded glow.

When he saw that it was the stables that were ablaze, he felt a fierce, sweeping relief. Mary could not be hurt. She would be safely in her bed away from this scene of disaster and pandemonium.

Then his thoughts turned to the horses he had worked so hard to raise. A number of the animals were racing about the courtyard in wild confusion. Several of the servants were making an attempt to capture them. Ian heard a group of men nearby shouting over the commotion about going back inside.

Looking at the blaze, Ian knew that to go back in would be to court death. The thatched roof looked ready to cave in at any moment. He leapt from his horse, running toward them. "No one is to go back in. I won't allow it."

They turned to him, their eyes filled with such stark sorrow that Ian felt an immediate stab of fear. One of them said, "We must go back in, my lord. Your wife and Miss Barbara..."

He grabbed the poor man by the front of his shirt. "What are you talking about?"

The young fellow raised harried eyes to Ian's. "They are inside, my lord. Neither one of them has come out."

"How do you know she was inside?"

"'Twas her that woke me," Lester said, wiping a hand over his damp eyes.

Broadsided by a pain so deep he staggered, Ian swung around and screamed, "No!"

The flames seemed to leap even higher as if fed by his agony. Dear God, he prayed as his leaden legs took him toward his wife, don't take her. Please don't take her. I love her, please don't take her.

The words repeated themselves over and over again in his mind as he burst into that hell of heat and flame. "Mary," he called, "Mary."

"Ian." Her voice answered so quickly he feared for a

moment that it was only in his imagination. But then he heard her again. "Ian, I am here."

The time it took him to reach his wife's side could have been seconds or an eternity. Ian had lost all sense of time and reality. He could think only of getting to her, of seeing that she was still alive.

When at last he came upon her he frowned in confusion, for she had her back to him and seemed to be dragging something heavy. When he put his hand on her back she straightened, but only briefly, as she called over the roar of the flames, "Help me, we must get her out of here."

He looked down, confusion and her own preoccupation keeping him from taking her into his arms and showing her how glad he was to find her alive. He saw that Mary had been dragging an unconscious Barbara.

Quickly he bent and took the prone woman into his arms. "Pull your cloak over your head and then put your head against my shoulder," he told his wife, waiting while she did so. Then he turned to race back through that wall of flame. Instinct alone helped him to bring them to safety.

Once out in the cool night air, he relinquished the unconscious woman to the care of others. But just as they swung around to take her away, Barbara opened her clouded eyes and said, "You saved my life. Will you forgive me, Mary? Tell me you forgive me, please?"

Ian watched as Mary lowered the cloak from her head and moved to the other woman's side. "I do forgive you, though I will never forget what you intended to do to me. You must leave here and try to make something better of your life."

Tears fell from her red-rimmed eyes. "I will."

"Take her inside," Ian ordered. "What happened here?" he then demanded, even as he placed a supporting arm around Mary's shoulders.

Mary did not look at him as she whispered, "She told me you were hurt, that you were in the stables, that you were asking for me. Then she tried to...the lantern fell when we struggled...the stable caught fire." She seemed dazed, her voice a colorless monotone as if she were speaking of some incident not connected to herself.

"Dear Lord in heaven," Ian gasped.

He only then realized that his father had joined them as he said, "Good God, Mary."

But he could spare no more than a moment for the older man. He could think only of his wife. He should have believed her, trusted her instincts. He had simply had no proof. Even the act of asking his cousin to leave had seemed somehow cruel.

And in spite of what Barbara had tried to do, Mary had risked her own life to save her. That his cousin had obviously finally come to see how wrong she had been did not absolve her—nor did the fact that Mary had survived absolve him.

Pain tightened his chest. What a fool he had been.

Mary swayed. Regret washed through him. She had been through too much to expect her to explain anything tonight. He swept her up in his arms, cradling her head against his shoulder. He then turned to his father. "The men will see that the fire spreads no farther." His gaze swept what was left of his stables. "I am going to take her away from here."

His father nodded, his dark eyes filled with sadness. "That would be best. I'll see to having the horses rounded up. The men don't believe even one of them perished in the fire."

"I think we have Mary to thank for that." Looking down at her, he saw that she had lost consciousness, and a great wave of tenderness crashed over him, bearing him down with the great depth of his love for her.

Love her he did, and with an intensity that was staggering. But he had realized it too late. His heart ached as though it were dying in his chest, for he knew he could never expect her to forgive him for not trusting her instincts this time. He would never forgive himself.

Two days later Ian went to his father's study. The earl was sitting listlessly, his papers spread out before him. He looked up as Ian entered, his expression welcoming. "Ian."

Ian sat down on one of the leather chairs, knowing his father was not going to like what he had come to say, but knowing his decision was the right one, the only decent one. "Father, I have to leave Sinclair Hall."

The earl looked at him in horror. "Whatever are you talking about? How can you leave when things have finally begun to work themselves out? Barbara has gone back to her family, though I do not believe she would ever be a threat to Mary again. She seemed concerned for nothing besides Mary's well-being as she was leaving, and this time I do not believe it was an act."

Ian scowled. "I care nothing for her. The only reason I did not bring in the authorities is that Mary would not have it. I did not wish to upset her more than she already is by disregarding her wishes. I have done so too much in the past. Which is why I must go from here. Mary has been through too much at my hands. I want her to be happy. The only way I can see to attain that is to go away."

"But you are my son, my heir. How can you abandon your birthright?" the older man asked him.

Ian shrugged. "Mary has earned her place here. After all I have done, my presence could not but give her pain. Under the circumstances we cannot remain in the same house.

Sinclair Hall is as much her home as mine, and if one of us should leave, I am the one who must do so.''

"Have you discussed this with your wife?"

"There is no need. She could not but resent me after the way I have treated her.''

Malcolm stood and came around the desk, placing his hand on Ian's shoulder. "Son, I know my advice is likely unwelcome and most justifiably so, but I must speak. I beg you not to duplicate my mistakes. I allowed my fears to keep me from reconciling with you. It was an error I can never correct. The pain of those years cannot be forgotten. If you believe this is what you must do, go to her and tell her you love her first. If she rejects you, then you will know that you have made the right decision in leaving her.''

Ian's voice was heavy with sadness. "How could she do otherwise?''

Malcolm tried again. "All you risk is your pride, Ian. Pride seems a small price to pay for the chance of being loved by a woman like Mary. She is so like your mother that I sometimes wonder if God sent her to you so you would know how dear and wonderful my—our—Laura was." His voice broke with sorrow. "I'm sorry it took me so long to see that you lost her, too. As I said, please do not follow in my footsteps, Ian. I have been a lonely and unhappy man. It has cost me dear.''

Was it true that he was afraid of risking his pride?

Ian did not know what to say, and thus said nothing. He heard the door close as his father left him to the torment of his thoughts.

Ian stood outside Mary's door, his hand poised to knock. He took a deep breath, then did so.

Her voice told him to enter.

When Ian opened the door, Mary was sitting in the up-

olstered chair near the tall windows, her hair spread out
around her like a golden halo. She looked up from the letter
he was reading, her pink lips forming an O. A flush rose
from the scooped neckline of her spring green morning
gown and spread across her lovely throat to her high cheekbones.

The surprise in her voice was evident as she said, "Ian."

Her reaction was not unexpected, considering the fact
that he had made no attempt to see her since the fire three
days ago. "Good morning, Mary," he said softly. "I hope
you are well."

She raised her left hand, which bore a light bandage. "I
received no serious injury. The burn on my hand is not
deep. I believe Barbara was more seriously burned."

He nodded. "That is what I am told, but I am sure she
is fine. We have not heard from her or her family since she
left."

Mary looked away, her profile cast in perfect lines
against the light. "She told me you had asked her to leave,
Ian." She turned, and her eyes met his. "Why did you not
tell me?"

"I did not want you to think I expected anything from
you in return. It was only what I should have done in the
beginning."

"You did that even though you did not suspect she had
tried to harm me." Her tone told him nothing of her feelings on this.

Ian made no reply. He certainly did not want her to think
he expected any thanks or accolades for this small and in-
effectual decision. Mary had still nearly been killed by the
woman.

She surprised him with her next comment. "You have
not been to see me since the fire."

He frowned. "I did not think you would want me t[o] come."

She only looked at him, her golden eyes giving nothing away. He drew himself up, realizing that he must sto[p] avoiding the real issue and carry through with what he ha[d] decided to do. "Mary," he said, "there is something [I] would like to show you."

She looked at him closely, a frown marring her brow[.] "What is it?"

Ian shook his head. "I cannot explain. It must be seen."

To his surprise she rose without further questions, he[r] golden eyes meeting his. "Then show me."

Mary had indeed been surprised to see her husband. I[n] the days since the burning of the stables she had thought [a] great deal. At first she had still been angry with Ian for n[ot] trusting in her judgment of Barbara, but then she had re[-] called the fact that she, too, had been fooled. How muc[h] more difficult would it be for Ian to believe that the woma[n] who seemed so very docile and easily cowed could be s[o] very vindictive?

As the days had passed she'd begun to focus on anothe[r] point. Ian had asked Barbara to leave, and the fact that h[e] had done this, had thought about her feelings in this matte[r,] allowed a faint glimmer of hope to rise in her breast.

When Ian had not come to see her, that hope had dwi[n-] dled. His appearance in her room now oddly did not see[m] real, especially after his telling her that he had not com[e] because he felt she would not want him. And his expla[-] nation for why he had not told her of his request for hi[s] cousin to leave was noncommittal at best.

When Ian reached into his pocket and produced a sno[w-] white handkerchief and said, "There is just one thing. [I] wonder if you would allow me to cover your eyes," h[e] sense of unreality only increased. He went on to add, "What I wish to show you is…" He halted. "Would you please let me cover your eyes?"

Mary stared at him for a long moment, knowing as she did so that her acquiescence would mean more than a simple yes to either of them, though she doubted that Ian realized how much.

Going to stand before him, Mary raised her face. "I will wear it."

When the blindfold was in place, Ian took Mary's hand in his and led her from the room. Once they had descended the staircase she lost all sense of where she might be until she felt the soft cushion of grass beneath her thin satin slippers.

Ian's hand left hers for a moment and she heard a soft scraping sound. Then he was back, urging her forward gently. He halted her unexpectedly, moving to stand behind her, his hands going to her shoulders as he said, "I want this first moment to be perfect. I have imagined just how it would be since I thought of giving you this gift. Now, keep your eyes closed and I will remove the blindfold."

She nodded, then felt Ian's fingers undoing the knot at the back of her head. When it was free, he stepped back and said, "Open them."

Mary lifted her lids and saw… She was in a garden, the likes of which she had never imagined. It was filled with beautiful blooming flowers of every kind, in neat little beds with flagstone walks between them. There were shrubbery and trees of every shade of green. Ivy and trailing vines hung from a high stone wall that encircled the whole, giving the impression that this was an old and established garden. There was even a swing hanging from the gnarled branch of an apple tree up ahead and to the left of the path.

But Mary knew it was not an old garden. This was what

had lain behind that mysterious wall. She turned to him slowly, her eyes and heart overflowing with awe of the beauty around her. "I don't understand, Ian. Why have you brought me here?"

"It is yours, Mary. I had it built for you. I wanted you to have something of your own, something of meaning to you, and I wanted you to know once and for all that I was not and have never been embarrassed by you or anything you would do."

Tears blurred her vision as he held out a large gold key. Taking it in her hand, she went forward, still not fully comprehending what he was saying to her, what such a gift would mean to her—to them. "It is mine."

He followed close behind her. "To do with as you please. No one may come or go here unless it is by your consent."

She went down the walk touching a clematis here, a rose there. "Mine."

"And the gardener has planted some cuttings from your mother's roses as well as those from my father's garden." He pointed to a sheltered spot along the wall.

Mary moved on until she came to a spot that must have been the center of the enclosure. Here there was a circular green with a statue and curved benches on either side. Ian reached out and took her hand, drawing Mary's gaze to his dark eyes. To her surprise she saw what looked to be nervousness in those compelling depths. "Ian?"

He said only, "Come."

He led her forward toward the statue. Looking more closely at this figure, Mary realized that it looked like…her. It was a perfect likeness. "But how…" Then the realization dawned. "The man who was watching me."

Ian nodded, still appearing strained. He pointed to the statue's outstretched hands, and Mary saw that it was holding an object that appeared to be carved from rose-colored marble. Stepping to examine it more closely, Mary saw that it was a heart, a rose-colored heart.

A shaft of sweet hope pierced her as she swung around toward him. "Ian, does this mean...?"

He squared his shoulders, facing her directly. "It is my humble sinner's heart, Mary, for what it is worth. For good and always, it is yours. If you don't want it, it is of no use to me, for it will be forever broken."

Joy, like a rushing tide, flowed through her as she said, "Not want it, Ian? There is nothing else on this earth that I do want."

She felt his strong arms close around her as she raised her face for his kiss. He whispered against her hair, "Oh, God, Mary, I can't believe you love me. I was ready to go away, to leave this place and not bring you any more pain. But my father convinced me to tell you how I feel. He said my pride was a small thing to risk in the hope of gaining everything." He looked down at her then, the early-morning sunlight shining in her golden eyes and hair. "You are so beautiful, so good, my Mary. I still can't believe you could care for me."

She closed the gap between their two mouths, telling him with her lips that the risk had indeed been wisely taken. She drew back, her breath coming more quickly from between her pink lips. "The letter I was reading when you came into my room—it was from Jedidiah. Victoria has delivered a son. They will call him Jedidiah William Thorn-McBride." Her voice took on a huskier tone, her eyes twinkling. "It made me think, hope...." A blush stole over her creamy cheeks. "I would be most happy to give you a son, my love, to make you happy."

A feeling of completeness swelled in him at the idea of his and Mary's child. His voice was husky with emotion.

"You, Mary Sinclair, make me happy." Ian pulled her close again, his lips finding hers as he realized that his sinner's heart had at last found its home.

* * * * *

The Jewels of Texas

Bestselling author

Ruth Langan

presents

Ruby

Book IV in
the exciting
Jewels of Texas
series.

The town marshal and the town flirt fall in love,
and join forces to save the little town of
Hanging Tree, Texas, from a killer.

The Jewels of Texas—four sisters as wild and vibrant
as the untamed land they're fighting to protect.

Available in September
wherever Harlequin Historicals are sold.

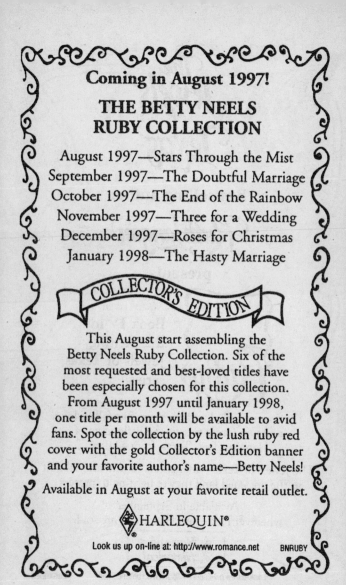

Coming in August 1997!

THE BETTY NEELS RUBY COLLECTION

August 1997—Stars Through the Mist
September 1997—The Doubtful Marriage
October 1997—The End of the Rainbow
November 1997—Three for a Wedding
December 1997—Roses for Christmas
January 1998—The Hasty Marriage

COLLECTOR'S EDITION

This August start assembling the
Betty Neels Ruby Collection. Six of the
most requested and best-loved titles have
been especially chosen for this collection.
From August 1997 until January 1998,
one title per month will be available to avid
fans. Spot the collection by the lush ruby red
cover with the gold Collector's Edition banner
and your favorite author's name—Betty Neels!

Available in August at your favorite retail outlet.

HARLEQUIN®

WELCOME TO *Love Inspired* ™

A brand-new series of contemporary inspirational love stories.

Join men and women as they learn valuable lessons about facing the challenges of today's world and learn valuable lessons about life, love and faith.

Look for:

The Risk of Loving
by Jane Peart

The Parson's Waiting
by Sherryl Woods

The Perfect Wedding
by Arlene James

Available in retail outlets
in August 1997.

LIFT YOUR SPIRITS AND
GLADDEN YOUR HEART with
Love Inspired™!

Steeple
Hill™

LI-997

HARLEQUIN WOMEN
KNOW ROMANCE
WHEN THEY SEE IT.

And they'll see it on **ROMANCE CLASSICS**, the new 24-hour TV channel devoted to romantic movies and original programs like the special **Romantically Speaking—Harlequin™ Goes Prime Time.**

Romantically Speaking—Harlequin™ Goes Prime Time introduces you to many of your favorite romance authors in a program developed exclusively for Harlequin® readers.

Watch for **Romantically Speaking—Harlequin™ Goes Prime Time** beginning in the summer of 1997.

If you're not receiving ROMANCE CLASSICS, call your local cable operator or satellite provider and ask for it today!

ROMANCE CLASSICS

Escape to the network of your dreams.

See Ingrid Bergman and Gregory Peck in *Spellbound* on Romance Classics.

FORTUNE COOKIE

Breathtaking romance is predicted in your future with Harlequin's newest collection: Fortune Cookie.

Three of your favorite Harlequin authors, Janice Kaiser, Margaret St. George and M.J. Rodgers will regale you with the romantic adventures of three heroines who are promised fame, fortune, danger and intrigue when they crack open their fortune cookies on a fateful night at a Chinese restaurant.

Join in the adventure with your own personalized fortune, inserted in every book!

Don't miss this exciting new collection!

Available in September wherever Harlequin books are sold.

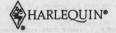
HARLEQUIN®